What the critics are saying...

"Second in her Saurellian Trilogy, Joanna Wylde's THE PRICE OF FREEDOM is a sexually explicit, wholly mesmerizing tale that entertains as much as it excites." - *Kelly Rae Cooper, Romantic Times Magazine*

"I was totally mesmerized with this story. Jess' finding of his woman was everything I had hopes it would be. I found the detail to each new place wonderfully described and, as always, the fierceness of the hero's love for his heroine sensual and erotic in its intimacy. I look forward to the next installment." - *Amy Turpin, Timeless Tales*

"Joanna Wylde pens a wonderfully wicked and erotic science fiction novel... If you're looking for something with strong characters, a little suspense and erotic love scenes, this one's for you." - *Missy Andrews, Blue Ribbon Reviews*

"Ms. Wylde weaves a wonderful story, one nearly impossible to put down. Bethany and Jess' by-play was so seamless it was unbelievable... The love scenes were touchingly emotional while holding an element of erotica exclusive to the Elloras Cave Authors." - *A Romance Review*

"Bethany and Jess sizzle in the bedroom. The sex is frequent and hot, hot, hot! If you haven't read Joanna Wylde yet, what are you waiting for?" - *Cat Cody, Romance Junkies*

Joanna Wylde

The Price
Of Freedom

Ellora's Cave
Romantica Publishing

An Ellora's Cave Romantica Publication

www.ellorascave.com

THE PRICE OF FREEDOM

ISBN # 1419950207
ALL RIGHTS RESERVED.
The Price of Freedom Copyright© 2003 Joanna Wylde
Edited by Martha Punches
Cover art by Darrell King

Trade paperback Publication January 2005

Excerpt from *Jerred's Price* Copyright © Joanna Wylde 2004

Warning:

The following material contains graphic sexual content meant for mature readers. *The Price of Freedom* has been rated *E-Rotic* by a minimum of three independent reviewers.

Ellora's Cave Publishing offers three levels of Romantica™ reading entertainment: S (S-ensuous), E (E-rotic), and X (X-treme).

S-ensuous love scenes are explicit and leave nothing to the imagination.

E-rotic love scenes are explicit, leave nothing to the imagination, and are high in volume per the overall word count. In addition, some E-rated titles might contain fantasy material that some readers find objectionable, such as bondage, submission, same sex encounters, forced seductions, etc. E-rated titles are the most graphic titles we carry; it is common, for instance, for an author to use words such as "fucking", "cock", "pussy", etc., within their work of literature.

X-treme titles differ from E-rated titles only in plot premise and storyline execution. Unlike E-rated titles, stories designated with the letter X tend to contain controversial subject matter not for the faint of heart.

Also by Joanna Wylde

❧

The Price Of Freedom

৪০

Part I

The Mine

Chapter One

✍

Damn, he ached.

Jess stared into the darkness above his bunk, willing himself to sleep. His body wasn't cooperating. He was exhausted from his work in the mines that shift—fourteen hours of pure hell. His cock didn't seem to understand that, though. He was rock hard, and his mind kept filling with pictures of *her*.

He had seen her for the first time a week earlier, pushing a cart loaded with food into the dormitories. She had been wearing a long, shapeless dress and a headscarf, like all those damn women did. She pushed the cart with slow, steady steps, refusing to look at any of them. A hundred men starved for food and sex surrounded her. No wonder she'd been afraid to look at them.

Their guards hadn't treated her with any respect. Of course, they never treated any of their women with respect, but this had been somehow different. It was as if she was an outcast even among her own people. They didn't speak to her, they didn't joke among themselves. They looked at her with disdain, as if she wasn't worthy to call herself a Pilgrim.

He had known she was different from the others, too. Even swathed in dark fabric, he had felt her presence across the room. He could sense her, smell her. She smelled like woman, and that first instant he saw her, he knew he wanted her.

Of course, they *all* wanted her. They wanted her even though her fear of them was palpable, as was the fear of every woman who brought them food. Twice a day, one of them would wheel a loaded cart in to the mass of starved, frustrated, angry men. The women would be escorted by two guards, men who carried instruments capable of killing any of the men instantly, but the fear was still there. After all, men under enough pressure will do desperate things, even if it leads to their own death. The women had to know that…

He had been at the far end of the barracks when she entered, but there was something about her that drew him to her. Maybe it was the way she carried herself. She was surrounded by a hundred men starved for a woman's touch, yet she remained calm and poised. Distant. As if she walked through a world of her own. He had moved through the ranks of waiting slaves until he was in front of her, taking the cart and pulling it away gently. She looked up at him, startled by his action. The guards watched in silence, hands on their weapons, but he did nothing threatening. He simply eased the cart out of her hands.

Her eyes had been wide with surprise when they met his. They were a brilliant green and almond-shaped, feline, like a cat. He had felt like he was falling into them. Her face was pale, slightly dirty, as if she had been working all day. Perhaps cleaning. There was exhaustion there, and a bit of defiance. She hadn't ducked his gaze, but met it head on. She might have been afraid of him, but she wasn't going to show it.

In that moment, he'd known she should be his. Of course, he had no idea how he'd ever get her. She was probably married—all Pilgrim women married young. She had to be in her mid-twenties, so she might even have several children, and a husband who had a right to touch her body whenever he wanted. Jess' fists clenched at the thought, and he pushed it from his mind, frowning into the darkness. He didn't want to think about another man with his woman. Instead, he imagined what she looked like under her robes. Her hair was dark brown, he knew that much. Her face was pretty, pale skin, luscious ripe lips. She was thin, her hands roughened from hard work.

What would her hair look like, loose and hanging around her naked body? He formed a mental image of her standing before him. Her breasts, high and pert, would peek out between the long locks. She would smile up at him, those green cat-eyes filled with secrets. She'd lick her lips and they would shine with her moisture. Then she would run her eyes up and down his own powerful, naked form, smiling at him with a sultry question written on her face. How did he want her? On her knees before him…under him…riding him?

Unable to help himself, Jess slipped one hand under his ragged blanket in the darkness of the barracks. Reaching into his pants, he found the long, smooth length of his cock. His eyes closed as his fingers grazed the head, a tingle of sensation stabbing through his groin. He touched the groove on the under side, rubbing one fingertip across it. His muscles clenched and he stiffened. The delicate touch was almost painful in its intensity.

He turned his thoughts to her again. She would kneel before him, and smile up at him with that peculiar look only a woman could give. As if she existed to rule and serve him at the same time. Then she would lift one hand and take his cock into her grasp, running her fingers over him. He moved his own hand against his skin, pretending he wasn't in a dark barrack, filled with a hundred slaves. Instead he was with her, and they had all the time in the world…

She gently touched her lips to the end of his cock, running her tongue around the head. He fought to control a gasp as she sucked his length into her hot, wet mouth. Then she started working her head back and forth. She raised one hand, firmly gripping the based of his erection and squeezing him in time with her movements. Her cheeks hollowed with each stroke, the suction of her mouth tugging on him in a slow, steady rhythm that was mesmerizing.

In the darkness of the barracks, it was easy to imagine that it wasn't his own hand stroking his hard length. Instead, she was with him, sucking him, pulling him. Each time her lips slid down the length of him, the pressure in his balls built a little higher. He imagined what it would feel like to pull her up until she stood before him. He would kiss her mouth with strong, penetrating strokes of his tongue. Then he would raise her in his arms and thrust his length into the hot, wet opening between her legs. Hard.

He could feel her wet lips, feel himself sinking into her again and again. His hand moved faster, roughly stroking up and down the length of his cock. He squeezed his fingers, imagining it was the pressure of her body around him. She would pulse under him, and when her own pleasure overtook her she would cry out in ecstasy. She'd go wild, muscles clenching his body. He pressed himself harder against his hand, imagining shooting his seed deep into her body. Again and again he stroked himself and with each touch the pressure grew until his balls tightened, ready to release. Orgasm hit, and his entire body stiffened. He stifled his moan, not willing to let the other men know what he was doing. Of course, it wasn't as if they weren't doing the same thing. There were very few secrets in the barracks.

Slowly, the pleasure of his release left him. Once again, he was alone in the darkness. Around him were the snores, sighs and soft moans of a hundred other men. For all he knew, they were sharing the same fantasy he had. In all likelihood he would never have sex with a woman again, let alone this woman he had come to think of as his. Hell, he didn't even know her name. He was a slave, and she belonged to one of his captors.

Morning would come all too soon, and with it another day of backbreaking labor in the mines. This was his life now, Jess told himself firmly. There was no room for self-pity, and there was no room for obsession with this woman. He closed his eyes and for the thousandth time, willed himself to sleep.

* * * * *

Bethany pulled the brush through her long hair. Every sleep cycle, since childhood, she had performed the same ritual. Her mother helped her when she was young. She had always imagined that some day she would do the same with her own daughters. There were no children, however. She had been her husband's third wife, and the first two had given him strapping boys and lovely girls. She had given him nothing…

Shaking off her thoughts, she separated her hair into three equal parts, braiding rapidly. When she finished, she stood and pulled off her drab brown dress, hanging it carefully on a peg near her door. Wearing only her shift, she padded softly across the room to her bed. It was small, and she was often cold, but she realized how lucky she was to sleep alone. For ten long years she had slept beside Avram, a man 30 years her senior. Every night, as she had prepared for bed, she had wondered if it would be one of the evenings when he reached for her. One of the times when he would pull up her shift and thrust his stiff penis into her unwilling flesh. As a frightened bride of 14 his touch was terrifying. In later years it simply became unpleasant. She could not bring herself to mourn his death as she slipped under the covers.

Avram was dead and she had other worries.

She was lucky to be back with her father, and in a way, she was lucky to be barren. She certainly didn't have to worry about getting married again. No Pilgrim man would have a wife who couldn't give him children. Her father may not be the most pleasant person to live with, but at least he ignored her most of the time. Of course, he would only keep her around as long as she could make herself useful.

She had almost fallen asleep when a harsh knock on her door startled her awake. She sat up in bed, breathing quickly. Was she in trouble?

"Bethany, get dressed and come out here," her father's voice growled outside the door. "The council meeting is over and I need to speak with you."

"Yes, I'll be right there," she answered automatically. Her father didn't like to be kept waiting. Bethany jumped out of bed, pulling one of her two dresses over her head. She wrapped her braid around her head in a coronet quickly, pinning it into place and making sure there were no loose strands. Her father had no patience for sloppy women. He would cane her if he saw a hair out of place.

Opening the door, she walked quickly down the hall to their living chamber. Her father's apartment was one of the largest in the mining community; as space in the habitation bubble on the asteroid's surface came at a premium. The fact that they had so much room was a testament to her father's influence with his fellow Pilgrims. Bose had been the official leader of their community for less than a year, but he had dictated policy long before that.

Her father was sitting in the one comfortable chair they owned, staring moodily at a report in front of him. His dark, swarthy face was mottled with color, his large nose flushed red. There was a bottle of the homemade *bakrah* he loved so much on the table next to him. She came to stand before him, eyes cast down modestly. He ignored her for several minutes, then looked at her with bloodshot eyes. He was drunk again.

"The council and I met tonight," he said. Bethany bit her lip, trying not to do anything that he might interpret as disrespectful. Bose was violent when he drank and she didn't want to provoke him. She'd had ample experience with his temper. He and the council met every cycle following dinner, mostly to drink, and he often came home in a foul mood.

Bose looked her up and down, an ugly look in his narrow, beady eyes. Her breath caught as fear washed through her. What was he thinking?

"It was brought to my attention—again—that a woman of your age should be married," he said. "But of course, that won't be possible. Your sinfulness is apparent to all of us. You have no children, despite ten years of trying with a good man who proved his virility with his other wives. The men are concerned that you might corrupt their women with your presence. Frankly, I'm inclined to agree with them. Since you came from your husband's home you've been nothing but trouble to me."

Bethany said nothing, eyes still cast downward. She kept her face impassive, biting back the angry words filling her thoughts. She had worked hard all her life, yet they all considered her a burden. Even now her fingers were raw from scrubbing the floor in Bose's room. He'd vomited there the night before, leaving the mess for her to clean.

"It was suggested that we expose you," Bose said, lifting his bottle to his lips and taking a long pull of the alcohol. Bethany stopped breathing. Exposure would mean death, slow and terrible from starvation. Assuming they *gave* her a pressure suit before shoving her out the airlock onto the asteroid's barren surface. If she was lucky, they wouldn't. At least that way death would come quickly. Would her father really do something like that to her? "After all, you have nothing to offer us, and it's a waste of good food to keep you around. Of course, I hate to think of doing something like that to my own child," he added, sighing piously. "But we do what we must for the good of the community. Sacrifices must be made."

Bitter fury welled up within her, but she kept her composure. If Bose sensed her anger, he would hurt her. She needed to stay calm, explore every option. Her mind worked quickly, trying to think of how to change his mind. She had talked her way out of difficult situations before…

"Then we had another idea," Bose said. Her heart leapt. "It occurs to me that good women are being exposed to the slaves every cycle, delivering food to them and caring for them when they're injured. Someone suggested that we have you work with the slaves instead. I know you've been part of the rotation, but from now on you would be in charge of them completely. That way no one will be further tainted by their presence. I'm inclined to see this as the best solution. What do you say?"

Bethany bit her lip, trying to think of a response that wouldn't set him off. Working with the slaves would make her valuable to the council. It meant survival, but she didn't want to look too eager.

"Whatever you feel is best for the community," she whispered, trying to look as submissive as possible. She dared to look at him, and he glared back at her. *Bastard*, she thought. She'd like to see him do half the work she did.

"Well, it's a good solution," he said. "We need someone to feed them, and we need someone to supervise their laundry and other womanly tasks. Decent women have been doing the work for too long."

"Yes, sir. Thank you," Bethany said meekly. She wasn't going to die after all, at least not for now. She could work with the slaves, she thought. They scared her, particularly the one who had taken the cart from her the last time she was there, but she would have guards to protect her from his intense gaze. To protect her from all of them.

"Go away," Bose said, taking another drink. "You'll start your new work during the next cycle. You'll follow the same schedule as the slaves. I suggest you get some sleep, because it may take you a while to get used to sleeping while the rest of us are awake. I don't want you shirking your duties because you're tired."

Nodding her head, Bethany moved quickly down the hall to her bedroom. She'd dodged disaster once again. Her life had been full of such crises since her husband's death, the first of which had been his family's decision to turn her out. She'd made it back to her father's house, and she was prepared to do whatever it took to survive. Bose and his council had no idea how determined she was to stay alive. She wouldn't go quietly. If they tried to expose her, she'd take as many of them as she could with her.

Pulling off her dress for the second time that night, Bethany hung it on the peg. She crawled into bed, pulling her knees up to her chest and staring into the darkness. She wasn't going to sleep for a long time. She was too filled with adrenaline for that. Her life had been in danger once again, simply because she didn't have a husband or children. It wasn't fair.

Bastards, she thought. Moisture welled up in her eyes, but she forced the tears back. She couldn't afford to show any weakness. She had to be as hard as a rock if she was going to survive.

* * * * *

Jess woke the next morning a few minutes before the bell rang, every muscle in his body tense. He always woke up like this, ready for a fight. His first sleep cycle in the barracks had been ugly—two men had tried to jump him. Since then he had slept lightly. The last three months had taught him a lot about protecting himself from all kinds of attacks.

Rolling out of his bunk, he moved quickly toward the back wall, where a fresher unit designed to serve ten men at a time was installed. His bunkmate, Logan, was already there. He nodded silently in greeting. A tall, quiet man, Logan rarely spoke to Jess—but they shared a certain respect. Jess got the feeling Logan would cover his back if needed, and tried to return the favor whenever possible. Both of them slept better for their shared vigilance, and occasionally they discussed escape. So far they hadn't come up with anything that seemed likely to succeed.

Jess relieved himself, then looked longingly at the sonic showers. Each man was allowed five minutes a day, and he had long since learned to save his time for after his return from the mines at the end of the shift. He never really felt clean, but he knew they were lucky to have the showers at all. Apparently the smell of a hundred unwashed men was enough to overwhelm the settlement's air filter system, so the Pilgrims had put in the units to control the stench.

Rinsing out his mouth, Jess strode back into the barracks. At the other end of the long room were several long tables, formed of plast-crete and bolted directly into the floor. The men were already starting to form lines in anticipation of their breakfast. The door opened and two guards walked into the room. They held their control wands before them, evil sticks with the power to kill any of the slaves instantly. Jess looked at them with hatred, but the guards didn't pay any more attention to the men before them than they would pay to animals.

The food cart came in with a rattling noise. They could always hear it coming since one of the wheels was loose. It was pushed by a woman, heavily draped as usual. But it wasn't just any woman, it was the woman he'd seen before. The one he'd dreamt of every night. His senses tingled as she approached. She walked slowly, carefully keeping her eyes pointed directly ahead. All around her the men watched with hungry eyes. They lusted for both the food and the body hidden under the folds of her clothing. His stomach clenched. He didn't like them looking at her like that. Gritting his teeth, Jess walked toward her, one eye on the guards. He had to get closer.

Her face was startled, wary, as he came and took the cart. His gaze met hers, and for one glorious moment he was sinking into those cat eyes again. Then she turned away and walked quickly out of the room, leaving the men to jostle for their food. Noise broke out and the tension eased.

The guards watched in sullen silence as the slaves ate, giving them fifteen minutes to complete their meal. Jess shoveled the tepid gruel without thought, grateful for the energy it would give him. Then one of the guards—a fat one they called Sluggo behind his back—gestured with his control wand, and the men made their way through the open door.

Jess was startled to see the woman in the outer room. She knelt in front of the large cabinet used to store medical supplies. Beside her was Bragan, a physician who had once been a free man. Now he tended to the slaves between shifts in the mine. Bragan was occasionally excused from working in the mines, so it was not all that uncommon to see him in the outer room. The sight of him with the woman, however, startled Jess. He'd never seen a Pilgrim woman talk to a slave before, yet these two seemed to be engrossed in conversation. She even smiled briefly at the man. Jealousy filled his heart. At that moment he could have happily smashed Bragan's skull in. His anger must have been written on his face, because Logan elbowed him, shaking his head in warning.

The guards didn't let them linger long enough for Jess to figure out what she was doing. They moved quickly through the room to a large staging area. Along one wall were lockers containing the pressure suits they wore to work the mines. Along the other wall—securely locked—were the lockers holding pressure suits and equipment used by the Pilgrims. Jess had never seen those lockers open.

Each man shrugged silently into his own suit. Then he and Logan took turns checking each other's suits to make sure they were sealed properly. A suit failure could mean death. Jess tried to have two different men check his—the week before one of the slaves had actually sabotaged another man's suit, killing him. None of them knew why he had done it, although Jess and Logan had been among those who had "questioned" him. Shortly afterwards he had perished in a mining accident. Justice among the slaves was swift and unforgiving.

Within minutes the men were suited. Under the watchful eyes of their guards, the line of workers trouped out the far end of the staging area. In groups of ten, they passed through an airlock and into the mouth of the mine. The walls gave way to rock, and the floor sloped noticeably as the tunnel went down into the asteroid's surface. They arrived at an elevator, and once again entered in groups of ten.

Jess waited his turn silently, gazing at the rusty, ancient elevator apparatus. Soon he would enter the metal box, which would carry him deep into the mine's depths. His partner, a young man name Trent, stood next to him quietly. Jess could hear his heavy breathing through the two-way radio they shared—their only way to communicate the entire time they were underground. Last week the radio had gone out shortly after they started work, and Trent had a panic attack. Jess had to work twice as hard to meet their quota, while his partner sat and cried. Trent was only 19 years old, enslaved for stealing.

Jess had already come to the conclusion that the kid probably wouldn't last too long. He wished Logan was his partner, but bunkmates weren't allowed to work together.

"Come on," he said, giving his partner a push when it was their turn to enter the elevator. "It's not going to be that bad. We're in one of the upper tunnels today. You can do this."

"I know," Trent said. He shuffled ahead of Jess, turning to face the front of the elevator with slumped shoulders. The elevator door made a screeching sound as it closed, then the car started its slow descent into the vast darkness of the mine. When they got to their stop, Jess flicked on his helmet light, and stepped out of the car. Trent followed him, then the car door slid shut with another screech and they were alone.

"Do you want to drill today, or do you want me to?" Jess asked, looking to his companion. They traded tasks off regularly, one running a powerful drill to prepare for the blasting the Pilgrims would do the next cycle while the slaves slept, while the other focused on removing the ore knocked loose from the previous cycle's blasts. When Jess had first arrived on the station, the sounds of blasting while he tried to sleep kept him up. Now he hardly noticed…working at "night" had become normal to him.

"You can drill," Trent said faintly. "I'll do the ore."

Jess nodded his agreement, then turned to the equipment they had left the day before. Picking up the heavy drill, he hefted it over his shoulder and started carrying it down the tunnel, the cords that powered it trailing behind him like a long, skinny tail. Normally he and Trent would work at the same end of the tunnel, drilling and hauling ore together. It was certainly safer that way. But they had been ordered to separate last week. Apparently their Pilgrims masters were having a disagreement over which direction they should be digging. Until they figured things out, the slaves were going both ways.

The whole thing—like so many of the situations the Pilgrims seemed to get into—was ludicrous. They were only accomplishing half as much as they could be, because they had to move the equipment and start over each day, but that didn't seem to matter to the idiots. Of course, Jess didn't really care. All he wanted to do was work just enough to meet his quotas and stay alive until he could figure out how to escape. The Goddess alone knew when he would find the chance, but until then he was laying low.

The morning went by fairly quickly, although after six hours of drilling he was getting a headache. He and Trent took several short breaks, discussing their progress each time on the radios. The last break, he hadn't heard anything from the kid. Finally, needing a rest from the drill anyway, Jess decided to go and find him. The radio must have gone out again. Trent was probably catatonic with fear by now, Jess thought wryly. He just didn't deal very well with being alone.

The darkness of the tunnel before him was absolute, the only light coming from his headlamp. As Jess walked down the tunnel he ducked his head several times to avoid overhanging chunks of rock. Here and there were metal struts they'd put in to hold the ceiling together, although in the three months he had been working in the mines there had been several times where the struts weren't enough.

Jess passed the landing area, where the elevator shaft and ore shafts passed through their tunnel into the mine's depths, then headed toward the far end where Trent was working. At first everything seemed to be the same as usual. Then he saw the first bits of rubble. Pulse quickening, Jess started jogging down the tunnel. His path was hindered, then blocked by rock and debris. Boulders filled the tunnel—a cave in. With a sinking feeling, Jess realized Trent was probably dead.

Jess keyed the com unit several times, trying to contact the boy. Quickly, he switched his transmitter to the emergency band, calling his fellow workers to come and help him look for his partner. It would take several minutes for them to arrive, though, assuming they could convince the guards it was a genuine emergency. The Pilgrims operated the elevators from above. Half the time when the men needed the elevators, their guards didn't respond. There was some speculation that they slept, although no one knew for sure. Jess looked at the ceiling carefully, trying to judge how safe he was. The normally solid rock overhead was cracked and every few seconds a small chunk would break off and crash to the tunnel's floor. Not good.

Without warning, several large blocks of rock crashed down within inches of Jess. Reacting instantly, he turned and sprinted down the tunnel toward the elevator. Behind him rock collapsed with a roar, the noise muted by the thin atmosphere in the mine. The rock beneath his feet shuddered. How could he have missed this terrible noise earlier? Was the drill he used really that loud?

He was only halfway back to the elevator shaft when the rock hit him. Pain exploded through his head, then everything went black.

Chapter Two

ℬ

Logan tore through the rubble, flinging rocks and debris behind him. It was almost impossible to hear anything on the radio because everyone talked at the same time. It occurred to him that if he found Jess, it would be best to have the doctor on hand. Turning, he grabbed another man's arm. Leaning in close, he toggled the man's radio to a new frequency.

"Find Bragan."

The man nodded, and took off toward the central corridor. It would be a while before he returned since the guards at the top weren't running the elevator very fast.

All along the tunnel, men were frantically screwing new supports into the rock walls. It had been nearly an hour since the cave-in, and they were all more than aware that another one could happen at any time. Logan had no idea if Jess and Trent were alive. In all honesty, he didn't care much about Trent. But Jess was his bunkmate, he had guarded Logan's back on more than one occasion. Logan wasn't going to leave him if there was even a chance he was still alive.

He pulled a medium sized rock out of the way and a spray of rubble showered down on him. He jumped back as a larger rock rolled toward him. Then he saw something, a stripe of reflective tape shining ever so slightly through the rubble. It was part of a man's pressure suit.

Logan gave a cry of triumph, and waved several of the others over to help him. Together they worked to free the man. Soon they had one arm loose. Following it, they dug toward his head. To Logan's relief, the faceplate was still intact. It was Jess. He was still alive. There was a slight clouding of moisture on the clear plastic in front of his mouth with each breath. But he didn't seem to be conscious.

The others worked to free his limbs as Logan carefully cleared the rubble from around his friend's head. He reached around to the back of Jess' neck, and his glove came back covered in blood. Jess was hurt. Even worse, there was a hole in the suit. The Goddess only knew if he was getting enough air…and the odds were pretty good that even if he was, his air tanks were depleting fast. They had to get him out of there or he would slowly smother in the thin atmosphere.

Logan felt something against his shoulder. He turned at the touch. It was Bragan. The doctor had an emergency medpack slung over one shoulder and Logan gave a sigh of relief. He toggled his radio.

"His suit has a slow leak and there's some kind of injury on the back of his neck."

"I've got a pressure tent," Bragan said. "If you get him free, we can put him in there. It should have enough oxygen for several hours. We'll need to keep his neck braced. He might have a spinal injury. If so, he'll be paralyzed if we move him wrong."

"If he has a spinal injury, he's dead anyway," Logan said, his voice tight. "They'll never give him enough time to recover from that. Where the hell did you get a pressure tent?"

"I have my ways," Bragan said, turning and setting the pack down. He started rummaging through it. Within seconds he had pulled out a long, orange tube. He laid it flat on the ground and unrolled it. Then he activated a switch and the thing started inflating.

"Pay attention to your digging" Bragan said sharply, turning back to Logan. "You do your job and I'll do mine. Get him out of there. I'll get things ready for him."

Logan turned back to Jess. Holding his head carefully still, he and the others cleared more of the rubble away. Then Bragan was back, pushing one of the men aside to get to Jess. Following his lead, Logan helped the doctor lift Jess away from the rubble, keeping his body as straight and stiff as they were able. It was a token effort, of course. If he were seriously injured he wouldn't be given a chance to recover. It was easier for their captors to import new slaves than care for the ones they already had.

The tent was fully inflated by now. There was a little tunnel at one end serving as a primitive airlock.

"There's not enough room for all three of us in the lock," Bragan said. "Help me get him in. I'll pull him into the tent, and then you can join us. The medpack is already inside."

Logan did as he was told, trying to gauge Jess' condition from Bragan's face. The faceplate on the man's suit made that impossible. Then the flap was closing and the little airlock sealed itself off. The pumps kicked in and Logan was left to watch and wait. The little tent was designed to provide safety in an emergency, but it was far from efficient. A full cycle of the lock would take at least 20 minutes.

Brooding, he turned to survey the scene in front of him. About 20 slaves were there, half still digging through the rubble to find Trent and the rest shoring up the walls of the tunnel. No sign of the guards. He assumed they were too frightened of another cave-in to come down and check on their workers. It was just as well since they might have called off the rescue efforts. The tunnel, seemingly identical to any other tunnel in the mine, offered no clues as to why it had collapsed. At least he could see well for once—every man present carried a powerful lantern on his helmet. The helmet had probably saved Jess' life, although it hadn't extended low enough to protect his neck. A small light on the tent's entrance turned from red to green, and he dropped to his knees. Time to go and see how Jess was faring.

Ever so slowly the lock cycled. Finally he was able to crawl into the tent. Bragan was kneeling next to Jess, examining him carefully.

"How is he?"

"The only injury I've found is to the back of his neck," Bragan said. "He got lucky. His suit was punctured, but the dirt and powdered rock kept it relatively well-contained until you freed him up. His oxygen levels are good, so that's one thing we don't have to worry about for now."

"So why isn't he awake?"

"I don't know," Bragan said. "But it isn't a good sign. He's got a concussion of some kind, and since the impact seems to have hit him right on the base of his skull, in the back, it could be very bad. His brain stem could be injured, particularly if the bones in there are shattered. There's no way of knowing, though, not without better equipment than I have here."

"What about his spinal cord?"

"As far as I can tell it's all right," Bragan replied. "We need to roll him over to get a better look. It will need cleaning, and probably some sutures. There's a risk that we'll cause further injury, but that's a moot point by now. For all I know he's brain dead. Can you help me?"

Logan nodded, and together they rolled Jess on to his side. Bragan turned the powerful lamp on to the wound, and Logan hissed. A sharp rock must have penetrated the man's neck. There was a deep gash and the entire wound was filled with a mixture of blood and dust, as well as tiny scraps of fabric.

"Fortunately I have antibiotics," Bragan said softly. "Their medic synthesizes them himself. He keeps me supplied. If we can clean this out we may be able to keep it from getting infected. If he's not brain damaged, he'll have a chance at survival. Doesn't look like it hit any arteries…Hold him for me."

Logan did as he was told, watching Bragan as the man muttered to himself. He pulled a small bottle of something out of the bag. Liquid of some kind…

"What is that?"

"It's a disinfectant," Bragan said, pulling the pressure suit's fabric away from Jess' wound with gentle fingers.

"What kind of disinfectant?"

"It's some of that Pilgrim moonshine," Bragan said. "*Bakrah.* I'll thank you to keep your mouth shut about the fact that I have it. It may save your friend's life, but I won't have much of it left if the men in the barracks find out about it. Antibiotics are easy to find, but alcohol comes at a premium."

"Is it strong enough to work on a wound?" Logan asked. "I thought you needed virtually pure alcohol for that."

"Let me put it this way," Bragan said, a note of dark humor in his voice. "I suspect that most of the Pilgrim men who don't die from liver disease die from alcohol poisoning. I take some comfort in that, actually. Think about it a lot…"

"How the hell did you get it?"

"I have my ways," Bragan said again. "You don't need to know."

Logan grunted, and turned his attention back to Jess. Slowly the wound was coming clean. Bragan had flushed it out, now he was picking out the larger pieces of dirt. He worked in silence for several minutes, then cursed.

"I need to take my helmet off," he said. "I'm starting to sweat in here. It's hard to see. Can you do it for me? I've already washed my hands, and I don't want to touch anything."

Logan lowered Jess' body carefully, then reached over and pulled the man's helmet off. He pulled off his own as well. Otherwise he wouldn't be able to talk to Bragan. Besides that, it was easier to see Jess. He lifted his friend again, and Bragan went back to work. Logan watched, mesmerized by the slow and patient way the man picked through Jess' flesh. Occasionally he would flush the wound, washing away the fresh blood that oozed up steadily. Then he saw something whitish, and his stomach heaved. It looked like…

"What's that?" he asked.

"His spinal column," Bragan said. "Don't worry, it looks like it's intact. The rock seems to have sheared right along it

29

without doing much damage. Practically shaved the flesh off..."

Logan stared, unable to stop himself. He had studied anatomy in school, but it was different to see it on a living, breathing person. Then something caught his eye. Right at the edge of the wound, atop the spinal cord, was something metallic.

"What's that?" he asked. Bragan paused, peering closely into the wound.

"It's the control implant," he said softly. "I'm sure you know what they are. We all have them."

"I know what it is," Logan said dryly. "At least in theory. They wave the wand at us, we die. Pretty damn simple. What's it doing on his spinal cord? I was told they were actually implanted within the cord. That's why you can't dig them out. But this is on the cord."

"It's probably the control unit," Bragan said, poking at it gently with the tiny metal pincers he was using. "This is what they implant. Then they activate it, and thousands of nano-machines expand out and go to work, spreading filaments through the nerves. That's why you can't remove it. Those filaments are braided directly into his nervous system on a molecular level."

Logan nodded, thinking. Bragan continued his work silently. After a moment, Logan spoke again.

"So that little unit is the hub, the processor, right?"

"Uh, huh," Bragan replied absently.

"So if that unit stops functioning, what happens to the filaments?"

Bragan looked up at him in surprise. "Nothing. They're still there."

"But are they active?"

"Define active," Bragan said, voice filled with dark humor. "They aren't active any time, unless they're activated by a control wand. The main unit serves as a control device and the filaments are what directly cause pain or death, depending how the wand is used. The rest of the time they just sit there."

"Does the wand activate the filaments directly, or does it simply interface with the control unit?"

"I would imagine it interfaces with the control unit," Bragan said. "The filaments are very simple constructions. They don't have any processing power of their own. Why?"

"I have an idea," Logan said quietly. "He's already unconscious, and there's already an opening on the back of his neck. I want you to take out the control unit."

Bragan grew still. Then he replied, very softly.

"I can't do that."

"Why not?"

"Because everything I've told you is hypothetical," Bragan said, his voice tense. "Just because I've speculated on how these things work doesn't give me the right to experiment on this man. And you don't have the right to make a decision like this for him. Taking this out could kill him. It could paralyze him, even stop his heart from beating. I don't know what the hell might happen. There could be a thousand different booby-traps built into the system to prevent tampering. It's wrong."

"It's *wrong*?" Logan asked, his voice harsh. "*Wrong* is working to death in a mine on an asteroid that doesn't even have a name. *Wrong* is never having sex again, never even eating real food. *Wrong* is slavery. If we can find a way to get rid of these implants we have a chance at escape. This is the best opportunity to find out if it's possible that we'll ever have."

"And what if it kills him?" Bragan asked, his voice caustic. "We don't have the right to make that decision for him."

"Do you know this man at all?" Logan asked, his expression intense. Bragan shook his head. "Well, I do know him. We've been bunkmates and we've talked. He wants to escape. He has a sister, he wants to get back to her."

"We all want to escape," Bragan replied. "And we all have families." He paused. "Or at least, we did."

"Yes, but he and I have been discussing escape plans from the moment we met," Logan continued. "This is an opportunity for him. He may die. He may live. But if he does live and he missed a chance to have his implant removed, I can guarantee that you'll hear about it. You have to do this."

"Just answer one question," Bragan said coldly. "And I want you to look me in the eye while you do it. If I did this, would I be doing it for him or for you?"

"You'd be doing it for all of us," Logan replied, meeting his gaze with cool certainty. "We're all going to die here, Bragan. And most of us will die within months, not years. We have a chance to save him, and ourselves. You have to take that chance."

Bragan closed his eyes without speaking. Then he nodded, once.

"I'll do it."

* * * * *

Bethany stared in horror as four of the slaves carried the man in from the mine.

He was covered in blood and black dust. His dark hair was matted with filth, and his breathing was fast and shallow. The guards had warned her that an injured man was coming, but nothing had prepared her for this...

His fellow slaves had found him in the rubble of the cave-in. Blood vessels in his face were broken from the low air pressure in his leaking suit, but somehow he was alive. It was nothing short of miraculous. His partner hadn't been so lucky. The other man's body had been crushed almost beyond recognition.

It was the same man who had taken the cart from her, the man with the penetrating stare. But he wasn't able to look at anything right now.

Bragan, the slave who was also a doctor, guided the men into the storage area where they carefully laid the man down on Bragan's own pallet. The doctor gestured for her to join him, then knelt by the man's side, carefully checking his vital signs. Standing over both of them was her father, Bose. He stared at the injured man with distaste, and Bethany felt cold fear for the slave.

"How soon will he be able to work again?" Bose asked Bragan. "If his recovery takes longer than two weeks, it's cheaper to import someone new."

"It's hard to know with a head wound," Bragan said, careful not to meet Bose's gaze. Bethany studied the doctor's face carefully, trying to determine how serious the man's condition really was. "He could wake up at any minute, and the rest of his injuries don't appear to be that serious."

Bethany looked at the patient again, then bit her lip. His condition looked pretty bad to her. Bose wouldn't hesitate to get rid of the slave if it was his cheapest option. The poor man had suffered through so much...he deserved a chance at life. Sudden determination to save him filled her.

"Father," she said quietly. Everyone around her went still. It was rare for a woman to speak in the presence of men on the station, and even more rare for one to speak to Bose. "I believe this man's survival may be a sign from the Celestial Pilgrim. How else would this man have lived, if our great leader didn't reach his hand out to save him?"

She held her breath, waiting for her father's reaction. Invoking the name of the Celestial Pilgrim, the prophet who had founded their sect a thousand years earlier, was not done lightly. Bose might react to her bold words with rage, or he might be moved by her bravery. His temper was too volatile to judge at times like these.

"How dare you speak of such a thing?" Bose asked her in a startled voice, the slave before him forgotten. "How are you worthy to speak the name of the Pilgrim?"

Bethany thought quickly. Bose was surprised, but didn't seem that angry. What should she say to him?

"Father, I do not know what moved me to speak," she said finally, trying to look as humble as she possibly could. "I can only imagine that the Pilgrim himself wishes this slave to live. Otherwise, why would he have compelled me to speak? I have never participated in such discussions before." She held her breath once she was finished speaking, staring at the floor and murmuring a silent prayer to the powers above her for mercy.

Bose stood silent for several seconds, then glared around the room at the open-mouthed slaves and guards.

"It is true that you are not one of those women who speak out of place," he said slowly. "But you are also a sinful woman. Why would the Pilgrim work through you?"

"I do not know, sir," Bethany whispered, truly filled with fear now. What had she been thinking, speaking up for the slave? Had she lost her mind? Her situation was tenuous enough as things stood…

"I do not believe that the Pilgrim would use a vessel such as you to communicate with his children," Bose said finally. "But it is truly miraculous that this slave survived. If the Pilgrim wishes him to live, then he will heal him. But if you're lying, and the man doesn't heal, then you will die with him. Do you understand me, daughter? We cannot tolerate a woman who would lie about something so important. You have two weeks."

Bethany breathed a sigh of relief as Bose turned and strode out of the room, gesturing for the guards to follow him. She was left alone with Bragan and the slave. Apparently she was no longer worth guarding, she realized. She'd never been alone with any of the slaves before.

"This man may die," Bragan said quietly. "You should have kept your mouth shut."

"How bad is it?"

"If he doesn't have brain damage or a skull fracture it won't be bad at all," Bragan replied. "I have no way of knowing whether he does or not, though. Not without better equipment than we have here. All I can do is treat the obvious wounds and try to keep him from getting an infection."

"Do you need anything?"

He gave a harsh bark of laughter, and she blushed. It was a foolish question.

"I need all kinds of things," he said finally. "But I doubt you can get them for me. How about some painkillers? If he wakes up he isn't going to be feeling very well."

"I don't think I can get that for you," she said softly. "My father has some, but he keeps a close eye on them. He would never give any to me."

"I didn't think you'd be able to get them," he replied with bitter humor. "I assume you're willing to help take care of him, given the little bargain you just made with your father?"

Bethany looked at the doctor and nodded. He seemed tired, and a little sad. He had been friendly enough in the days since she had started working with the slaves, showing her supplies and helping lift the heavy trays of food from the communal kitchen. Now his eyes were filled with compassion, and she realized he didn't believe the man was going to live.

"What's his name?" she asked, turning to the man again. He hadn't moved since he'd been brought up from the mines, not even when the doctor had pried his eyes open and gazed at his pupils.

Bragan seemed startled by her question. With a wry smile, he said, "I have no idea. I try not to get to know the new slaves any more, because they don't last very long. It's hard enough to survive, let alone waste energy on friends."

"I know what you mean," she said bitterly. Bragan lifted one eyebrow questioningly.

"That's a strange sentiment for a young woman like you," he said slowly. "Although I've noticed the guards don't treat you with much respect..."

"Why should they?" Bethany asked darkly. "My husband is dead, and I have no children. I don't serve any purpose here and they all know it."

"Couldn't you get married again?"

"No," she said, closing her eyes against a sudden rush of tears that threatened. "You don't understand. I *can't* have children. My husband had two other wives, both of whom had children. There's something wrong with me. No Pilgrim would ever take a woman like me to wife, and there's not much else for me here," she added. "I was living on borrowed time before this."

"I see," Bragan said quietly, looking uncomfortable. Changing the subject, he said, "Let's get him cleaned up. Want to help? I'm sure he'll be more interested in a woman's touch than mine. He might still be able to hear, so you should speak to him. Encourage him to wake up. It just might save your life."

"All right," she said, looking uncertainly at the slave. "Hello, there, um...well, whatever your name is. You'll have to wake and tell me."

"I'll make up a second pallet here on the floor," Bragan said. "That way, if he needs anything during the sleep cycle, I'll be there for him. You'll have to watch him while we're all at work."

"All right," Bethany said. She rose to her feet, moving out into the main room to get water. The slave complex was simple in design, a barracks area, a main room, a storage area and two tunnels. One went into the mines, and the other led to the main habitation complex and was heavily guarded. Taking a bucket, she filled it with hot water and grabbed several clean rags. Then she went back into the storage room, where Bragan was checking the bandage on the back of the slave's neck. He nodded at her, then moved out of her way. Kneeling beside the man, she daubed carefully at his face, wiping away the bloodstains.

"I'll just move my things out of the way," Bragan said. "I usually keep them on the shelf right next to my pallet, but if he does wake up and start thrashing he might knock them over."

"What about *his* things?" she asked, looking down at the injured man.

"I doubt he has any," Bragan said with a sad smile. "I'm treated differently because I'm a physician. I'm more valuable than the others, so they let me keep some odds and ends I've scavenged around. I have to go now, though. Just clean him up and keep an eye on him. When I get back at the end of the shift, I'll check him again."

Bethany nodded, then set back to work. Bragan walked out into the main room. She heard the squeaky sound of a locker opening, then heard him grunting as he pulled on a fresh suit. Within a few minutes, he had disappeared down the tunnel leading to the mine. She was alone with the slave.

"I wonder who you are?" she asked, wiping at the man's face. His features were becoming clearer as she worked. His skin tones were darker than hers, although his face held an unnatural pallor from his injuries. He had thick, black lashes, high cheekbones and full lips. There was something about his lips that drew her attention—her husband's lips hadn't been like those at all. She touched the bottom one briefly, wondering at its soft feel. Then she shook her head, and blushed at her thoughts. The man was injured, and a slave. She had no business touching him.

She managed to get his face and neck clean, and even sluiced some of the water through his dark hair until it was relatively free of blood. The rest of him presented a problem, though. He still wore the mangled remains of his pressure suit, which had been quickly patched in the mine so they could bring him to the surface. His helmet was already off, but she would have to get the rest of the suit off him before she could clean him up any further. She shouldn't have let Bragan leave so quickly...

She looked at the suit carefully and realized there was no way it would ever be usable again. Bragan had already pulled the suit apart where it had been taped at the neck. There were other taped spots, too. She might as well cut it off him, she realized.

Bragan had showed her a storage locker earlier that held his limited supply of medical implements. It was locked, of course, but the guards had coded her fingerprint into all the locks when Bose first announced she would be working in the slave complex. Pressing her finger against the plate, she pulled the door open and started looking for scissors. She found a pair, re-locked the cabinet and returned to her patient.

Moving quickly, she cut through the suit's reinforced fabric easily enough. Bragan's scissors were very sharp, sharper than any she had ever used before. They also seemed to be of higher quality...where had he gotten them?

The scissors blade slipped and cut her finger. For a minute it didn't hurt, then blood welled up and it started to sting. She stared at it, startled by the pain. Without thinking she stuck it in her mouth, then got up to look for something to bandage it with. The blood, warm and salty, filled her mouth. She wondered if he was in pain, too. Probably not, at least not yet. But he would be when he woke up. If he woke up... Was there any way she could steal some pain tabs from her father? She'd have to think about it.

She found a small strip of fabric to wind around her finger. She wrapped it tight, and the pain seemed to recede a little. *Nothing like a little pressure to make the blood stop,* she thought. Time to get back to her patient. She finished cutting apart the suit and peeled it to either side. It was still trapped under his body though, and now she faced another challenge. Underneath the suit his clothes were soaked with sweat and stained with blood—they looked and smelled disgusting, and she knew she had to get them off of him. She would have to cut them off just like the suit. It was a waste of good material, she realized, but if she cut carefully she would be able to salvage some of it. Unlike the suit, it was still largely intact. If she destroyed his clothing, she had no idea what he would wear if he survived. Such cloth was precious...

She started with his right arm, carefully slitting the seam of his shirtsleeve. She took care not to jostle him as she cut, following the seam to his armpit and down the side of his shirt. The rough fabric was stiff with dried blood, hard to maneuver. She finished one side, then carefully cut the seam around the arm and across the shoulder.

She moved to his other arm, repeating her actions. Finally, she was able to pull the entire front of the shirt off him. Then, cradling his head in her arms, she lifted his upper torso just enough to slide the filthy fabric out from under his back. Lowering his head again, she rocked back on her heels to look at him.

His chest was like nothing she'd ever seen before. He was banded with strong, lean muscle, the result of his manual labor in the mine, she supposed. Lying against it was a crude necklace, a string holding a shiny round pendant. Lifting it in one hand, she looked at it curiously for a moment, then let it drop. His necklace was none of her business, she reminded herself firmly. His stomach was rippled, and a line of dark hair trailed from beneath his pants up and across his chest. His upper chest was covered in the dark, curly hair, another thing that was new to her. Her husband had been old—she had never even seen him without a shirt, she realized. This man was young, and his body was strong... The sight of him was compelling. She felt her cheeks growing warm.

Unable to control her curiosity, she dropped one finger to his stomach, trailing it along the line of hair. His skin was soft, but the hair were stiff and wiry. The sensation was intriguing. She flattened her palm just above his skin, allowing the tiny hairs to tickle her hand as she moved it. A shiver went through her, and for some reason she felt tense. She snatched her hand back from his body, stood up quickly and picked up the bucket. It was time to clean him.

Moving as efficiently as possible, she wiped down his upper body. It was hard not to touch him with her bare skin, but she managed to keep the rag between them the entire time. His arms were thick with ropy muscles, his stomach tight and hard. Just slooking at him made her feel dizzy. All too soon, his upper body was clean. Time to deal with the rest of him.

She looked speculatively at his lower body, still clothed in filthy trousers. She was going to have to cut those off, too. Stifling a sigh, she started cutting carefully along the right seam. As she moved down the length of his leg with her scissors, his flesh was revealed. Like his arms, his legs were thick with muscles, and small dark hairs bristled against the backs of her fingers whenever she touched him by accident.

She finished the seam, then moved around to the other side of his body. Once again she attacked the rough threads of his garment, determined to preserve the fabric. She would wash it and stitch it back together for him.

When both sides were cut, she gathered a deep breath and started to pull the fabric off his limp body. Fortunately, she was able to get the pants off without moving him too much, although she did have to reach one arm under his back to lift his lower body slightly. She kept her eyes averted from his genitals, embarrassed by how much she wanted to look at him. The air was chilly, and before her eyes small bumps rose on his leg. He was cold, she realized. She needed to get him covered.

She looked around the storeroom and found a blanket, folded neatly beside the pallet Bragan had made up for himself. She brought it back out to her patient, and draped it across his upper body and groin. In doing so, she couldn't help but notice the smooth length of his soft penis. Even at rest, it was much larger than her husband's had been. What would it look like fully aroused, she wondered? A shiver passed through her at the thought. Blushing, she forced herself to look away. Then she attacked his lower legs with her water-soaked rag.

His feet were huge. That was her first thought—so much bigger than her own. Her husband's had been smaller than this, too. This slave was tall, she remembered, from when she'd seen him the barracks. Much taller than any of the Pilgrim men. Around each ankle were vicious scars. The manacles used to restrain him must have caused them, she realized. She trailed one finger along the ridge of twisted skin, a mixture of old, white scars over-laid with newer red ones. He had suffered a long time. She shuddered, thinking of the pain those scars represented. *Don't think about it*, she reminded herself. *There's nothing you can do about that. It's just the way things are.*

Both feet clean, she started working her way up. His calves were lean and tight. The tiny hairs bristled at her touch as she washed him. The further she moved up his body, the more mesmerizing she found her task. His skin was smooth, but still much rougher than hers. She shivered, wondering what was wrong with her. It was hardly cold. She felt hot and restless. If anything, she wanted to loosen her collar and get some fresh air.

By the time she reached his knees she had grown short of breath. There was something about the feel of his skin that made her feel almost lightheaded. Each muscle in his leg was sharply defined. Not an ounce of extra skin to be found anywhere.

All too quickly she reached the point where she had to move the blanket aside, exposing his groin. She tried not to look at his penis, moving briskly and efficiently. But her eye kept catching on it, and she just had to find something out…was it as soft and smooth as it looked? Glancing behind her quickly to make sure no one had magically appeared to watch her, she touched the length of it. The skin was incredibly soft. Much softer than she would have dreamt possible on a man as hard as this one. It was longer than her hand, and she allowed her fingers to drift down the length toward the smooth head.

Tracing the flared tip, she realized that it was changing slightly. He was hardening under her touch, and she jerked her fingers back in horror. But when she looked at his face, she realized he was still completely unconscious.

Of course, touching him was wrong, but when would she ever have another chance like this one? For all she knew he would never wake up again. And if he didn't, she would be dead in two weeks. Startled by her own daring, Bethany reached toward his penis again, lifting it gently with her fingers. She stroked it up and down several times, and was rewarded by the sight of it growing longer and harder under her ministrations. To her fascination, the head turned dark red, and then a small bead of moisture welled from the tip.

She was feeling fluttery, her breath coming quickly. Under the harsh fabric of her tunic, she could feel her nipples peaking. They were so sensitive that they almost hurt as she leaned further across the man to examine his face. The fabric of her dress was intolerably rough. She shook her head, trying to regain control of herself. But instead she leaned in closer to his face, studying it. It remained completely blank, but his lips looked so soft and inviting she couldn't prevent herself from wanting to touch them again. Without pausing to consider her actions, she lowered her lips to his, kissing them gently. She brushed against them once, twice, then sat up and pulled the blanket over his body. Flushing deeply, she took a few deep breaths and sat back on her heels.

She knew what she had done was wrong. She sat there, examining her feelings for a few minutes, and realized that she didn't regret her actions one bit. In fact, just thinking about touching him excited her in a way that was totally different from anything she'd ever felt with her aging husband. This man was young, and strong. He was sick, but he was still more interesting than any of the Pilgrim men she'd ever met. Saving him had been the right thing to do. A sensation of calm came over her. Whatever happened in two weeks, she wouldn't regret her decision.

* * * * *

It took more than an hour to ferry all three carts of food to the barracks at the end of the slaves' work cycle. It would be cold by the time the men came in from the mines, but that didn't really matter. It was still food, and they would be hungry. She had their dinner ready and waiting by the time they arrived back from work, escorted by several Pilgrim men she had known in her childhood. Of course the men didn't even bother to acknowledge her presence now. Several of the slaves looked toward the storage room with vague curiosity, but none seemed inclined to go over and visit. They seemed too tired to care about their fallen comrade.

Bragan came over to check on him as soon as he pulled off his pressure suit and stowed it in a locker. She could see the fatigue in his face, but the doctor still took his time while looking over the injured man. Bethany searched his face anxiously for some sign of what to expect.

"There's no real change," Bragan said, sitting back on his heels. "He's dehydrated though, and if he doesn't wake up soon he never will. Of course, if we had even the simplest of equipment here I could do something about that, but I don't even have a way to get fluids down him as it stands."

He sat back and sighed heavily. "I'm too old for working in the mines. Usually I don't have to do the heavy labor, but they've got me substituting for him right now." He gestured toward the man with his chin. "I'm going to get my food now. Is it all right if his bunkmate visits him for a minute, before they lock the barracks down for the cycle?"

"Sure," Bethany said. She stood and stretched tiredly. "It's been a long day. You must be eager to sleep."

"That's the truth," Bragan said. He stood and walked out of the room. A few seconds later a tall, muscular man with deep black hair came in. His face was streaked with dirt, and he scowled at Bethany. She shivered, and suddenly realized she was alone with him. His eyes roamed up and down her body, stripping her naked, then looked away from her dismissively.

"How is he?" he asked in a low voice.

"Bragan doesn't know how he's doing," she replied. To her disgust, her voice cracked. There was something about this man that scared the hell out of her, but she stood her ground, watching as he knelt beside the man and touched his face with surprising gentleness. Then he stood again and walked out of the room without speaking. Bethany exhaled heavily, and sagged against the wall. It was all too much, she thought. Far too much for one day.

She shook herself, then turned to her patient and made sure he was tucked in for the night. She went back out into the main room and started hauling the empty food carts back to the kitchen. The few men who weren't in the barracks watched her with blank eyes as they patched their pressure suits and checked their equipment. Finally, her work completed, she watched in silence as the guards locked the men in. Then, walking behind them as a good woman should, she made her way out the main door of the slave compound and into the tunnel connecting it to the main habitation bubble. Another cycle was over.

* * * * *

That night as she slept, she dreamt again and again of the man's injuries. Each time they were slightly different. At one point, his leg was crushed, and he was crawling toward her, one hand outstretched and pleading for help. Another time he was blind, stumbling through the mine, trying to find her. She tossed and turned as dream after dream hit her, buffeting her with their intensity. Every time his injuries were worse and she never managed to help him. All the dreams ended the same way, though. Her father, leading a group of Pilgrim guards, would drag them to an airlock. The doors would slide shut and the air would be pumped out with a wheezing, hissing sound.

Then, their lungs bursting within them, she and the slave would die.

Chapter Three
One cycle after the mine collapse

&

Logan had trouble settling down that night, his mind spinning with possibilities. If removing Jess' implant worked and Jess survived, they had a whole new hope for survival. If Bragan could remove one in an oxygen tent in the mines, he could remove more. They could escape.

He forced himself to stay in his bunk, conserving his energy despite the restless tension that filled him. When the wake-up sounded, he jumped to his feet. Time to find Bragan. The doctor came into the main barracks to get his food a few minutes later, and Logan pulled him to one side.

"How is he doing?"

"He's doing great," Bragan said. "He woke up in the night. Seemed a little confused and in a lot of pain, but I managed to get some water into him. I told him about the implant, too."

"What did he say?"

"He was glad we'd done it," Bragan said, wiping one hand across his forehead nervously. "Started talking about escape right away, about rescuing his sister. I was relieved to hear it, I have to admit."

Logan nodded. No point in rubbing it in.

"How long was he awake?"

"For about an hour, on and off," Bragan said. "He woke up several times during the night. We've decided that we'll keep him 'unconscious' for a couple days. That way he'll be completely free to listen and spy on them without any suspicion. He'll report what he finds out through me, and together we can come up with a plan."

"That's great," Logan said, grinning fiercely. "I want you to take out my implant today. We'll switch partners in the lift. I know someone who owes me a favor. He'll cover for us."

Bragan stared at him.

"I won't do that," he said. "It's completely irresponsible. For one thing, I'm not a surgeon. We don't even have any anesthetic. There's a good chance I could kill you!"

"I don't need anesthetic," Logan said coldly. Bragan laughed.

"You think you're pretty tough, don't you?" he asked. "Well I won't do the surgery without some way of sedating you. You think you don't need any painkillers. You're wrong. Even the slightest movement during the surgery could be disastrous, and then I'd have a body on my hands. Not only that, you need to be able to work the next day. There is no way you'd be able to do that without some kind of medication. Even *with* medication, you'd be doing well to be up and walking around."

"How did you get the alcohol?" Logan asked. "Wouldn't that work?"

"It's a very poor substitute and I doubt I could get any more," Bragan said. "And what little I do have needs to be saved for emergencies"

Logan smiled at him, baring his teeth.

"I think you should reconsider," he said. "I know what I'm capable of handling. Life could get very unpleasant for you if you refuse to help me with this."

Bragan shrugged.

"Life is already very unpleasant for me," he said. "And you can't force me to do anything. Remember, if I don't like you all I have to do is agree to the surgery. You have no way of controlling what I do inside that tent. I could have you dead in seconds, and don't think I wouldn't do it. No anesthetic, no surgery."

"What about the girl?" Logan asked suddenly. "She seems to like you. Can you convince her you need pain medication for Jess?"

"I *do* need pain medication for Jess," Bragan said. "And I've already asked her about it. She says she can't help, but I'll keep working on it."

"Do that," Logan said. "And be prepared. If we're going to do this, you'll have to operate on all the men eventually. And we'll have to do as many as possible before the escape attempt. I'm starting to put a plan together, but we'll need Jess on the outside to help us. That means we have less than two weeks to pull this off…"

* * * * *

Third cycle after the mine collapse

Beth brushed out her hair and braided it quickly before leaving her room. It was strange, getting used to her new schedule. She was waking up just as everyone else got ready to sleep. But in many ways she enjoyed that. The less she saw of her father, for one, the better.

She was early, but she needed to get breakfast for the slaves before they left for the mine. Fortunately she wasn't responsible for actually cooking it—that was done in the communal kitchen which served most of the station. Still, carting enough food for a hundred men took quite a bit of time. She was also eager to check on her patient. Would he show any improvement after resting?

For the past three days she had checked him carefully each morning, wishing desperately to see some sign that he might wake up. He was getting painfully dehydrated, at least that's what Bragan told her. She actually thought he was looking quite well, given his situation. According to Bragan, there was little hope for him if he didn't wake up within the next day. Her hands trembled momentarily as she raised a hand to open the apartment door. If the man died, would Bose have her killed immediately? She glanced around the room. It was bare, gray, anything but comfortable. At the same time, it was her home. Would this be the last time she saw it?

As she stood there, a woman padded softly out of Bose's room toward the fresher. It was Moriah, a young widow who worked in the kitchens. Beth stared at her, shocked by her presence. What had she been doing there?

Moriah seemed equally horrified to see Beth. She was caught, and she knew it. Regardless of Bose's stature as station leader, Moriah's punishment for being caught in his apartment would be terrible if she were discovered. Beth tried to think of why the woman would do such a foolish thing. Moriah raised one hand tentatively, pushing a lock of black hair behind one ear. She fingered the side of her neck softly, and then Bethany saw it. An ugly bruise, red and new, circled Moriah's throat. A wave of nausea came over as she realized Bose had forced the girl.

Walking quickly across room, she silently took Moriah into her arms. The woman trembled and silent sobs shook her body.

"He says I have to marry him," she whispered into Beth's shoulder. "I don't have a choice. He says I could be pregnant already, and if that happens while I'm unmarried we all know what will happen to me."

There was nothing to say, so Bethany simply held her a moment longer. Then Moriah pushed away from her and wiped her eyes.

"We need to get to the kitchens," she said. "I'm supposed to help prepare the slaves' meal tonight. If I'm late, someone might suspect. Will you help me leave? If you can check the corridor to make sure no one is out there, I can slip away…"

"Of course," Bethany said quickly. "I'll check for you."

They crept softly across the room, and Bethany opened the door. She stepped out into the corridor and looked carefully each way. No one.

"It's safe to come out," she whispered, and Moriah crept out behind her. Quickly, the younger woman scuttled down the hallway toward her own apartments. She had a child, a daughter less than a year old, Bethany remembered. Hopefully someone she could trust had been with her. Another wave of nausea came over her as she realized it was entirely possible that Moriah had been forced to leave the baby all alone. Forced to do so by Bose, her own father.

She started toward the slave complex to pick up the food carts. It was better not to think about these things. They were entirely out of her control. The day guards were still on duty, lounging outside the main entrance to the complex. The men had been locked in the barracks the cycle before, so there was no reason to leave anyone stationed in the main room or the mine. The two men opened the locked and barricaded doors for her without comment, closing them behind her with a loud, clanging noise.

She made her way quickly down the short corridor into the main room. To one side was the tunnel leading to the mines, but all she could think of was checking on the slave. Opening the storage room door, she flicked on the light and moved quickly to his pallet. Bragan groaned, rolling over to cover his eyes with his arm.

"Couldn't you knock first?" he moaned.

"I'm sorry," she said softly. "I didn't mean to startle you. How is he doing this cycle?"

"He's fine," Bragan muttered. "I'm going back to sleep. I've still got several minutes before I need to be up and I'm going to use them."

She nodded, and stepped over the sleeping man to check on the slave. His name was Jess, she reminded herself. Bragan had told her the cycle before. Calling him by name was infinitely better than "the slave". He was lying in the same position she had left him, looking so weak and pale that it scared her. How could he still be alive? He hadn't had any food or water for days, yet when she checked his pulse, it was still strong. She gave a sigh of relief for that—she had at least one more day to live. She shook her head, clearing away the morbid thoughts, then stood and left the storeroom.

There was no time to waste. She had to get the carts to the main kitchen. They would wake the slaves in less than an hour, and the food had to be ready for them. Pushing the first of the three large carts, she made her way back through the main room and down the corridor. The guards let her back through the re-enforced doors, and she walked briskly toward the communal kitchen area.

Unlike her father's apartment or the slave complex, the kitchen was a sea of activity. All around her, women and young girls were chatting and laughing together as they cleaned up from the last meal of the day. The kitchen was usually like this, at least as long as the kitchen supervisor, a stern and humorless woman named Magda, wasn't around. She usually left just as the evening meal was being served. For many of the women— Bethany included—hours spent in the kitchen following that meal were the most pleasant on the station.

She didn't have many female friends here. She had left so many years ago to be married that few of the girls she grew up with were still around. Most had moved to various other mining stations to be with their husbands. As a widow without children, she didn't fit in with the rest of them. Some of them scorned her, but others looked on her with kindness. She might not have friends, but certainly she wasn't among enemies in the kitchen. At least not in the evening, when the younger women worked.

Out of the corner of her eye she saw Moriah. She was wearing a high-necked tunic which completely covered the bruises Bethany knew were on her neck. Moriah shot her a quick smile, and Bethany gave a sigh of relief. If someone had caught her sneaking out of the apartment she wouldn't be smiling.

Pushing the cart over toward the big kettles at one end of the kitchen, she steadied it as two of the women poured nutritional gruel into the large tubs. As soon as they were full, she headed back with the cart. It was heavy now, but she didn't allow herself to think about how hard it was to push. She still had two more trips to make before she ate her own breakfast, and then it would be time to wash everything again.

* * * * *

She was back. Jess forced himself to lay utterly motionless, in the same position he had been when she left him earlier. It was hard to ignore the smell of the hot food she wheeled into the main room.

Her name was Bethany. Her presence had filled his senses from the moment he'd awakened three days earlier. Everything about her was beautiful to him—amazing. Bragan seemed to have no appreciation for the beauty of her name when he'd mentioned it, yet Jess repeated it to himself over and over like a mantra. Bethany. He loved her clean smell, loved listening to the soft songs she would hum as she cleaned and worked. He also loved the occasional touches she gave him, checking his forehead or wiping his face as he feigned sleep.

Bragan said she was an outcast among her own people. He seemed to feel she could be trusted, and the story of how she'd saved his life was certainly amazing to Jess. Still, he wanted her to believe he was unconscious for another day. The longer he was incapacitated, the more likely he was to learn valuable information. Bragan had often tried to spy on the guards at night, but he was too tired to stay up much. Fatigue could kill a man in the mines. Jess' injury had given him the perfect excuse to rest all day and plot all night.

He waited quietly while she wheeled the heavy carts of food in to the men. He could hear their activity. Fifteen minutes to eat. Then they were pouring out of the barracks and suiting up for their work in the mine. Another day, just like all the others before it.

Bragan stopped in, followed by the woman. Jess laid still as he took his pulse, then spoke to the woman.

"He seems to be stronger," Bragan said cautiously. Jess held back a snort of amusement. He was better all right. Last night he and Bragan had talked for an hour, planning his slow process of "recovery" and the escape they hoped would follow. In all honesty, he was still weak. But there wasn't any reason he couldn't have gone back to the mine in a day or so.

Instead, they were going to keep him out for almost the entire two weeks. It was a delicate balance. If he were too sick the Pilgrims would give up on him. But he couldn't go back to work until the last minute. He needed every moment of precious freedom to plan and plot the escape. If things went well, he would be free in less than two weeks. Free or dead.

Jess was relatively certain that if he could come up with a decent escape plan, the men would follow him. Logan was covering his end. Already they had ten volunteers who wanted their implants removed. If everything went off just right, that might be enough. They were willing to risk death to get out. But up to this point, no one had been able to find an avenue of escape that had even a chance of success.

He was determined to do it, or die trying.

The men had left for the mine now. She was moving around in the room, and he could hear the rattling of the carts. He was so damn hungry — Bragan had promised to leave him some food in his locker. He had to wait until the men were all in the mines and she was gone to get it, though. The carts rattled again, and he could hear her washing the trays. It seemed like forever. He imagined the tiny bits of porridge left on them, being washed into the station's recycler. They would be used again, perhaps for dinner that night. But he needed food now…

Finally, she finished. She loaded the carts up and then rapped on the outer door. The guards on the other side opened it, letting her out. He heard the door slam shut, and slowly raised himself from the pallet.

Opening the door slowly, he peeked out to make sure the room was empty. It was.

He crept over to Bragan's locker. Nothing. He pawed through the contents, and then he found it. Damn, but the man was resourceful.

There was an empty blast casing, the type the Pilgrims used to form the plastic explosives used in the mining. They were careful never to allow the slaves access to the explosives, of course. All the blasting was done during the slaves' sleep cycle.

But the forms they used sometimes got lost. There was a bounty for returning them, an extra ration of food at night. But many of the slaves kept them, using them for other things.

Bragan had filled this one with porridge.

It was cold and gelatinous. It wouldn't flow out freely, so he dug his finger in, digging at it and stuffing it into his mouth. Nothing had ever tasted better in the history of time. *Nothing.*

All too soon it was gone. Bragan had warned him he needed to be cautious about over-eating, and his stomach was full. Hunger satiated, he was suddenly aware of the low, painful throbbing in the back of his neck. There was nothing they could do about the pain. He gritted his teeth, willing himself to ignore it. Quickly, he cleaned out the empty tube and put it back in Bragan's locker. They would need it again that night.

He crept back to the storage room, uncertain of how much longer he had before she returned. He needed to find a way to time the guards' movements during the work cycle. The bastards had to have a weakness, and Jess was going to find it.

* * * * *

Bethany ate her own small bowl of porridge in the kitchen. The kitchen crew was cleaning up the last of the main evening meal, as well as preparing special food for the blasters returning from the mine. They worked in two shifts, blasting by day and guarding the slaves by night. Of course, the elders, such as her father, weren't directly involved in the mining efforts. That would hardly be appropriate for their dignity. There were also groups who traveled between settlements, and a very small number who traveled to Discovery Station, where the ore was processed.

Eventually, even that small bit of contact would be curtailed.

The cost of the ore-refining equipment was very high, but for a decade the elders had been saving and planning for the day when they could start their own refining operation. Then they would be able to send shipments directly to the central temple on Karos, where the Celestial Pilgrim himself had lived. All part of some glorious plan she had never been worthy of sharing, she thought darkly. How many women like herself had spent their entire lives working in service of that plan? Did any of them ever really understand what they were working for?

Her train of thought was broken when someone sat down beside her. It was Moriah. The girl smiled at her nervously.

"Thank you for your help earlier," Moriah said quietly. "I hope you don't mind me sitting with you."

She looked unsure of herself, almost as if she were afraid Bethany might stand up then and there to accuse her of immoral behavior. Bethany smiled, wanting to ease the younger woman's fear.

"It's nice to have company," she said softly. "I grew up here, but I left when I was fourteen. I don't feel like I really know the people here anymore."

"Yes, I remember hearing that your husband had passed," Moriah replied. "Was it terribly hard for you? I felt like my life was over when they told me Ger—my husband—had died in the mines. I was seven months pregnant…"

"I'm so sorry," Bethany said. She could see the girl was still troubled. It was hard to understand why a woman would be sad over losing a husband. Then again, not all husbands were like Avram had been... "I take it you had a love match?"

"Yes," she replied softly. "I was betrothed to his older brother, but he died before we could marry. I practically grew up with Ger. I fostered with his family after the betrothal. I hate to admit it, but part of me was happy when I heard his brother was dead. I don't think I could have stood living so close to Ger as his sister-in-law...I guess I should just be glad for the time we had."

"Was he a blaster?" Bethany asked. Setting explosives in the mine was one of the most dangerous jobs on the station. Unlike other dangerous jobs, it couldn't be given to slaves. As an elder, her own father had managed to avoid working the mines for many years.

"Yes, a blaster," Moriah said, her voice trailing off. "I never thought things would turn out like this," she added in a bitter voice.

Bethany nodded. There was nothing else to say. Her father had hurt this woman and would probably hurt her again. There was nothing either of them could do to prevent that from happening.

They sat without speaking for several minutes. Finally, her food finished, Bethany set down her spoon and looked intently at Moriah.

"I realize I can't help you much," she said quietly. "But I just wanted to let you know that you aren't totally alone here."

"I realize that," Moriah said smiling at her shyly.

Bethany nodded. They shared a situation, and now they shared a secret. It was good to have a friend.

* * * * *

Jess laid quietly. He'd been resting, and listening, all day. One time she'd nearly caught him. She'd been cleaning out in the main room, and had abruptly walked into the storage room to get something. Fortunately, he had just returned to his pallet after getting a drink of water. If she caught him up and moving the game would be over.

It was easy enough to track movements through the area during the day. There were very few visitors. The blasters wouldn't come through until the slaves had returned from the mines. To Jess' surprise, there didn't seem to be any regular guard patrols. Just two men who stood outside the slave quarters, and those stationed at the head of the mineshaft.

Of course, the slaves were usually far too tired to do anything that might upset their captors in the first place...

A plan was starting to take shape in his mind, but he still had quite a few details to work out. He had realized not long after he'd first arrived that it would be relatively easy to overpower the guards watching the mine if their slave implants were out of commission. While armed, they were vastly outnumbered. Their communication equipment was poorly maintained. Failures had become commonplace, and no one gave it any thought if they fell out of touch with each other. If he and the other slaves could jump the guards one by one, no one would notice their absence for an hour or more.

But once they got rid of the guards, they faced a whole new set of challenges. There were only two ways out of the mine. One was with the ore, which ran on a large conveyor up and out to the transport ship, where it was loaded and taken to the processing plant. Unfortunately for the slaves, the conveyor ran through the same area that housed much of the equipment used to produce a protective force shield over the settlement. It kept them from being destroyed by other asteroids. But the base equipment also produced a disruptive electro-magnetic field that would kill any human who came too close to it. The entire system had to be powered down before it could be serviced. There was no way they'd be able to get out that way. Of course, if they could disable it somehow... So far, he hadn't been able to come up with a way to do that.

But their other option, the main doorway, was a great deal more promising. It was locked from the outside, and guarded by two men. The tunnel was narrow, designed so those two men could defend it easily against a large group of escaping slaves.

Assuming those men were paying attention to their duties.

But every time Bethany went to the doorway and knocked to be let out of the slave quarters, he noticed that they took several minutes to respond. What were they doing? He suspected they abandoned their post regularly. After all, it had to be incredibly boring to simply stand guard at the end of a narrow tunnel day in and day out. That boredom could make all the difference for the slaves as they tried to escape.

Yes, there were possibilities all right. It wasn't time to give up and die just yet...

* * * * *

Fifth cycle after the mine collapse

"Can I have some water?" Jess whispered as she came into the storage area at the beginning of the next work cycle.

She gasped, and dropped the bucket she carried.

He was awake.

She realized Bragan was sitting up next to him, smiling.

"Look who woke up during the night," Bragan said, waving an arm toward Jess. "I'm out of water, though. He needs more and I have to get ready for work. Can you help him?"

"Of course," she said, eyes lighting up.

The sudden relief was incredible. She felt light, almost giddy, so excited that she could hardly think. He was awake, and he was going to live.

She was going to live, too. Until that moment, she hadn't quite realized just how much she wanted to.

"Water," he whispered again. She laughed, and pulled herself together.

"Of course," she said. "I'll be right back with water for you."

She turned and hurried out to the main room. He would have to drink water out of the sink. Foul stuff, compared to the filtered drinking water they drank in the main compound. She'd always assumed the slaves got filtered water, too, but if that was the case, she didn't know where it came from. All she'd been able to find was water straight from the recycler, the kind she only used to clean at home...

None of that mattered. He was alive.

But he wouldn't be for long if she didn't get some fluids into him. He must be terribly dehydrated. Not to mention hungry. With that thought, she realized she was already running late with breakfast for the slaves. And if she were late, they would be late to start their work for the day. Perhaps more likely, they might end up having to work without food. That was no good.

Moving quickly, she brought him the water. He leaned up feebly on one arm, but wasn't able to take the cup himself.

"I'm sorry, but I'll have to help you with this in a few minutes," she said. "Otherwise no one will get their food. I'll be back soon."

With that, she darted back out of the room and headed toward the entrance.

She had to get going with those carts.

* * * * *

He had made a tactical error, Jess thought. He'd wanted her to help him drink the water. It would maintain the fiction that he was still desperately ill. More importantly, she would be forced to touch him.

He wanted her to touch him very much…

He had listened to her, watched her movements as much as possible, all day yesterday. Her smell hung in the air around him. Her skin was pale, very white. It looked creamy and clean. He wanted to know if it tasted as good as he thought it might.

He liked her voice, too. It was soft, and she liked to sing little songs as she cleaned. They sounded sad to him, and he wondered what her life was like. Was her husband good to her? A wave of resentment washed over him. He didn't want to think about her husband. If she had one, it was likely he'd be killed during their escape attempt. For a brief moment he hoped he might be the one to kill him. Hardly the way to win her affections, he thought wryly.

He could hear her coming back. First there was the screech of the outer door opening, and then there was the rattling noise the food cart made as she pushed it. A moment of silence, and the door screeched again. She would make the same trip three times, bring enough food for a hundred men. And the guards wouldn't lift a finger to help her — they never helped the women.

Finally she came for the third time. This time, there were others with her. They joked and laughed among themselves. Noises in the outer room grew louder, and Jess realized the night shift — the blasters — must be passing through, finished with their work. Blasting had ended quite a while back, though. Why had it taken them so long to come up from the mine? He had no idea if this was the normal schedule. The slaves were never allowed out until after the blasters were gone, and the entire complex was locked tight.

The noise died down, and then a new noise began. The main door to the slave barracks was opened, and suddenly the bustle of a hundred men preparing themselves for a day of work flooded the air. The barracks were fully soundproofed, he realized. Interesting…

The door opened suddenly. He barely managed to drop his head in time, and for one minute he thought she'd caught him sitting up.

"You're safe, it's just me," Bragan said. "I've come to check on you. She's very excited that you're awake, you know...and concerned," he added with a laugh. "She wanted to make sure that I helped you with any 'personal' needs you might have before I leave for the mine."

Jess looked at him, startled. Then a sly grin stole across his face.

"I hadn't thought about that," he said slowly. "This is going to be even better than I thought."

"She's a sweet little thing," he said. "I have to admit, I like her. I don't want you hurting her..."

"I don't plan on hurting her," Jess said. "But remember, she's one of them. And they're the reason we're here. Don't be getting too soft on her just because she's a woman. If we're going to escape this place, people are going to get hurt. Some of them may be women, you know."

"I know," Bragan said. "And I understand what you're saying. I want to get out of here, too. But we're a long way from any kind of successful escape attempt. And remember, you're the only one who doesn't have an implant. We still need to figure out how we're going to be dealing with those, too...Logan wants me to do the surgery. I can't do anything without some kind of pain killer, and she insists she can't get any."

"I have great faith in your abilities, Bragan," Jess said. "You managed to get it out of me without killing me. I'm sure you'll be able to do the same for the others when the time comes."

"And suppose we pull this all off," Bragan said. "What am I supposed to do? There's no one to remove my implant."

Jess stared hard at him.

"We'll find a way to get you out too," he said. Then he grinned. "Look on the bright side. We probably won't survive the escape attempt. Don't borrow trouble, Bragan."

The doctor snorted, then looked to the door.

"I need to get going," he said. "How are you feeling?"

"Pretty good, all things considered," Jess said. "My head still aches, and I don't have all my strength yet. But I'm doing considerably better than you'd think"

"Well, try and pretend you're in terrible pain today. I want her to be worried about you, so worried that she'll risk stealing those pain meds," Bragan said. "Before I go, do you want me to help you with your 'personal needs'?" he asked, grinning. Jess glared at him in response.

"I'm fine, thanks," he said. "I'll take care of myself."

"Just don't let her catch you doing it."

"I know what I'm doing," he replied. "You let me and Logan worry about the escape. You think about the best way to remove the implants."

"I hope you know what you're doing," Bragan replied, his tone turning serious. "Otherwise we're all going to die here."

"We're going to die here anyway," Jess said quietly. "I don't know about you, but I'd rather die fighting."

* * * * *

The slaves had eaten and were starting to put on their suits by the time she was able to get back to Jess. He looked so pale and weak…At least the bandage on the back of his head had stopped oozing. Bragan said he would need to continue using the antibiotics for the next two weeks.

"How are you?" she asked softly as she came into the room.

"My mouth is dry," he whispered. "I can't drink by myself."

"Didn't Bragan come in to see you?" she asked. "I thought I saw him in here."

"Yes, he did," Jess replied. "But I'm thirsty again. Can you help me?"

"Of course," she said, kneeling next to him. Her breath caught, and she blushed. He was still naked under the covers and she was going to have to touch him. Not that she hadn't touched him before, but this time he was awake and alert. It was totally different.

"Can you raise your head at all?" she asked.

"No," he said, his voice thready. "My neck feels so weak. And it hurts. Bragan says I nearly died."

"Yes, you did," she replied. "It was horrible when they brought you up from the mine. I was sure you were dead."

"Can you lift my head a bit so I can drink?" he asked, his eyes meeting hers. They were dark blue. Her breathing stopped. He was so handsome, better to look at than any man she'd ever met before. Without thinking, she raised her hand and pushed his black hair away from his eyes. He gave a feeble smile, and she smiled back. Even the scruff of hair along his chin was mesmerizing.

"Water?" he whispered again. She started in surprise. She'd forgotten all about the water.

"Sorry," she replied, feeling a hot blush start up her cheeks. For some reason she just didn't seem to think very well around this man.

Now, how to do this? She was going to have to raise him, and support his head somehow with her arm. Otherwise the water would just choke him.

"Bragan tells me you don't have any paralysis. You're lucky," she said, leaning over him. He nodded, closing his eyes in exhaustion. Moving carefully, she rolled him to one side and slid her arm under his back. She lifted a bit, allowing his head to rest against her shoulder. It worked and he would be able to drink now. But his cheek was pressed squarely against her breast…

She grabbed the water with her other hand, roughly sloshing some of it onto the floor. He didn't seem to notice, she realized with relief. Instead, he drank deeply as she held the cup to his mouth, lifting his head slightly as he did so.

Even though the cloth of her dress separated his body from hers, it felt as if a red-hot brand were touching her chest. She knew she must be blushing brightly. Fortunately, he didn't seem to be noticing. He was focused on the water.

Then his head sank back against her softness. She started to lower him, but he spoke.

"No, I want more water," he said. "But even this is very tiring, and I'm in a lot of pain. Can I just rest for a moment?"

"Of course," she said, feeling guilty. She'd been so eager to get away from his touch that she hadn't even thought of his needs. Some nurse she was turning out to be.

They sat there like that for at least five minutes. At first she was tense, but he seemed to be completely unaware of the inappropriateness of their position. *He might be naked*, she reminded herself, *but only because he's so sick*. She must be some kind of pervert for reacting so strongly to his body. *Why, he could be no more interested in her than a newborn baby was interested in its mother,* she told herself. He needed food, water and care. She would provide it for him. If she did a good enough job, they would both survive this ordeal.

He was breathing slowly and steadily against her breast. Was he asleep? It seemed strange that he would drop off so quickly, and while he was thirsty. On the other hand, he did have a serious head injury, she reminded herself. Probably maintaining consciousness even briefly was difficult for him. She looked down at him with interest. He certainly seemed to be asleep.

She should really lay him down and get back to work.

But his breath against her breast was warm. Not warm, hot. She could feel his heat penetrating her clothing each time he exhaled. Her nipples hardened in response and she felt a tingle of sensation start right at the tip. Giving in to temptation, she closed her own eyes and leaned back against a storage unit, still holding him cradled against her body.

She told herself she was just taking care of him. She knew she was lying. Each breath sent a new tingle of sensation winding through her. They started at the peak of each breast, then shimmered down through her stomach toward that secret spot between her legs. Oh, it was wrong. He was sick and he wasn't even conscious. But just holding him was so good she couldn't make herself stop.

Feeling very daring, she raised her free hand and touched a strand of his hair. It was soft, and would hang around his shoulders when he was upright. Of course, she knew that from before. But somehow seeing it so close was different. Each strand was like silk. Bragan must have been helping him keep it clean somehow, she realized. She rubbed the lock of hair between her fingers. It was thick…what would it feel like to stick her fingers into it? She shivered.

He gave a little moan in his sleep. Guilt washed over her.

The poor man was probably in pain. His neck was injured. There was a terrible wound on the back of it. What kind of sick person would hold him this way and hurt him more?

Moving carefully, she lowered him to the pallet. He was difficult to maneuver, and at one point she accidentally pressed both breasts against his face. He moaned again. Such suffering… She felt so bad for him. Perhaps she *could* find a way to steal some painkillers like Bragan had suggested. They were locked up, but still, she owed it to him after the way she'd hurt him.

Leaving the cup of water next to him, she stood and brushed herself off.

She had work to do. And when she finished, she was going to find him some painkillers. It was the least she could do, under the circumstances.

* * * * *

Jess gave a moan of relief when she closed the door behind her. Touching her was heaven and damnation all at once. The softness of her breasts against his cheek was the most wonderful thing he'd felt since he'd come to this hellhole. And when she'd almost dropped him she'd crushed his face against both of her breasts. It had taken everything he had in his body to keep from reaching his arms around her, pulling her down to him.

Of course, his neck still hurt. He was weak. But he wasn't dead.

She was incredibly naive. She had no idea the effect her touch had on his body. No one could have missed an erection the size of his under the blanket, yet she had been oblivious. It was a good sign. She may not be a virgin, but she wasn't used to a man's body. That meant she probably wasn't married. It had been a long time since she had had sex, if ever.

One less person for him to kill, he thought darkly.

Because if she did have a husband, he would kill him. Of course, if their escape plan worked he'd have to kill a lot of the Pilgrims. This was about survival. But killing Bethany's husband would have been more.

He reached down under the blanket, feeling his rock-hard cock. He was swollen, close to exploding. It was a mixture of exquisite pain and terrifying pleasure to be near her. Hopefully she would be checking on him regularly during the day, he thought with a grin. He had a feeling he would be very thirsty, and he would need a lot of help with his slow recovery. A part of him—the part that used to be human rather than a disposable life on a mining station—reminded him that he probably shouldn't manipulate her like this.

Fortunately, that part of him was no longer in charge. She was all his, whether she knew it or not.

Chapter Four

⋅⋅∽⋅⋅

Stealing the painkillers was much easier than she'd thought it would be. Just as she was waking the next cycle, her father came home drunk. Within seconds, he was bellowing at her to find "something to make his damn head stop hurting." She had her excuse.

There were a few pain tabs in fresher, but she quickly pocketed them and went out into the living area. Careful to keep her eyes downcast, she folded her hands before her and waited for permission to speak.

"Where the hell are my pain tabs?" Bose demanded.

"You used them all last cycle," she said quietly.

"You're lying," he said, words slurring together. "I would have remembered to get more. I never forget them. There were two left."

"I'm sorry, Father," she replied quietly. Her heart raced. If she got caught in her lie, she was done for. But she owed it to Jess to help him… "But you called me late last cycle and had me bring you the rest of them. I believe you had more to drink."

Bose wrinkled his forehead. She knew from experience that he had occasional blackouts.

"Oh, I remember now," he said expansively, and she gave a sigh of relief. He was too proud to admit he might have blacked out. How much of his life was he missing, she wondered? He drank every night. What else could she get away with?

"But that's no excuse for not having pain tabs when I need them," he said, his voice growing angry.

"Father, I am not authorized to get pain tabs from the medical storage area," she replied quietly. "I want only to serve you, but I can't get you the medicine unless you give me that authority."

He glared at her.

"I'll take care of it," he finally said, his voice tight. "You go to the infirmary and get the damn drugs. I'll call ahead and let them know you're coming."

"I believe they're closed for the cycle," she added in a soft voice. He threw his glass at her, grunting in disgust. She ducked, and the clear liquid splattered against the wall behind her. It had been a mistake to provoke him, but failing to bring back his pain tabs would be a bigger mistake.

"I'll call the medic in his rooms," Bose said. "Now get my pain tabs, and then clean up this damn mess."

"Yes, sir," she said, making for the door. She had to hide a smile. The first part of her plan was working out just fine.

Most of the corridors were deserted as she made her way to the infirmary. The only people still awake were the women who prepared food for the returning blasters. They also prepared the gruel for the slaves. Bethany knew the tasteless mixture that formed their entire diet was nutritious. But it was also disgusting. Until she had started caring for the slaves on a regular basis, she hadn't realized how good her life was, she mused. They certainly had a more difficult time of it than she did.

Garand, the station's medic, didn't look happy to see her when she arrived. He paced nervously outside the infirmary door, pausing only to glare at her.

"You shouldn't have let your father run out of pain tabs," he said tightly. "He's a dangerous man when he's angry."

"I realize that," she said dryly. "But if I had come to you before now, would you have given me pain meds? I was under the impression that all narcotics are restricted."

"Well, they are," he acknowledged. "But in your case I would have made an exception. We both know your father goes through a lot of them. From now on you can come here and get what you need. I'll key your thumbprint to the lock. I can't afford to have your father angry at me again."

Bethany stared at him, shocked. Without thinking, she blurted out a question.

"What did he say to you?"

"He threatened to have me put outside the airlock," Garand said, hands trembling. "He said he'd do it without taking me to the council first. I believe him too."

"I didn't realize that," she said slowly, mind spinning. Bose's actions were completely out of line, even for an elder. "I can't believe he'd do that. It would be crazy. It could cost him his seat on the council."

"Do you really think he's still sane?" Garand asked, his voice bitter. "I don't."

"I can't believe you just said that," she replied. "If Bose heard that he'd…"

"What? He'd go crazy?" Garand gave a harsh bark of laughter. "Too late. Beside that, you're the only one who's heard me say it. It would be my word against yours. Bose hates you and the entire station knows it. I don't have anything to fear from you. You'd better keep him happy or you'll be the first to go."

With that, he thrust a bottle of pills into her hand. She backed out of the infirmary, shivering. Garand hated her father, and he seemed to hate her, too. How many others here shared that malevolence?

Suddenly, she didn't want to know.

Turning away, she started walking quickly back toward her father's quarters. She palmed the door open, only to find her father holding Moriah in a tight embrace. She gave a little gasp of surprise, and he turned to her.

"Good, you're back," he said. He wore a broad smile, seemingly unaware of the impropriety of the situation. His features were flushed red, and he wobbled unsteadily. Moriah looked terrified, but she stood beside him, propping him up as best she could.

"I have good news for you," Bose said. "You're going to have a new mother. Moriah and I will be marrying soon."

Bethany looked at Moriah, compassion for the younger woman filling her heart. She didn't deserve this. But there was nothing she could do about it...

"Congratulations, Father," Bethany said. "I look forward to your wedding."

"Oh, you won't be there," Bose said. Her heart froze. Why wouldn't she be there? Was he planning to put her outside the airlock already? Had he changed his mind about giving her two weeks?

"You'll be sleeping," he said. "You've got work to do while the rest of us sleep. I won't have you neglecting your chores because of a wedding. Now where are my pain tabs?"

"Here they are, Father," she said, quickly taking two out of the bottle. "Shall I get you something to wash them down with?"

"No, Moriah will do that," Bose said. He wavered, then stumbled over to his chair. Collapsing in it, he leaned his head back and closed his eyes. "Moriah will be taking care of me from now on. You'll stay here for now. Until I find a better place for you. Now get to work."

Shivering, Bethany handed Moriah the two tabs and then quietly opened the door to leave. Moriah clutched her hand, and leaned over to whisper, "Please don't tell anyone I'm here. You know what will happen if they find out."

"I won't tell," Bethany said, squeezing the younger woman's hand. "Don't worry about me. Worry about him."

"I do," Moriah said, a tear welling up in her eye. "I worry about him all the time."

There was nothing Bethany could say in response. Moriah would have to find her own way through this.

* * * * *

Sixth cycle after the mine collapse

Jess had just about figured out the routine. Bethany would arrive each cycle as the blasters were coming up from the mine. She would check on him briefly and then go to get the food.

By the time she came back with the second cart the guards would have arrived. They sounded the wake-up, and the men would hurry to get out of bed and get ready. Then she would arrive with the third cart and they would eat.

Fifteen minutes later the men spilled out of the barracks and suited up. They would go down into the mine for the day's work and stay there for the next fourteen hours.

The most valuable piece of information he had gleaned was that even as the slaves were working, the majority of the Pilgrims slept. And there were very few guards at the mine. He'd always assumed that the entire contingent was there throughout the cycle. But within minutes of the last slave entering the mine, all but two of the guards left. Halfway through the slaves' work cycle the guards were relieved by two new men. Other than that, the compound was left empty.

Empty except for him and Bethany.

It was perfect for his plans.

She popped her head in to check on him even before the blasters came up. He heard her coming, and pretended to sleep. She was more likely to touch him if she thought he was unconscious. When he was awake she seemed nervous. If he had been less honest with himself, he could have rationalized pretending to sleep by saying it was so he could spy on her. But he was more than willing to admit his real purpose. He wanted her to touch him. He wanted to smell her scent, to feel her soft warm flesh against his. When she'd given him the water the night before, it had been like touching heaven. He wanted more of that heaven.

He could hear the faint swish of her skirts as she approached his pallet. Her breathing was light, as if she were afraid to disturb him even in so small a way. Then she was kneeling next to him, and her cool fingers were touching his forehead.

It was all he could do to keep from moaning aloud.

Instead, he fluttered his lashes and looked up at her sleepily. Her green eyes blinked, and a soft smile stole across her face.

"How are you today?" she asked, her voice a smooth purr in his ears. As always in her presence, he hardened. How much more of this torture could he take? He didn't care how difficult it was. He wanted to listen to her talk forever.

"I'm all right," he whispered, voice raspy. "Can you help me with some water? I'd really like something to eat, too, if you've got it."

"I'll help you with the water," she said. "But we'll have to wait for Bragan to make sure it's all right for you to eat. I don't want to do anything that might hurt you."

"You could never hurt me," he said without thinking. She blushed, then looked away from him. She was like a beautiful flower he'd once seen, grown hydroponically in a station greenhouse. Shy and flushed, almost afraid to look straight at him. So lovely…

"I have good news for you," she said. "I managed to get some pain pills. Once Bragan says it's all right you'll be able to take some for your neck. I'm sure that will help."

"I'm sure it will, too," he replied.

"I need to get more water, I'll be right back."

She stood and left the small room. He closed his eyes and breathed deeply. Her smell was still in the room. Soon she would be touching him again. If there was one thing he'd learned during his time in the mines, it was to take each moment and savor it.

Being with her was definitely worth savoring.

She came back after a second with the water and knelt beside him again. Then she was lifting him in her arms again, cradling his head against her breast just as she had the night before. It was wonderful, even better than he remembered.

This time he sipped slowly at the water she held to his lips. The longer it took him to drink, the longer it would be before she left. At least that was the theory. Unfortunately they were interrupted all too soon by the sounds of the blasters returning from work. She gave a startled little gasp, then lowered him quickly to his pallet. Of course, there was one good thing about her self-consciousness, he told himself. She was clearly as aware of him as he was of her. He liked that idea.

"I have to go and get the food," she said, standing. "Bragan will be in to check on you soon. We'll find out about the food and the painkillers then. I'll be back."

With that she was gone, scurrying off to get the carts.

He listened quietly as she brought each cart. Then the noise level rose as the men came out to suit up. The door opened, and Bragan stepped in.

"We've only got a minute or so, she's coming back," Bragan said. "I have good news. She had no idea how much pain medication you might need, so she's brought ten tabs. She says she can get more if we need them."

"Will that be enough?" Jess asked.

"It will be enough for five men," Bragan said. "You'll have to convince her you're in more pain so she'll keep giving them to us."

"When are you going to start removing the implants?" Jess asked.

"I'm doing Logan's today," Bragan said. "It's the most risky, because I'll have to do it in the mine in a pressure tent. We've decided we can't risk doing this first one in the barracks.

Once Logan's done, he can stand guard while I do the others during the sleep cycle. We don't know if this will work. If he doesn't recover enough in one cycle to keep working, they'll get suspicious"

"What if he doesn't recover?" Jess asked.

"Then he'll have a mining accident," Bragan said grimly. "I'm not willing to sacrifice myself for your plot. You know that already."

"Does Logan know?"

"Yes, he knows," Bragan answered. "And he's willing to take the chance. Remember, his wound won't be as serious as yours. Of course, taking out the implant may paralyze him completely, but I've been able to study yours. It wasn't as hard to remove as you'd think. I guess someone was feeling cheap when they ordered supplies."

Bragan started to say more, but he was cut off as Bethany entered the room.

"How is he doing, Bragan?" she asked quietly.

"He's doing all right, but I'm a little concerned," Bragan said, his face serious. "I've looked under his bandage and the flesh around the wound appears to be a little red and flushed. There's a bit of infection there. We'll have to keep a close eye on him."

"I think I can do that," she said slowly.

"How about the pain meds?" Jess whispered weakly. "Will I be able to take those, Bragan?"

"Yes, you will," Bragan said. He turned to Bethany. "I want you to give him one every two hours. Preferably with food. Will that be a problem?"

"No," she said, looking surprised. "But isn't that an awful lot of pain medication? I've seen my father take two before, but they knock him out for hours at a time."

Bragan looked serious.

"The type of infection he's developing can be very serious," he replied. "And very painful. If he isn't given the meds he may hurt himself as it grows worse."

"Should I be crushing them and putting them in his food?" she asked quietly. "It might make it easier for him."

"No," Bragan said quickly. He exchanged a quick glance with Jess. "No, in fact you should let him take the pills himself. It will help him moderate his consumption of them. We don't want him to become addicted."

She frowned.

"Bragan, I don't want to seem difficult, but that doesn't make any sense to me. He can't even drink by himself, how will he take the pill?"

"You can place it in his hand and help him lift it to his mouth," Bragan said quickly.

"How does that keep him from getting addicted?" she asked skeptically. Bragan snorted, and stood up abruptly. His face grew cold.

"Are you an Imperially-trained physician?"

"No," she said quickly.

"Do you have any medical training at all?"

"No," she whispered. Jess bit his lip, trying not to laugh. Bragan was bluffing so hard it was almost pitiable.

"Well, then I suggest you don't question my methods," Bragan said coldly. "I saved this man's life and I'm keeping him alive now. I performed surgery on him in a pressurized tent, for love of the Goddess. How can I possibly be expected to explain years of training and theory on addiction to you? You don't even have the vocabulary to understand the scientific reasons he needs to be taking his own medication. Give me one of them right now and I'll show you how to do it. No, give me two. He's suffered all the past cycle. This will help get the pain under control."

She gulped, then nodded. Bragan took the tabs from her and knelt beside Jess.

"Place them in his hand like this," Bragan said, pretending to give Jess the pills. Jess played along, clutching his fingers around the imaginary drugs. As Bragan lifted his head, Jess winced. Somehow being helped by the doctor wasn't the same as being helped by Bethany. It would be nice to take one of those pain pills, although he wouldn't dream of doing it. If they were going to escape, they'd need every one of them.

"Then raise his hand to his mouth," Bragan continued. "This allows him to have control over the medication, to make a choice about taking it."

Jess obligingly pretended to drop the pills into his mouth. Next time he'd have to find a way to hide them in his hand during this…perhaps between his fingers? That might work.

"Now lift the water and let him wash it down," Bragan said in a condescending tone. "Can you do that, or is it too complex for you?"

"Yes, of course," she said, her voice tight. "I'm perfectly capable of helping him do that."

She sounded upset, and to his surprise he felt compassion for her. Ruthlessly he pushed the feeling aside, forcing his heart to grow cold. He couldn't afford to have warm feelings toward any Pilgrim.

"You see," Bragan said, lowering Jess' head. "It's relatively straightforward. I'm sure you can handle this. Remember, two pills every hour."

"I'll remember," she said, her voice soft. She stood and left the room quickly. Bragan shook his head.

"I feel so bad for treating her like this."

"Don't," Jess said. "She's one of them. She may be beautiful and she may be kind, but her people are the reason we're working ourselves to death here. I don't want to hurt her any more than you do, but I won't let compassion for her stop me from getting out of here. I would advise you to do the same."

"You're right," Bragan answered. "She is one of them. I just wish that she wasn't."

"So do I," Jess replied softly. "So do I."

* * * * *

It was a long day for Bethany. She helped Jess drink and take his medications. She fed him several times, always cradling his head against her body and feeding him herself. The cold porridge seemed disgusting to her, but he was happy enough to eat it. Of course it was slow going for him. Each session took at least twenty minutes, all of it spent with him lying against her breasts. She was so embarrassed. Every time he touched her it seemed as if her heartbeat grew fast and fluttery. Her nipples responded to each movement he made. She was terrified that he would notice the two tight nubs under her clothing. Thankfully, he seemed completely unaware of her discomfort. It was one small blessing.

By the time the day ended she was exhausted. Between trying to get all her chores done and caring for Jess, she'd barely had time to run to the infirmary and get more pain meds. He was getting sicker over the course of the day. She could see it in the confusion on his face, the way he turned to her without recognition. Several times he spoke, rambling and saying things she couldn't understand. At one point he started thrashing about, and she'd been forced to throw herself over his body, pressing him to the pallet with all her weight. He'd settled down after that, at least for a while, although he grew worse whenever she tried to leave him. Finally she simply gave up and snuggled down with him in the pallet.

The strange thing was that he didn't feel particularly warm or feverish to her. But then again, she wasn't a doctor, she reminded herself. Bragan knew what he was talking about. It wasn't her place to question.

Part II

The Revolt

Chapter Five

80

Jess was growing restless. It was so hard to keep up his pretense of being an invalid. Ten cycles had passed since his accident and the men were nearly ready for their revolt. He could tell that if they didn't move soon they'd have problems. Bose had been in to check on him once already. Something about the man's manner, standing over him in utter silence as his hands twitched uncontrollably, made Jess even more nervous than he'd been before. He wasn't sure the station leader would give him the full two weeks.

Bethany wasn't making things any easier for him. Initially she had been so attentive. Something he'd done changed that. He suspected she'd seen him hiding one of the pain tabs. Now she watched him like a hawk, and their supply of painkillers had stopped. She might not know what was up, but she certainly no longer trusted Jess and Bragan. That was clear enough. She wasn't willing to touch him any more. Jess missed those touches more than he cared to admit. It had been so wonderful to feel her against his skin. From the gentle sensation of her fingers against his cheek to the softness of her breast against his head, everything about her mesmerized him. Watching her every day without once being able to touch her was unbearable.

Even more unbearable was the fact that he couldn't do anything to counteract her newfound caution. If he pinned her against a wall, took her in the storeroom, she would know he was much stronger than he pretended to be. The game would be over.

Still, he burned for her. He pretended he was tired of staying in the close confines of the storage room, told her he needed to get out and move a bit. Every morning she watched with hooded eyes while he slowly and painfully walked out into the main room, settling on a pallet he made from his blankets. She never offered to help him, although she took care to make sure he had water at all times.

Fortunately, she didn't seem to mind leaving him alone in the room as she ran her errands. Whatever she was afraid of, it never occurred to her that he might steal her supplies, he thought grimly. He now had a wickedly sharp pair of scissors in his possession, as well as a small knife. They might be small but he figured they would be more than enough to slit a man's throat. All he had to do was kill the two guards at the head of the mineshaft. Then he could free Logan and the twenty-eight other men who had volunteered to have their implants removed…

He closed his eyes in sadness for a moment. There were supposed to be thirty men. Two had died under Bragan's knife. Officially, the Pilgrims believed they'd been killed in mining accidents. Everything was ready and it was time to make their move. One more cycle and he would creep softly down the tunnel toward the guards. He would slit their throats slowly and deliberately, then send the elevator down for Logan and the men. Timing was everything. He had to move right after the guards changed shifts, mid-cycle. This meant the men he had to kill would be relatively fresh, which concerned him. But the added benefits of striking while the entire station slept and no change of guard was expected seemed worth the risk. He and Logan had gone over the escape a hundred times over the past few cycles, while he was ostensibly "showering" in the slave barracks with Bragan's help.

Their plans were clear.

Bethany was the key to those plans. He would take her hostage, then they'd use her to trick the guards into opening the locked door to the mining complex. He didn't like the idea, of course. She would be in some danger right at the beginning. But they were at war and she was his enemy's daughter. After the next cycle he would never be a slave again. She was a necessary part of that. It was too late for regrets.

She came into the room with the first of the food carts, interrupting his thoughts. He nodded at her. It still amazed him that they would leave her alone with him for hours at a time, no sign of a guard. Just one more example that she was of little value to her people. He thought of his sister Calla, and his heart ached. No matter what she did, whatever personal failings she might have, he would never have treated her the way Bethany's family treated her.

It simply wasn't right.

"How are you feeling?" she asked him courteously. She used her foot to kick down the cart's brake and walked over to the counter.

He already knew what she was doing—she was getting him his bowl of gruel before it got cold. Why she did it he had no idea. His company seemed to make her nervous. For all she knew his very existence could cost her life. Yet she still took the time to bring him his food before it had time to cool.

"Enjoy your dinner," she said, giving him a brief smile. "I have to go and get the other carts."

"Thank you," he said politely, reaching out to take the bowl from her. He deliberately stretched his fingers so he could touch her hand. That spark of awareness leapt between them, and he tried to capture her gaze with his. He loved looking deep into those cat eyes. Too bad she was afraid to meet his stare.

"I have to go," she said, her voice cracking.

Jess smiled. She could pretend all she wanted but there was no way she could deny their attraction. She wanted him just as much as he wanted her. Once the revolt was over and the station belonged to the slaves, he was going to make her admit it.

* * * * *

Bethany put both hands against the small of her back, enjoying the way it stretched her aching spine. The carts were so heavy… at least she was done with them for now. The men were locked in their barracks. Soon the blasting crews would enter the mine, and she should get some sleep.

But even as she walked toward her father's apartment, she couldn't stop thinking about Jess. It was getting harder and harder to ignore him. She'd realized fairly early on, within the first few days of his waking up, that he was taking advantage of her.

And to think she'd felt so dirty and wicked for having thoughts about him. After all, he was an injured man who relied on her for his very survival. That was until he'd shifted position as she was feeding him, pressing his erection against her rather blatantly. Suddenly she had realized the attraction wasn't one sided. It hadn't taken long after that to understand he was milking her for all she was worth. Every time she helped him, he was doing his best to feel her up. Worse, he was hoarding his pain pills. She had to put a stop to it or he might end up addicted. This kind of complication was the last thing she needed in her life.

Of course, she understood he was still very sick. Privately she wondered if he would be able to return to the mine in time to meet their deadline. They'd only discussed it once and he had told her not to worry. He would make it somehow.

The words haven't been reassuring enough for her.

At least he was tucked in for the cycle, and it was time for her to go home and rest. All the slaves were fed and locked in the barracks. Jess and Bragan were secured in the storeroom. Everything was clean and ready for the next work cycle. She sighed, enjoying the fact that she had eight blessed hours to rest and be alone. Her father probably wasn't even out of bed yet.

She made her way through the quiet station. The only signs of life were a few of the younger women who had helped prepare dinner for the slaves. Now they were hard at work on breakfast for the rest of the station. Fortunately, Bethany had managed to scavenge some bread earlier so she wouldn't have to waste precious sleep time waiting for the food to be readied.

She arrived at her father's apartment, amused as always to see the small surveillance camera above the door. It swept slowly back and forth, recording everything in a continuous loop, all cycle every cycle. It was relatively new and with his elevation to the head of the council he'd become convinced that he needed such security.

Bethany considered him utterly paranoid. Of course, her opinion didn't really count, she thought wryly. Pompous ass.

She placed her hand on the palm plate and the door slid open silently. She crept into the apartment as quietly as she could. She knew from experience that waking him wasn't a very good idea. She moved quickly to the fresher, but to her surprise the door wouldn't open. It seemed to be jammed, and there was a tangy, almost metallic smell in the air. What was going on?

"Is there someone in there?" she asked, keeping her voice low. If he was still asleep she didn't want to risk waking him.

"Bethany, is that you?" Moriah's voice came though the door. For a moment Bethany didn't recognize it, the sound was hoarse and painful.

"Moriah?" she asked. "It's me, Bethany. Open the door. What's wrong?"

The door slid open and Bethany sucked her breath in. Moriah stood shakily in the center of the small room. She was naked, her pale body streaked with blood. Around her neck were fresh bruises and her eyes looked dead.

"Moriah, what happened?" Bethany asked in a shocked whisper.

"I think I killed your father," Moriah said, her voice harsh and painful. Bethany's mouth dropped.

"What do you mean?"

"He was strangling me," Moriah said. Her gaze fixed on a point somewhere over Bethany's shoulder. "I thought I was going to die. He was drunk and saying crazy things. He was going to kill me," she added. "I could hardly breathe. My arms were flailing around and then I felt something…"

"What was it?"

"It was the lamp," she said tonelessly. "You know, the one in his bedroom? Made out of plast-crete? I grabbed it and hit him over the head."

"Are you sure he's dead?" Bethany asked, filled with dread. "If you just injured him, he might not remember what happened. We could tell him he had an accident."

"No, I'm pretty sure he's dead," Moriah said, her tone flat. "I didn't stop hitting him until I could see parts of his brain. I splattered them."

Bethany gasped and swayed. She grabbed the door for support.

"I suppose you're going to turn me in now." Moriah said softly. "Will you let me shower first, and get dressed? I don't want them taking me away while I'm still naked."

Bethany nodded her head, stunned.

"Um, yes, you can shower," she said. "But we have to figure out what to do."

"What's there to figure out?"

"How we're going to get rid of the body. And explain his absence. I have to admit, I don't have any ideas right off."

"You aren't going to turn me in?" Moriah asked, voice hollow. The woman was in complete shock. She didn't have a clue what she was saying.

"No, I'm not," Bethany said. "It's obvious that you did it self-defense. I know what Bose is like. You aren't the first woman he's abused, and he's certainly threatened my life more than once," she added with a bitter laugh.

"There's no way you'd get a fair hearing, though," she continued. "And in all honesty, there's no reason they wouldn't blame me for what happened. With Bose gone I won't even have anyone to live with. I wouldn't be surprised if they punished me instead of you," she mused. "Makes a certain amount of sick sense. If they blame me, they get to punish someone who doesn't have any value to the community. They won't want to kill you. You can still have children."

"So what do we do?" Moriah asked. "People are going to be looking for him today. There's a body in the bedroom. What should we do?"

"Well, first you need to get cleaned up," Bethany replied. "I need you to go home to your baby. I'll tell everyone that Bose is sick—that will buy us some time. Then we'll think of what to do next. Maybe we can rig some kind of accident?" she muttered, thinking out loud. "If his body's destroyed in it, they won't know when he died. He's been drinking a lot lately, more than usual. They might blame the *bakrah* for the accident."

"What kind of accident could you rig?" Moriah asked. "How are you going to pull that off?"

"I have no idea," Bethany said grimly. "If you have any suggestions I'd love to hear them."

* * * * *

It took her hours to clean up the bedroom. It was the most horrible, disgusting thing she'd ever had to do in her life. She wrapped his body in some blankets and managed to shove it into one corner, then attacked the blood in the floor and walls. She'd sent Moriah home as soon as she had showered. It wouldn't do either of them any good if she were caught leaving the apartment.

To her surprise, the lamp itself cleaned up easily enough. The plast-crete was strong, far stronger than her father's head had been. She examined her feelings as she cleaned, looking for grief. Her father was dead. It was his blood staining her hands. Shouldn't she feel something?

She felt fear. Fear she would be caught, fear that Moriah's child would be left without a mother. She also felt anger. Anger at her father for bringing her to this point. Anger for the drinking, the abuse.

But no matter how deep she looked within herself, she couldn't find any grief. There was a secret exaltation in his death. He would never hurt her again, never hurt any woman.

She was glad he was dead. There was a good chance it would lead to her own end, but she didn't care. Seeing him dead was worth it, and for a brief moment she wished she had been able to do it herself.

The cycle was almost over by the time she finished cleaning. She still didn't know what she would do in the long term. She had no way to explain what had happened to him and no way to dispose of the body.

She took a long shower, washing every trace of blood from her body. Then she scrubbed her clothes out in the sink. Strange, she wasn't very tired. Must be the adrenaline…She was shaky, though. It was going to be a long cycle.

* * * * *

Jess and Bragan had been up for more than an hour by the time they heard Bethany arrive with the first food cart. Both men were tense. Today was the day. Whether they would live as free men or die as slaves would be decided in the next few hours. Logan and Jess had briefed their men the night before. Everything was ready. Now they sat, chatting anxiously and waiting to be let out for the cycle.

Usually she opened the storeroom as soon as she arrived with the first food cart. Today she didn't, and Jess looked at Bragan questioningly. Had she somehow guessed what they were going to do? Would they be greeted by guards instead of Bethany that morning?

By the time she came back with the second cart, Jess was getting restless.

"Go and knock on the door," he told Bragan. "Find out why she hasn't let us out. I'll stay here on the pallet looking sick."

Bragan nodded, and made his way over to the door. He knocked, softly at first, and then harder.

"Bethany?" he called out. "Are you there? Are you going to let us out to eat?"

A second later the door opened and Jess smothered a gasp of surprise at the sight of her. She looked horrible...Her face was drawn and white with stress. Her hands shook, and she seemed unable to look directly at either of them.

"What's the matter with you?" he asked without thinking, his voice sounding stronger than it had in weeks. She jumped, startled. Jess cursed silently and she wasn't used to hearing him talk that way.

"My father was sick during the last cycle," she said. She held her hands tightly together, as if to keep them from shaking.

It was obvious that something was very wrong.

"I didn't get much sleep," she continued.

"I see," Bragan said. "What kind of illness is it? Have you called the station medic?"

"No," she said quickly. "I think he had too much *bakrah*. I don't have time to talk about it right now. I need to get the last cart."

She turned and moved away from them quickly. Bragan and Jess exchanged glances.

"I wonder what's going on?" Bragan asked. "I doubt the station's medic could help, anyway. The man has almost no training. They're fools to trust him with their health."

"What, you haven't volunteered to help them?" Jess asked with dark humor.

"They wouldn't let me touch them," Bragan said with a laugh. "I'm good enough for my fellow slaves, but I guess they consider my techniques unclean or something. Ignorant fools."

"I suppose they get what's coming to them," Jess said.

"Does any woman really deserve to die in childbirth?" Bragan asked, some of the humor fading from his voice. "You asked how I earned my alcohol. Sometimes I *do* help them. Their fool of a medic has called me several times to try and salvage his mistakes. He usually waits too long, though. I've seen a lot of young Pilgrim girls die since I've come here."

Jess didn't reply. There was nothing he could say. Bragan's pain spoke for itself.

"After tonight you won't have to do that anymore," Jess said finally. "We'll escape or we'll die. Either way it will be over."

"Thank the Goddess for that," Bragan said. "I'm ready for it to be over."

* * * * *

It took every bit of strength Bethany had to keep moving. She had worked only half way through the cycle, but she felt exhausted. The guards had just changed shifts, and she still had no idea how she was going to get rid of her father's body, let alone what she would say about his disappearance. They wouldn't believe he was sick forever... Perhaps she could say he got drunk and decided to take one of the ships out. If she managed to launch one of the smaller transports and set it on a course to impact an asteroid, they would think it was an accident. No body, no questions. He certainly had enough of a drinking history to justify such a foolish thing.

Of course, she had no idea how to launch a transport, let alone program it to collide with an asteroid. She didn't even know that she could get to one. They were usually guarded.

She weighed her options as she worked, ignoring the curious looks Jess shot her way. Finally she realized she only had one choice. She would have to confess to killing her father. Someone was going to pay for his death, and Moriah had a child.

A sense of peace came over her. She was going to die soon, but at least she wouldn't die without a purpose. Moriah was a good girl. She loved her child, and with Bose out of the way she might even be able to make another love match.

Bethany dropped her cleaning rag, stood up in the center of the room and stretched. Jess stared at her from his pallet, obviously confused by her sudden change in demeanor. She laughed out loud, feeling happier and freer than she had in years.

"How are you feeling, Jess?" she asked, walking over to him. She knelt beside him, reaching out to touch his forehead with one hand. He looked so confused by her actions that she just had to laugh again. Life was so strange…

"Do you think you'll be able to rejoin the men after this cycle?" she asked softly. "I know you thought you'd have a couple more days, but I think time may have run out for you."

"What do you mean?" he asked.

"I mean I won't be back," she said. "Not after this cycle. You'll need to rejoin the men or you may end up joining me. And I don't think you want that to happen."

"What's going on?" he asked, sitting up abruptly. She sat back on her heels.

"I thought you might be in better shape than you were pretending," she said, appraising him carefully. "I didn't want to say anything, because I figured this was as close to a vacation as you'll ever get. I'm not stupid, I know you've been playing games. But I'm glad you're strong enough to go back to work. I don't want to see you killed, Jess."

He looked so startled, so confused, that she couldn't help but laugh again. She would really miss his company, she realized. Caring for him was one small part of her life that was pleasant. She looked forward to seeing him, although she hadn't allowed herself to trust him. Now she didn't have anything to fear.

Without pausing to think about it, she leaned forward and kissed him softly on the lips. She could feel his quick inhalation of breath. Then he groaned and his arms were winding around her. He pulled her to one side, rolling her under his body. His hips pressed urgently against her. Every part of his body was hard and ready.

She was ready for him, too.

He opened her mouth with his, plunging his tongue into her even as he pinned her body to the pallet. The floor was hard beneath the thin blankets but she didn't care. So what if she had bruises later? Later she would be dead. This was the last chance she'd ever have to feel a man's touch. And what a man. She'd ached for him for weeks. He'd ached for her, too. Once she'd realized he wanted her, she had felt that desire in his eyes. He was always watching her, his gaze intense and penetrating. Burning.

Now she would feel his penetration in other ways.

He was moving frantically against her, and she squirmed. She felt wild, like an animal. She wanted to rip off his clothes and take him. She wanted to grunt and sweat and bite him. Who was she? She'd never felt like this before, but she knew in her heart that it was right. Before she died she wanted to feel him everywhere. Especially deep inside.

Jess rucked her skirt up around her waist, tearing at her undergarment with desperate hands. She reveled in the power. This man, this slave she had nursed back to health, wanted her and he was going to take her. She shivered as the cool air hit her heated skin. This was completely different than anything she could have imagined—so urgent, so incredibly intense—as if a fire burned out of control through her body.

This was going to be good.

Acting on instinct, she lifted her legs and wrapped them around his waist. He groaned.

"Damn, I can't believe this," he muttered. Then he took her lips again.

She twisted against him, seeking something she didn't even fully understand. Everything was happening so fast. She could smell him, feel his hard muscles under her fingers. She wanted to dig her nails into him, raking them down his back and mark him as hers.

Why not?

With a laugh, she did it. He groaned, then he lifting his hips, reached down between their bodies. At first she fought him. She didn't want him to stop touching her for even a second. Then his fingers found the spot between her legs and she exploded.

It was like nothing she'd ever felt before in her entire life. One second she was twisting against him, yearning for something she couldn't explain. Everything in her body was tight and tense. Then she shattered, convulsed. He smothered her scream with his mouth the instant it hit her, wrapping himself around her like a shield. At that moment she was completely safe.

She came back to herself to find him kissing her gently. One of his fingers trailed along her cheek, then dropped along the line of her chin. Little tingles followed it and she gave a sleepy smile.

"That was incredible," she said softly. "I've never felt anything like it before."

"We've just started," he whispered. "I have other things to show you."

She closed her eyes, expecting him to kiss her again. To her surprise, he lifted himself away, scooting down her body. What was he doing?

A second later she realized. He was kissing her, but this time between her legs. It was amazing. First his lips touched her softly and she shivered as his warm breath brushed across her most sensitive spot. She'd never dreamed of anything like this, something so wonderful and exciting. Then his tongue touched her clit and she stiffened. It was soft, wet, slick. He probed the folds of her labia, then flicked his tongue back and forth across something that made her want to scream. She bit her lip, trying to stay silent. The tension was building inside her again. She wanted to stay relaxed, to continue basking in the afterglow of her pleasure, but each time his tongue flickered and stabbed, she couldn't help but twitch in response. At first the twitches felt good. Then she grew frustrated. She wanted more than that light, teasing tongue. He'd pressed her hard before and she needed something hard now, too.

"Please," she whimpered. He gave a low, throaty laugh. She felt the vibration of it through his mouth. It twisted deep down inside her.

He pulled away from her and she whimpered as if in pain. How dare he do this to her? He couldn't stop now. She was so close to…whatever it was, she was very close. It had been so incredible before. She wanted to feel those incredible explosions again, and she wanted to feel them *now.*

Still, the weight of his body as he lowered himself back over her was good. She twisted against him, enjoying the rough sensation of her clothing against her nipples. His legs were bare against hers, at least between her thighs. To her shock and delight, she realized he'd lowered his trousers. He was naked down there. He was going to come into her.

She felt the head of his penis against her wet lips. It was wide, larger than her husband's had been. For a moment she tensed. Avram had hurt her so many times…would this lovely sensation turn painful before it ended? Jess murmured something in her ear. She couldn't understand what he said, but she understood the tone. It was soft and soothing. He was stretching her now, slowly lowering himself into her body. He might be larger than Avram, but something here was very different. Avram had felt dry and painful as he pushed into her but she was wet and slick for Jess. He was stretching her, yes. But it was a smooth, delicious stretch. She could feel him inching in, and willed her muscles to relax as he penetrated her. With aching slowness he filled her. She shivered, and as she did so, she could feel her stretched muscles tightening around him within her body. He stilled, groaning.

"You are so beautiful," he whispered. "If you only knew how good that feels..."

She tightened her muscles again, reveling in the sensation of power it gave her. He gave a little gasp, his breath coming heavily.

He was all the way inside her now. His body had come to rest, cradled between her legs. He lay still for a moment, then whispered, "Look at me."

She did as he asked. There he was, midnight blue eyes gazing into hers. Oh, she liked looking at him. He was mesmerizing, every line of his face perfect. For one excruciating moment she allowed herself to wonder what it might have been like if he had been one of her people. What if their parents had arranged a marriage between them? They could have had this all the time.

She could feel tears welling up at the thought, and then she closed her eyes. She could feel moisture running down her face, little rivers of grief over what might have been. Instead, she was going to die. He would work for a few more months or years in the mine, and he would die too.

They would never see each other again after this cycle. The pain was too great.

She felt something soft and warm against her face. He was kissing the tears away. Slowly, his hips started pumping in and out of her body. Without thinking, she found herself lifting her pelvis in answer to his motions, unconsciously mimicking his movements. That tension was still inside her, and now it leapt to angry life. She wanted this, she wanted him. For the first time in her life, she understood what the restless ache she sometimes felt in her body was supposed to be for.

Mating.

Again and again their bodies met. Thrust after thrust, grinding and coming together with a power that would have seemed violent to anyone watching. But the violence felt good to her. The urgency, the tension. She wanted to pull him down into her womb, to take him prisoner and keep him there. She wanted to own him, mark him, make him *hers.*

Impossibly, he was moving faster, and that hard part of him, his penis, she thought in satisfaction, was rubbing her in a way that was almost intolerable. She tilted her hips, creating a slightly different angle, and then she exploded for the second time.

Every muscle in her body went tense. Her legs clutched him, making it all but impossible for him to move. She squeezed him so hard he gasped. At first she thought he was in pain, that she'd hurt him. Then he was convulsing over her and she could feel his seed entering her body in hot streams. Again and again he shot into her. It was so satisfying, so amazing. Such a beautiful way to say goodbye to life.

They lay there on the floor, trying to recover for several minutes. Finally she noticed how hard the floor was beneath her. She would have bruises from this, she realized. He had marked her in more ways than one, she thought with a little smile. He kissed her gently on the mouth, then lifted himself just enough to pull her skirts down. His pants were still down around his knees but he didn't seem to care.

He took each of her hands in his, then drew them to his mouth. He kissed her softly, then folded them tenderly together in his right hand. He reached up with his left hand, pushing a few stray locks of hair away from her forehead before dropping it to the blankets beneath her.

"Bethany," he said, his voice a sigh. "That was a wonderful gift. I'm so sorry I have to do this to you."

What? What was he talking about? Before she could even ask, she felt something against her throat. Something cold, metallic. Sharp.

"Don't move," he said, and cold betrayal filled her. She realized his body was completely covering hers, his right hand imprisoning both of hers with ease. She tried to squirm and felt the bite of the blade against her neck.

"I'm going to tie you up," he said without emotion. "And put you in the storage room. You'll need to stay very quiet. I don't want to hurt you, but if you try and call the guards I'll have to. Do you understand me?"

"What the hell do you think you're doing?" she asked.

"Escaping," he replied coolly.

"You're crazy," she whispered, searching his face for some sign this was a bizarre joke. "Do you realize there are at least fifty armed men on this station? They can kill you with their control wands, they don't even need their blasters!"

"Not if I kill them first," he said coldly.

"You're going to kill everyone?" she asked, blood chilling.

"No," he said. "Just those who get in my way. Don't get in my way, Bethany."

Chapter Six

ɞ

The look on Bethany's face as he closed the storage room door burned him. She looked so scared, so confused.

He shouldn't have fucked her before betraying her.

But she had been willing and he'd dreamt of doing it for so long. She'd felt even better than his dreams, better than anything he could imagine. Even now, as adrenaline for the revolt was pumping through him, he felt a kind of calm and relaxation that he knew could only be there because he'd had sex with her. She might be carrying his child, he thought with primitive satisfaction. He hadn't had a birth control shot since he'd arrived at the mines. The Pilgrims sure as hell didn't use them.

Of course, she thought she was barren. At least that's what she'd told Bragan. But her husband had been old. He'd probably barely been able to get it up. Things would be different for them, Jess thought in satisfaction. If they survived this he wanted to have fifteen children with her, all adorable little girls who would grow into beautiful women like their mother. He shook his head to clear away the fantasy. He needed to focus on the task at hand.

He pulled on a pressure suit, carefully checking the seals, then loped down the tunnel to the mine. Fortunately, the airlock was well out of sight of the mineshaft head. That, combined with a thin atmosphere barely capable of transferring sound, would make it easy for him to sneak up on the guards.

At least that was the theory.

Once there, all he had to do was overpower and kill them. *Easier said than done*, he thought, grinning fiercely inside his helmet. But damned if he wasn't going to try. He waited patiently as the airlock cycled, careful to keep his breathing slow and steady. When the light flickered from red to green, he pressed the button opening the door. He was in the tunnel.

Normally he would turn on his headlamp at this point, but any light would help them to see him coming. Instead, he stepped out into the pool of light thrown by the airlock and placed his left hand against the tunnel wall. It would guide him to the guards. The airlock door closed behind him and he was alone in the blackness.

There was something about being alone in absolute darkness that made him want to run, to scream. Perhaps it was instinct, harkening back to the days when his earliest ancestors had prowled through the trees, hunting for food and seeking to hide from predators. The primitive parts of his brain screamed a warning that there was danger ahead. *Run.*

He forced the thought away. This was no time for fear of the dark. He knew what the tunnel looked like, knew every twist and turn. It didn't matter that the darkness pressed down on him like a living thing. He couldn't allow himself to think about what kinds of creatures might dwell in such a place, what monsters would thrive in blackness so intense that a man couldn't see his own hands before his face.

Closing his eyes, Jess forced himself to breath deeply and move forward. First the right leg, then the left. Repeat. He started making progress, and felt a surge of satisfaction when he rounded he first corner. Only two more turns to go, and then he would be upon them.

By the time he reached the last corner he could see a trace of their light spilling out. It seemed bright to him, and he realized his eyes had so fully adjusted to the blackness that he would be blinded if he wasn't careful. He peeked around the corner, forcing himself to stare directly into the light. His eyes watered, but they adjusted. The two guards were there all right. Sleeping. Sluggo was one of them.

Joanna Wylde

The Goddess must be watching out for him, Jess thought with dark satisfaction. This was going to be easier than he'd dared dream.

Moving steadily and quietly, he came up and stood over Sluggo. He reached out and gently toggled the man's radio to the "off" position, then unlatched his helmet. He woke instantly, and Jess found himself in a deadly, strangely silent struggle. The man gasped for breath, his face turning purple. Jess knew that if he merely held him for several minutes he'd die of asphyxiation, but cutting his throat would be far more humane.

In an instant it was done. Blood poured down the front of the man's suit in a red river. It splashed on Jess, and to his surprise he felt a slight twinge of remorse.

Ruthlessly he pushed the emotion back. This man deserved whatever happened to him.

He dispatched the second guard with ease. It was almost too simple…they were completely unprepared for anything like this. They hadn't even had a chance to try the wand on him. In a way that was unfortunate. Bragan hadn't been able to say with one hundred percent certainty that the wands wouldn't somehow activate the remaining filaments still in his spinal cord. He'd find out soon enough, though. During the course of the revolt a wand was bound to be activated…

Toggling his radio on, he spoke quickly.

"Logan, things are going well in this sector," he said. Hopefully any Pilgrims who might hear them would think they were simply two slaves talking about their work. That was the theory, at least. "I'm ready to move on to the next blast site."

"I've got that," Logan replied, his voice casual. "I'll see you there in a minute."

"I'll be waiting," Jess replied. He turned to the elevator controls, pressing the button to send the car down to Logan's level. It took two trips to get all the men who had had their implants removed to the shaft head. Bragan came up top, too.

He would be in charge of the elevator, allowing the slaves who still had their implants to come to the surface. They would barricade themselves on the mine-side of the airlock until they knew whether the revolt was a success. No one wanted to risk being trapped down in the mine. A quick death from a wand was infinitely preferable.

Jess, Logan, and the first eight men went through the airlock together. They stayed silent as it cycled, unwilling to risk being overheard on their radios. Then the light was turning green and they stepped out into the corridor leading to the slave quarters. As soon as they were out, the door slid shut. It would take two more cycles to bring the others through.

Logan pulled off his helmet, speaking for the first time. There was a wild, almost primitive look in his eyes.

"How did it go?" he asked.

"Good so far," Jess replied, wishing he felt as confident as Logan looked. "The guard change was just like normal. Bethany's tied up in the storage room. I haven't tried getting into the blasters' lockers yet, though. Figured we'd do better to try it together, once we have something to open them with."

"Makes sense," Logan grunted. He signaled all but one of the men to follow him, and they took off down the tunnel toward the main complex.

"Remember," Jess reminded them as they pulled off their helmets. "No radio talk unless the station loses pressure. Keep your helmets attached, ready to pull closed. Anything can happen at this point."

The men nodded. They'd been over the drill a thousand times already. The locker room was blessedly empty when they arrived. Logan and Jess went over to the Pilgrims' lockers and studied them. They were made of thick metal imbedded in plast-crete. The locks were forged from heavy steel, but they narrowed at one point.

"I think we could get this open with a blaster," Logan said. Jess nodded.

"If we do this right, we'll be able to get one off the guards outside the tunnel."

"Go get the girl," Logan said. "It's time."

Things started to seem a bit surreal to Jess as he walked toward the storage room. He hadn't been entirely sure they'd make it this far. He had left her knowing there was a good chance he might fail at the mineshaft. He would get to see her again. A feeling of fierce, possessive joy came over him, tempered immediately with fear for her safety. He stopped at the door and turned to the others.

"Remember," he said coldly. "No matter what happens, she's mine. Any of you touch her, you're dead. Understand?"

The men nodded, although it was small comfort. Jess was less worried about this handpicked group then he was about the remaining slaves in the mine. There were some rough characters. Life could get ugly for the women of the station if they weren't very careful.

He opened the door slowly. She was still tied and gagged, although her eyes shot hate-filled beams in his direction. He knew without a doubt that if she had a weapon, he'd be dead.

"Calm down and you won't get hurt," he said softly. "I'm going to untie your legs and help you out into the main room. There are some other men out there. Don't do anything stupid."

She continued glaring at him as he freed her legs. He pulled her to her feet and she stumbled. He must have cut the circulation off in her feet.

They hobbled into the main room together, and he felt her body stiffen as she saw the other men. For the first time he saw them as they appeared to her. Tall, muscular. Their eyes were filled with hate, and their hair was shaggy. Some of the men no longer bothered with such niceties as removing facial hair.

They were terrifying.

"I'm going to pull off your gag," he said quietly. "If you make any noise, they'll kill you. Do you understand?"

She nodded, not taking her eyes off the men before her. He could feel her heart racing, and a part of him wanted to cuddle her close, comfort her. He pushed it down. They needed her fear as it was their ticket out of the mine.

Slowly he pulled off the gag. She spoke, her words hardly more than a whisper.

"Are you crazy?" she asked. "Don't you realize that all they have to do is activate the wand and you'll be dead?"

"That's not your problem," Logan said roughly. He started toward her, and she shrank back against Jess in fear. Logan raised an eyebrow at Jess, who shook his head in warning.

"In a minute you're going to walk through the tunnel to the door with me and Logan," Jess said. "He and I are going to stand to either side of the door. You are going to tell the guards that you need their help inside. Then you're going to get out of the way. Do you understand?"

"What are you going to do to the people on the station?" she asked in a low voice. "You're going to kill them, aren't you?"

"We're only going to kill those we have to kill," Logan replied coolly. "If they give up, we'll spare their lives."

"What about the women?" she asked, voice quavering. "What will happen to them, and the children?"

"We'll try to keep them safe," Jess said.

"And if they get in the way?"

"We'll kill them," Logan said, his voice icy. "Just like we'll kill you if you don't help us. We *will* take control of this asteroid. What you have to help choose is how we'll take it. If you help us get out quietly, we can disable the men and take control peacefully. If you don't help us, we'll use explosives from the mine to blow the whole place up. Believe me when I tell you I'd rather kill everyone on this Goddess-forsaken hellhole than go back to the mine."

"You're bluffing," she said. "You can't access the blasting clay. You can't break into those lockers."

"Am I?' Logan asked. "Try me."

The two glared at each other for long seconds. Jess kept one arm wrapped around her waist, simultaneously supporting her weight and squeezing her to reinforce Logan's words. Then she gave in.

"I'll do it," she said. "But I want your word—every man's word—that you'll do this as peacefully as you can."

All the men nodded.

"And I want you to promise no women will be raped."

Jess froze, wishing she hadn't asked that of him.

"We can't promise that," he said softly. "We can try to control the men, and we plan to isolate the female prisoners. But mistakes happen."

Logan nodded, his face serious.

"Nobody gets raped by *mistake*," she hissed. "It's always deliberate."

"Preventing something like that from happening is why it's so important we do this in an orderly way," Logan said in a harsh, urgent voice. "I can control these men here. I can't speak for all the men still down at the mine. This will have to be good enough."

She nodded, and a single tear rolled down her face. Jess' gut clenched.

"Let's get on with this," he said, his voice gritty. "We're wasting time."

"You weren't so worried about wasting time before," Bethany muttered. Logan gave Jess a long look, then started toward the tunnel entrance.

"Let's go," he said.

* * * * *

Bethany shivered as she walked slowly up the tunnel between the two men. They were both about the same height, and both had black hair. Logan had the same midnight blue eyes as Jess, too. Perhaps they were brothers? How long had they been planning this? Was Jess' attraction to her just one more part of the plan?

She knew almost nothing about this man she'd had sex with…

She'd done it because she though she would die. With sudden insight, she realized that this revolt they planned could save her. She could blame her father's death on the slaves. Relief swept over her, only to be followed by self-disgust. How could she consider betraying her people just to save her own pathetic life? Granted, she didn't feel much kinship with most of the people on the station. But the women were nice, at least some of them. Moriah, for one. And the children. They were innocent of any wrongdoing. Her gut twisted as she realized that Moriah and her baby could very well end up dead before this was over.

She had to do something to stop that from happening. She had to get away and warn the others. She had to find a way to save Moriah…

They reached the end of the tunnel and she took a deep breath.

"Don't make a mistake," Jess said, his tone deadly. She nodded her head quickly, not needing to feign fear. Jess hardly seemed like the same man who had been so tender with her earlier.

She raised one trembling hand and knocked on the door.

"Guards, I need you," she said, her voice quavering. There was no answer at first.

Jess and Logan looked at her with questions in their eyes. She shrugged.

"Sometimes they don't stay by the door," she whispered. "I think they get bored."

"Try again," Jess said, his tone harsh. "Louder this time."

She did as she was told, calling out the same message. This time one of the men replied.

"What do you need?"

It was her moment, and at that second she knew what she had to do.

"Get help! The-" She was abruptly cut off by Jess' hand coming down across her mouth so hard she bit her lips. Instantly she could taste salty fluid that had to be her own blood. Logan looked at her with hatred in his eyes.

"Bitch," he hissed.

"What was that?" the guard called. "I couldn't hear you. Just a minute."

There was some muttering, and then they could hear the bolt sliding through on the other side. Logan poised to move while Jess pushed her roughly behind his body. She drew breath to scream, but it was too late.

The door swung inward. In a flash, Jess slammed it back, hitting the guard in the head. The man dropped like a stone. Logan jumped through the doorway looking for his companion. There was no one there. Jess followed him quickly, ready to move.

"Where the hell is the other guy?" Jess whispered harshly. Bethany stepped through the door hesitantly, following Jess. He and Logan were looking up and down the corridor, but neither of them seemed to notice the small alcove that held the table where the guards usually sat. There was a bottle of *bakrah*, and some kind of board game set up. And a blaster.

Moving quickly and silently, she crept toward the table, hoping desperately she could stop this revolt here and now. Someone tackled her from behind. She went down, hard. A man's heavy body hit her, and suddenly she couldn't breathe.

"Stop pulling crap like this or I won't be able to guarantee your safety," Jess whispered in her ear. "I don't want you to get hurt, but I'm the only one who feels that way right now. Shut up and do as I say if you want to live."

She gasped, trying to catch her breath. He couldn't guarantee her safety no matter what, she though darkly. He couldn't guarantee *anyone's* safety.

"I've got the blaster," Logan said quietly. "We need to get her out of the way, and get rid of that guard, too. His friend could come back at any minute."

"You get the guard," Jess said grimly, his voice a rumble against her back. She had to get away from him, she thought desperately. She forced herself to go limp, not fighting as he pulled her to her feet. She raised one hand to her head, wobbling. He'd fooled her about his physical condition for ten cycles. Time for him to learn what it felt like to be the fool.

Watching out of the corner of her eye, she waited until Logan was dragging the guard's body through the door to strike. She raised her knee with all the force in her body, slamming it into Jess' crotch. He dropped to the floor and she was off. She was around the corner before either man realized what happened. They'd come after her, of course, but they had a serious disadvantage. She knew her way around the station, had played in these corridors as a child. There were a thousand hiding places. No way they'd be able to catch her now.

Behind her she heard a startled cry. The other guard must have returned. There was the sound of blaster fire and the smell of burning plastic. Everything was suddenly far more real than it had been just seconds earlier. If she didn't warn them, every woman on the station could end up raped, even dead. She didn't even like thinking what might happen to the children.

Then she heard footsteps behind her. Someone was following her, running hard. It had to be Jess. She ducked around another corner, desperately pushing into a small storeroom. If she remembered correctly, there was an air vent at the back. As a child, she and her friends had crawled through it. Would she be too big to fit through now? If he found her, he'd probably kill her.

She scrabbled frantically through piles of debris. Old blast casings, torn pressure suits, parts for mining tools. There it was, the grating that covered the vent. She felt the corners for the fasteners and found them gone.

The children must still play here, she thought with satisfaction.

Pulling off the grate, she started crawling into it, feet first. It seemed like she would fit, although her skirts would make it tight. Why hadn't she thought of that? She started to pull her legs back out to take off the bulky clothing, but then she heard someone out in the corridor. He could find her any minute. She slithered into the vent as quickly as she could. When she was all the way in, she reached out and pulled one of the pressure suits across the open space she'd cleared. She pulled the vent casing into place behind her and started scooting backwards. There should be a wider vent about ten meters back. Once she was there, she would be able to turn around and crawl more easily.

Time to go and warn her people.

* * * * *

Jess cursed, opening door after door along the corridor trying to find her. She'd simply disappeared, and now he was wasting valuable time looking for her. They had hoped to take on the Pilgrims slowly and steadily as they slept.

That wasn't going to be an option now. More people would have to die. It was only a matter of time before she brought help, and all they had to show for their efforts so far were two blasters.

Disgusted, he jogged back to the main entrance of the mining complex. Two slaves stood over the dead guard's body. When the second Pilgrim had come wandering back up to the corridor, he'd seen Logan, and raised his blaster to fire. Logan had reacted instantly, shooting the blaster like a seasoned soldier. In those seconds, Jess had realized how little he really knew about the man. They had never discussed their backgrounds or their families. He didn't even know what

Logan had done before he'd become a slave. After seeing him attack the guard, Jess had a few suspicions.

He jogged past the men guarding the door, moving quickly down the corridor to the main room outside the barracks. Logan and the others already had one of the lockers open. He was handing out small cubes of explosives, while another man—Kresn—was showing them how to use the detonators.

"Remember," Kresn said. "You blow this in the wrong place and the dome looses pressure. We don't want that to happen, but keep your helmets ready. If something goes wrong you'll only have a few seconds to pull them on."

"Why don't we just blow the dome and kill 'em all?" another man muttered, his voice harsh.

"Because we're better than them," Logan said, staring at him with cold eyes. "We don't want to kill the women and children if we don't have to. Those children are completely innocent."

"Not only that," Kresn added, his voice filled with dark humor. "I don't know about you, but I'm looking forward to getting my hands on some of those women. It's been a long time since I've had myself a piece of tail."

"No rapes," Jess said. The men all turned to look at him. "If I catch any man raping a woman, I'll kill him. Do you understand?"

"The same goes for me," Logan added. "We are *better* than them—remember that. It's the only thing keeping us human. Their women are hardly more than slaves as it is. They're victims, too, and I want them to be treated well, or you'll answer to me and Jess."

"Oh, I understand," Kresn said, his voice light. "But I have a feeling some of those Pilgrim women might enjoy the chance to take up with a new kind of man. This could be as much of an escape for them as it is for us."

"We can talk about that later," Jess said. "We need to get moving now. Bethany got away, and Goddess knows how long we've got before she finds help. Remember the plan. Now let's move."

The men stowed the small blocks of explosive in their pockets and clipped their helmets to the backs of their suits. Then the group started jogging out the tunnel into the main station. Logan and Jess took the point positions, covering each other with the blasters as they made their way into unfamiliar territory. Fortunately, the corridors were clearly marked with color-coded strips.

The Pilgrims were even stupider than they'd thought.

* * * * *

Bethany crawled along the ventilation shaft as quickly as she could. She must be almost out of the mining complex by now. It was just one of four domes making up the settlement. They were connected by four intersecting tunnels, with ventilation shafts running above each. It seemed like every movement she made was noisy. How could they not hear her in the tunnel below? She could hear them. They'd run beneath her just seconds earlier.

After what seemed like an eternity of crawling through the darkness, she felt a change in the vent's surface. Where it had been smooth plast-crete before, there appeared to be a slot. She had reached one of the recessed shields that would snap closed if a dome lost pressure. That meant she was almost to the junction where her vent would meet up with vents from the other domes.

She slowed, feeling her way carefully. The vents got confusing at this point. She had to find just the right one. If she remembered correctly, it was the one on the right, and she would have to boost herself up several feet to climb into it. There it was. She climbed up into the new tunnel, moving quickly over another of the blast shields. They always frightened her. As a child she'd been warned that if a human was standing in the way when a dome lost pressure, the powerful shields could cut them in half. She'd had nightmares about it for years.

She moved safely past the shield and then came to another junction. She tried to remember the fastest way out to the kitchen. It was the closest place she could think of that would have communication equipment. Everyone would be asleep and she had no idea how to trigger a general alarm. But she knew if she called one of the elders, he would know what to do.

Unfortunately, making her way to the kitchen wasn't as easy as she remembered. The shaft narrowed as she crawled, and finally she could go no further. All but crying in frustration, she realized that while she had been able to pass this way easily as a child, she was simply too large now. She would have to go back. She backed up carefully, trying to remember what her other options might be. An instant later she felt her skirt catch on something, and her leg was pinned. She couldn't see anything, and the shaft was far too tight for her to reach down and free it.

Shit.

She closed her eyes, forcing herself to calm down and think for a minute. She had to get free and she had to get out of there quickly. She moved one leg experimentally, and felt the fabric pulling against whatever had it hooked. If it was rough, she might be able to saw through the fabric and free herself.

Bethany moved her leg slowly back and forth, rubbing the fabric against whatever had caught it. Then she pulled, testing to see if anything would happen. She felt a small piece of it tear. She twisted her leg a bit and managed to hook one foot in the hem of her dress. She pulled down, slowly and steadily, and was rewarded with a ripping sound. She was free.

She started scooting backward again, taking care to avoid the rough spot that had caught her in the first place. Then she was past it. She had no idea how long it had been since she'd made her escape. They could already be in the main station, and she had no idea where to go next.

She'd have to risk coming out in the first room she could find that had a vent large enough for an adult to crawl through, and take things from there.

It took her several tries to find a way out. She was hopelessly confused by now. As a child she had never gone through these shafts alone, and certainly never without a light. Finally she found what looked like it might be a way out. She could see a faint light at the end of one of the shafts. It looked large enough for her to pass through, so she went for it.

She moved as quickly as she could, but it still took several minutes to reach the vent. By the end, she was scooting along on her belly, moving mere inches at a time. When she reached the vent, she peered out of the grill to find that she'd stumbled across someone's fresher. The light was a small one to help the occupants find their way in the dark.

Some family is going to get a big surprise, she thought grimly.

She had pushed open the vent and was halfway through before she realized she had another problem, a big one. This vent was nearly six feet from the floor, and all she had to break her fall were her own hands.

"Hello?" she called, trying to maintain her balance as she hung halfway out the opening. "Is anyone here? I need help."

She called several times, but there was no response. Suddenly an explosion rocked through the dome, knocking her out of the vent. Instantly the air was filled with sirens and she heard someone in the apartment scream. Even with the noise around her, the crash she made as she landed was loud enough to catch the attention of the apartment's occupants. The door swung open, and a man dressed only in his drawers brandished a blaster at her.

"Don't move," he said, his voice harsh. A woman peeked around behind him, one hand held to her mouth.

"The slaves," Bethany gasped out. "The slaves are escaping. I got away from them. You have to do something."

Another blast rocked the building and the lights flickered out. Then they came back on as the emergency power supply kicked in.

"It's Bethany, Dom," the woman said, plucking at the man's arm. He slowly lowered the blaster, giving her a suspicious glare. Then he turned to his wife, running his fingers through his hair nervously.

"I need to join the men," he said. "If the slaves are escaping they'll need me. Marta, you get dressed and get ready to defend the children. And you," he said, turning to Bethany. "You get to your father's apartment. Once we get this taken care of, the elders will want to talk to you."

Bethany nodded, and stood up rather shakily. Marta led her quickly through their rooms to the door, her daughter clinging to her mother's side.

"Be careful," she whispered. "I don't know what's going on out there, but the men will be quick to shoot."

"I will," Bethany said, trying to smile at her. Another blast rocked the station and both women winced. Marta was one of the younger women who worked in the kitchen. She had often slipped a roll with some meat in it to Bethany when the older women weren't watching. Visions of what her dead body might look like rolled through Bethany's mind and she quickly turned away. She couldn't think about that right now.

Marta unlatched the door and Bethany slipped out into the hallway. She had done her best to sound a warning. Now she needed to get home, where her father's body was still wrapped in a sheet in his bedroom. The traitorous thought she'd had earlier crept back into her thoughts—if the revolt succeeded, the slaves might not be the only ones to escape the hellhole that was Bethesda Station.

Chapter Seven

෨

The escaping slaves worked their way through the dome that housed the mining complex as quickly as they could. They kept expecting to hear alarms. There was only silence. Jess murmured a prayer of thanks to the Goddess for that. Something had happened to slow Bethany down. Briefly he wondered if she was all right, and a pang of fear went through him.

He pushed it out of his mind.

People would die on both sides before this was over. If she had stayed with him, she'd be perfectly safe right now. He had planned to leave her locked in the slave barracks. Eventually all the prisoners would end up there. If she got caught in the middle of the fighting at this point, that was beyond his control.

They had decided to stick with their original plan for now. They were betting that the mining station had been built using standard, pre-fabricated domes set in a pinwheel formation. It was the most likely set up. The main question was how many domes there were and how many people lived on the station. He'd probed Bethany for information as much as he could. They calculated the station had a population of about one hundred and seventy. About fifty were men. The slaves were outnumbered, but they had the element of surprise on their side, at least for the moment. They also had decent firepower. The Pilgrims had rather foolishly located their arsenal right outside the slave complex. Logan had actually burst out laughing when he'd found it, amazed by their shortsighted stupidity.

In record time they made their way through the mining complex and reached an area that could only be the central hub of the pinwheel. Jess noted with satisfaction that there were four portals leading into the hub, each of which had a large shield capable of cutting off the corridors if there were an emergency. The mining dome was already theirs. If they could close the doors, they would be able to pick off the inhabitants of the other domes at their leisure. One of the domes appeared to be a greenhouse. The second public rooms and the kitchen. The third housed the apartments, and would be their primary target. Jess marveled at the foolish arrogance the Pilgrims showed yet again. Everything was clearly labeled. It had simply never occurred to them that they might have a security risk in their slave compound. They'd made moving through the station laughably easy for the escapees.

The men split into their pre-assigned teams and prepared themselves to storm the apartment block. A small group of four men would remain behind, ready to close the blast doors if needed. There probably wasn't anyone in the other domes right now anyway, but they didn't want to take any chances. Logan gave the signal, and they started their assault.

Jess and his men split off from Logan almost immediately, heading to the right side of the dome. Moving silently, they forced open the first apartment door. Two of the men slipped in, prepared to capture or kill the inhabitants. Jess waved the rest of the men on. There were more apartments to enter. Everything was going off without a hitch. No alarms. What had happened to Bethany? Had she changed her mind about alerting the station? Maybe she hadn't even found her way out of the mining dome, he realized. He was surprised how much relief the thought gave him. He wanted her to live with emotion bordering on desperation.

He and his men had just reached the fourth apartment when a blast rocked the station. Alarms shrieked to life around them.

"Get back to the central chamber and see if they need help," he yelled to two of his team members. "We'll keep moving through the apartments. If you get the blast shields closed we'll be able to take them out one dome at a time."

He grunted as he pushed his way into the next apartment. There was a man stumbling out of his room. Without thinking Jess shot him, and a little girl screamed. He gritted his teeth, ignoring the wave of horror that washed through him. Grimly, he pointed the blaster at the child and her mother, directing them out into the hallway. There was already a small group of women and children huddling there against the wall. One of his men watched over them grimly. Would he be able to keep them safe? He turned to look down the hallway, assessing their next move.

He heard a scuffle, then the little girl ran by him. He jumped after her, missing the fabric of her nightshirt by inches. She darted around the corner and was gone. Already Jess could hear blaster fire breaking out in the distance. What if the Pilgrims managed to get organized and mounted an assault on their position? He and his fellow slaves were hopelessly outnumbered, but they did have one thing on their side, he thought. They were desperate. They weren't going back to slavery, even if it meant blowing apart the entire station.

Somehow the thought was small comfort in the face of a child running for her life…

* * * * *

Smoke billowed through the corridor as Bethany ran toward her apartment. Immediately the air scrubbers kicked into action, adding a high-pitched whine to the noise around her. Men were spilling out of their apartments, some pulling their pants on as they ran. Each and every one of their faces held an expression of grim purpose. They were preparing to fight for their lives.

She turned the corner to her father's apartment at a run, and flung herself against the door. It slid open. She stepped in and locked it behind her.

Now what?

Before she had time to think, someone was pounding on the door. She looked at the small monitor next to it, the one connected to the security camera, to see who it was. Amador, captain of the station's guards. She opened the door.

"Where is your father?" he asked, his voice tight.

Without thinking, she replied, "He's dead."

The words startled her. She should have lied. Now she would be caught. The thought was cut off as another explosion rocked the station.

Amador cursed, running a hand through his hair.

"I didn't realize they'd gotten this far in yet," he said. "What happened?"

She looked at him, startled. Then it fell into place. Naturally, he assumed Bose had been killed by the slaves. Relief washed through her and a detached part of her mind noted that her entire body seemed to be trembling.

"I don't know," she said quickly. "I escaped the mining compound and came to warn everyone. By the time I got here he was already dead. They killed him in his bed," she added for good measure, trying to inject a sense of outrage into her voice.

"It's horrible," she added in a strained whisper.

Amador looked at her sharply, then turned as another man called his name.

"Lock your door and stay hidden," he said quickly. "We're going to fight them. Be prepared to defend yourself."

He turned and ran down the hall. She closed the door behind him and leaned heavily against the wall. Suddenly her strength gave out, and she felt herself sliding to the floor.

It was too much. Tears welled up in her eyes, but before she could give in to hysterics there was more frantic beating on the door. She looked to the monitor, but didn't see anyone. The camera was sweeping across the hallway, and to her disgust she realized she must have activated a "search" sequence. Some good the damn thing would do her now.

"Who is it?" she asked anxiously.

"Let me in!" a little girl's voice called. Bethany jumped up and opened the door, pulling in a child who could be no more than six or seven years old. She was a wearing a nightgown. Her brown braids had come loose, and her cheek was streaked with black soot. Bethany took one look at her and picked her up, hugging her fiercely.

"It's okay, I'll take care of you," she whispered into the little girl's ear. The child's body shook as she burst into tears. Bethany searched her memory, trying to remember the girl's name. Was it Sara? Dara?

Before she could ask there was more pounding on the door.

"It's me, Moriah!"

She set the girl down and opened the door a third time. The younger woman stumbled in, baby clutched in her arms.

"It's horrible out there," she said, voice high-pitched with fear. "I don't know what's happening. They're fighting in the hallways, and someone came to my door and told me to run while I still could. I think that our men are losing control of the dome."

"The slaves are escaping," Bethany said quietly. "I tried to warn the elders, but I couldn't get here fast enough. Do you have any idea how many people have died? Are they hurting the children?"

"I have no idea. We've got to find a place to hide," Moriah said. "They were coming this way. Where can we go?"

"I tried crawling through the air ducts earlier," Bethany said tightly. "But that won't work now. The air scrubbers are on. If we go up there now we might smother."

"There's no way in or out of the apartment except the front door, is there?"

"No," Bethany said slowly. "I think we're trapped here."

"Let's barricade ourselves in your bedroom," Moriah said in desperation. "They'll come looking for your father. Maybe they won't look there."

She and Bethany exchanged a long look, and Bethany smiled gently. They both knew her bedroom wouldn't be safe. There weren't any safe places left to hide.

"All right," Bethany said finally. She turned to the child, suddenly remembering her name. Zara. It was Zara.

"Zara, we're going to go back here now," she said, reaching out a hand. The girl took it slowly, and together they walked toward the back room. All they could do now was wait.

They sat in the back room, huddled, for what seemed like hours. Explosions continued to rock the station. Zara cried and moaned while the baby grew fussy. Moriah tried nursing her, but she was too afraid to eat. Bethany held Zara tightly, and watched her small clock.

Less than ten minutes had passed since they'd gone into the back room together, but those minutes had lasted a lifetime.

They started hearing noises out in their own hallway. Bethany and Moriah looked at each other, and finally Bethany spoke.

"I have to know what's going on," she whispered. "I'll be back in a minute."

"Don't," Moriah said. "It's too dangerous."

"It's dangerous no matter what we do," Bethany replied grimly.

She stood and walked shakily out into the main living room. The noises outside were growing louder. She could hear men calling to each other, and the sounds of blasters firing. The worst of the fighting seemed to be right outside the apartment.

She walked up to the door and looked at the small screen next to it. Now she could see into the hallway through her father's ridiculous security camera. Jess was standing directly outside the apartment door, face twisted with rage and triumph. His pressure suit hung in tatters around him. His arms, strong and roped with muscle, held a blaster pointed at the locking mechanism. Terrified, Bethany ran toward the back of the apartment. They would be inside any minute. She had no idea what would happen to them. Jess had told her the women wouldn't be hurt but she didn't believe him. She'd seen the bloodlust in his eyes.

She and Moriah pushed into the closet, pulling an old blanket over themselves and the children. Would the slaves realize they had found her father's apartment? Of course, she thought in disgust. The door was clearly labeled. Everything was labeled, she realized, shaking her head. How much easier had the Pilgrims made it for the slaves?

Yet another explosion rocked the apartment, and then they could hear the men's triumphant cries as they came inside. Jess' voice sounded above the others, giving an order.

"I want Bose," he said. "And I want him alive."

The men hooted in response, their voices sounding triumphant.

"Good news, Jess," one of them called. "Logan just radioed a message. The second dome is fully under our control. The men over there have surrendered and they're being locked up right now."

"Jess, get in here," another man called. "Bose is dead. Looks like someone did him in a while ago, a day at least"

"What?"

Bethany shivered in the closet, pulling Zara closer to her body.

"Stay quiet," she whispered to the child. Zara nodded.

Then the baby sneezed, and all hell broke loose.

Chapter Eight

 හ

Jess stood over Bose's body, his moment of triumph feeling empty. The bastard was already dead. Someone had gotten to him first.

A baby sneezed.

"There's someone in the other room," he said, voice tight. Two of the men nodded, and went into the smaller room in back. They had already cleared out nearly twenty apartments. They had come to realize just how important it was to keep each other covered.

An instant later one of the men gave a startled yelp. Jess brought his blaster up, ready to fire. A small child streaked through the room, hair flying behind her, teeth grimly clenched. Jess gasped—he'd almost shot her. Just one more close call. One of the men took off after her.

"Zara!" a woman's voice called. Bethany's voice. The child was forgotten—Bethany was in there. Hiding from him. He could feel a fierce grin spreading across his face, blood surged through his body to his groin.

The station was all but theirs. Now she would be, too.

He stalked into the room to find two women huddled in the closet. One of them clutched a baby. The other one was Bethany.

He nodded at Kresn.

"Take her and the kid out to the other prisoners," he said in a grim voice, pointing to the other woman. "I'll take care of this one."

Kresn gave him a knowing look.

"Remember, we aren't finished yet," he murmured.

"I know," Jess said. "I'll just be a minute."

Kresn reached down and pulled the other woman to her feet. He wrapped one hand around her upper arm, but she shook it off.

"I'll go with you," she said, her voice dignified and quiet. Kresn quirked an eyebrow and bowed to her mockingly.

"Of course," he said.

She stiffened, but didn't reply. Together they left the room.

Jess was left alone with Bethany. She was dirty. Her hair had come loose from its braids, flowing down her back in a river of brown waves. He'd dreamt of touching that hair, wrapping it around his fingers a thousand times and now she was his. He'd kill any man who tried to take her away from him, and he'd be damned if he'd tolerate her running away from him again.

"Get up," he said. She stood, eyes darting around the room. Looking for escape? He laughed at her mockingly.

"You aren't getting away this time," he said. "The station is ours. Your father is dead. How did that happen, by the way? I was looking forward to doing it myself…"

She shivered, then lifted her chin defiantly.

"I don't know what you're talking about," she said. "You must be mistaken."

"Is that why you were so friendly earlier?" he asked coolly. "You killed him, didn't you? You thought you were going to die. That's why you fucked me."

She refused to meet his gaze and he laughed. Without warning, she leapt for the door. He blocked her, wrenching a hand into her hair and pulling hard as she tried to knee him.

"Oh, no," he whispered. "We're not going to go through *that* again."

He wound his fist tightly into her hair and pulled her through the apartment. As much as he was enjoying his moment of triumph, there was more work to be done. By his estimates, there were probably at least ten Pilgrim men unaccounted for in this dome. His hand clenched her hair tighter. She yelped in pain once, but any sympathy for her evaporated when he thought about the way she'd run from him earlier.

She had endangered herself recklessly and that was unforgivable. She belonged to *him* now and he wouldn't tolerate losing her again. She would have to learn to behave from now on, to do as he told her.

As they came closer to the door, she started to struggle against him. There was a lingering smell of blaster fire and burnt flesh in the air. He shook her roughly, forcing her to keep moving. Then they were in the doorway. For one brief second her body pressed against his. Something in him snapped, he had to touch her. He pushed her up against the door-frame and kissed her. Not a tender kiss, his mouth *claimed* hers. He'd fought and killed to get her, now she was his. Forever. He knew he'd never let her go.

She twisted against him, fighting and scratching to get free. She was panicked. He could feel it in the way her heart pounded. Her fingers clawed at his chest, and she ripped something loose. His necklace? Before he could fully formulate the thought, incredible mind-bending pain flashed through him and he dropped to the floor. He rolled there, his entire being pulsing with deep red agony. She had caught him in the groin with her knee. Again.

He forced himself to breathe, to push the pain to the back of his mind. He had to stand. Had to get Bethany. Had to continue the fight. Ignoring the agony that washed over him, he stood and faced her.

She was still at the doorframe, trapped by her own hair. It had wound around the destroyed locking mechanism. Smiling, he pulled a large knife from a sheath on his leg. He'd taken it off a dead Pilgrim just moments earlier. He raised the knife, and she blanched, whimpering. Her green cat eyes turned to his, and she whispered, "Please, don't kill me."

He laughed, the adrenaline in his veins turning to lust. Despite the lingering pain in his groin, he could feel himself swell with need.

"Oh, I won't kill you," he said, his voice low and threatening. "I'm going to fuck you. We've got a lot of lost time to make up for."

Then he raised the knife and sliced it neatly through the locks of hair that held her to the door. She quivered against him and he felt the power that was his. He was hard and ready for her. Without thinking, he lowered his mouth to hers again. His tongue pushed roughly into her mouth, branding her. He took no chances this time. His arms held her so tightly against his body that she could barely breathe, let alone attack. Finally he pulled away.

As much as he'd like to take her right then and there, he had work to do. Lifting her easily, he threw her across his shoulder and started back down the hall. She'd be safe enough with the other women for now. They'd have plenty of time to finish what they'd started later.

* * * * *

Bethany and Moriah sat huddled together in the slave barracks. They were surrounded by women and children. Almost all of them, actually. As far as she could tell, only two women were missing and none of the children. Somehow they had all managed to survive the attack.

There were no men, however. No one seemed to know what was happening to the men, although rumors were running rampant.

They were all dead.

The other domes had been blown up.

They were going to be left here to starve to death.

They would be raped and then tortured, then they would be sold as slaves.

The list went on and on…

It had been hours since the last group had been brought in. They had heard several explosions, including one massive one that had to have destroyed at least one of the domes. Hopefully not the greenhouse, Bethany thought. If they destroyed that there was no way they'd have enough food to survive. What wasn't grown in the greenhouse had been stored there.

Finally, the door opened. Two of the former slaves, heavily armed, stepped through. Behind them were Jess and Logan. The women quieted, holding each other and waiting to discover what their fate would be

"Your men are dead," Logan said, his voice devoid of emotion. A wave of alarm spread across the group of prisoners. A couple of the women burst out in tears, but others remained suspiciously dry-eyed.

More than one unhappy marriage had just been dissolved, Bethany thought.

"We didn't want to kill them all," Logan continued. "We had gathered them in the third dome and were holding them there. They found some weapons and attacked us. We had no choice but to blow the dome open to space."

Bethany shivered. It was a quick but unpleasant death, one she had feared all her life. Anyone who lived in space feared a loss of pressure.

"I tell you this because I want you to understand your situation," Logan continued. "We don't want to kill you. I consider many of you to be as much victims of your men as we were. I can see from some of your faces that you don't believe me. Ask yourselves this… If we didn't want to spare your lives, why didn't we just blow up the entire station? We had pressure suits and explosives. It would have been the safest and easiest way for us to make our escape.

"We didn't do that because we have a sense of humanity, of dignity," he continued. "Unlike your people, we respect life. But I speak for all of the former slaves here when I tell you I'm not willing to go back into captivity. If we have to kill all of you and your children to escape, we will. I would suggest that you be very, very careful over the next few days. You will do exactly as we tell you, and you will do it when we tell you. Do not push us."

The room fell silent, except for the occasional whimper from one of the captives. Bethany shivered, she had no doubt Logan meant what he said.

Jess stepped forward. His hair was slicked back with sweat, and she was struck again by the resemblance between him and Logan. Were they brothers? Had they known each other before arriving at the mining station? It was uncanny — they could have been twins.

"Bethany, you'll be coming with me," Jess said. All around her, the women started whispering. For a moment, she considered defying him, but the look on his face told her she would regret it if she did. She stood and started slowly walking toward Jess. Several gave her looks of sympathy, but even more gave her looks of hatred.

They thought she was part of the revolt, she realized. In that instant she knew she could never be safe with them again.

They would kill her.

Jess took her arm, leading her from the room. She soon found herself out of the barracks, surrounded by jubilant, newly freed slaves. She knew the room well, had brought the food carts here every day and watched as the men donned their pressure suits, and cleaned up after them in this room.

Today was different, though. Today there were no guards.

Instead there were at least seventy-five men watching her with hungry eyes. She recognized many of them, but they looked different now — more threatening. Her eyes darted quickly around the room. In one corner of the room there were bodies, laid out in neat rows. Ten of them.

"They died in the revolt," Jess said quietly, his left hand holding her upper arm tightly. He walked them quickly through the watching crowd of men, right hand resting lightly on his blaster. "We were lucky. Your men were taken almost completely off guard. Six of our dead died after we were almost finished. One of the guards got back in here with a control wand. They hadn't had their implants taken out yet."

How the hell had he gotten rid of his, she wondered? They must have removed it in the mine. She thought of all those pain pills she'd smuggled in to him and gasped.

"You used those drugs for your friends, to remove the implants."

"Of course I did," he said reasonably. "I was lucky enough to be unconscious when Bragan operated on me. They needed something for the pain. Every single one of those men had to go back to work after Bragan finished with them."

They passed out of the slave quarters as he spoke, then they were in the warren of storage rooms that made up the rest of the mining complex. Jess pulled her along, without speaking, down first one hall and then another. Finally he stopped in front of a room and opened the door.

"This is my room for now," he said. "You'll be staying here. I've installed a lock inside as well as outside. Nobody will be able to get in unless you let them."

"Aren't you worried that I'll lock you out?" she asked.

"You'll get hungry eventually," he replied lightly. He looked happier than she'd ever seen him, she thought wistfully, and even more handsome than before.

He pulled her into the room and the door slid shut behind them. She looked around, noting that he had stacked the room's contents—boxes of some kind of mechanical equipment—against one wall. Along the other was a pallet made of several blankets layered together.

"Why have you brought me here?" she asked, trying to keep her voice steady. He gave a bark of laughter.

"Don't be naive," he said. "You're mine now. I've claimed you, and every man left on this asteroid knows it."

"So, you're going to rape me?"

Jess looked at her steadily.

"I'm not going to do anything you don't agree to," he said. "But I don't think you're going to fight me, not if you're honest with yourself. When you thought you were going to die—when there weren't any consequences to your actions—you wanted to be with me. What's different now?"

"You used me to betray my people," she whispered. He laughed again, shaking his head.

"*Your* people?" he asked. "Sounds to me like *your* people would have executed you just as soon as they found your father. They were going to kill you if I couldn't go back to work, right? Excuse me if I'm off here, but can you explain exactly what about their treatment of you makes them *your* people?"

"What about the other women?" she asked, unwilling to acknowledge he was right. "The women aren't guilty…at least not all of them. What's going to happen to them?"

"Logan's working on that," he said. "We decided it would be hypocritical for me to tell the men they couldn't have them if I was taking you. But we're not animals, you know. We're not *Pilgrims*. I don't think any of us believes in slavery as an institution," he added mockingly. "We're a little too familiar with it. Logan wanted me to leave you alone, but I will never do that. I've known you were mine from the first moment I saw you. I'll be damned if I let anyone stand between us."

She closed her eyes, wondering what to say next. He seemed so different from the man she had come to know in the slave quarters. There he had been weak, polite. He was much larger standing up. She hadn't realized how tall he was. He towered over her by at least a foot.

He was massive, too. She'd seen his body, touched those muscles on his shoulders and thighs. But she'd had no idea what he could do with them. His arms were strong, roped with muscle. He'd used them to kill men. Men who would have killed her, she realized. Men who had killed slaves without thinking twice.

Their blood stained his clothing…

He closed in on her, pulling her into his arms.

"I've waited for this forever," he said, kissing the side of her neck softly. "Do you have any idea what kind of hell I've been through? Now I'm a free man, with a woman of my own. I can't tell you how much this means to me, Bethany. Just being alone here with you seemed like an impossible dream. Now we can build a life together."

She tried to ignore him, focus on the things he had done. He was a violent man, a controlling man who was taking away her freedom.

But none of that mattered as he touched her.

His hands clutched her shoulders, then ran up and down her arms. He seemed to be reassuring himself she was real, that this was actually happening.

He kissed her neck again, then nibbled his way to her lips. She expected an assault, a follow- up to the brutal kisses he'd given her outside her father's apartment. But he was so soft, so gentle. His lips nipped at hers, coaxing them to respond to his touch. She shivered, and he reached his arms around her. Her body brushed against his lightly. The tips of her breasts touched his chest, and the bulge of his swelling cock grazed her stomach.

She remembered what that monster felt like inside her body. *So good…*

Against her will she responded, opening her lips just a bit. She could taste him now. Salty with sweat. He *smelled* sweaty, too. Normally she would have found it distasteful, but there was something so masculine about his smell. Something raw and new.

She wanted to taste him. Bethany opened her lips further and her tongue darted out. He stilled, then pulled her forcefully against his body. Now he was giving her the kiss she expected, the ravaging follow-up to his earlier touch. He was hungry for her, he wanted her, and he was going to take her. She could feel it in the tension of his arms, the thrust of his cock against her soft belly. She shivered, moaning deep within her throat. It was a moan of need and fear combined, a moan of submission. In her heart she knew he was right, she did belong to him. A thrill ran through her as she realized he belonged to her, too.

He groaned in return, every pore of his body oozing masculine triumph. The captor was about to take his spoils.

Then he pulled away from her, and put his hands on her shoulders.

"I've been thinking about this for along time," he said softly. His dark blue eyes burned, like those of a being possessed by some dark force. Slowly he started pressing down against her shoulders. She whimpered as she realized what he intended.

"On your knees," he whispered. "I want you to start on your knees. I've thought about your lips every moment, dreamt of having them on me every night. I've already pleasured you with my mouth. Will you do the same for me?"

She shivered, remembering how it had felt when he'd kissed her between her legs. It had been hot and pulsing, pleasure and pain more exquisite than anything she'd ever imagined. She understood all too well why he wanted her to do the same to him.

Without speaking, she dropped to her knees before him. He leaned back against the door, both hands pressed flat against it. She looked up at him and his eyes burned through her, feverish in his need. Then she turned her attention to the bulge straining his pants.

Raising one finger, she traced the length of it through the cloth. It was so strong and warm, it leapt under her touch, a creature with a mind all its own.

She could feel its shape. There was the shaft, straight and true. It stretched upward toward his belly, narrowing just a bit before her fingers reached the flare at the end. The head was broad and rounded. It had seemed too big as it pressed into her body earlier and it seemed even bigger now. How had she managed to take it into her womb? And how would she manage to take it into her mouth?

She remembered performing this same act on her aging husband with a shudder of disgust, but this was different. As much as she wanted to tell herself that she didn't want to touch him, that he was forcing her to do this, she couldn't. She wondered, with every fiber of her being, what he tasted like. She could smell him, musky and masculine, and she wanted more. She wanted him as much as he wanted her.

She reached for the fastening of his pants, slowly pulling them open. He wasn't wearing anything beneath. With a start she realized he probably didn't own anything else. Even his pants were the same ones she had cut off him, then stitched back together while he lay ill. She pulled the pants down a bit and all thoughts of his clothing disappeared. There it was, his cock. It stood proud and large, waiting for her touch. He grunted, catching her attention.

"Keep moving," he said softly. She nodded.

She peeled back his trousers and pulled them down his legs a bit. Now she could see all of him. His long, hard cock. His balls, hanging just below in their sack. Already they pulled up, tight and tense. Despite the limitations of her experience, she knew he wasn't going to last that long once she touched him. What would he taste like, coming in her mouth?

Once again she traced his length with her hand, but this time there was no fabric between them. He was soft, and oh-so-warm to the touch. She followed the vein along the underside, first trailing one finger up it and then reaching out with the tip of her tongue. She traveled up the shaft slowly, exploring every bump and wrinkle with her tongue. Then she reached the top. There was a little dip in the skin there, a spot where the ridge of his cock-head came together. She tickled it with her tongue and he gasped.

She looked up at him, eyes wide, and touched her tongue to that spot again. He gazed back at her, eyes bright as deep blue coals, then he dropped his head back against the door and moaned.

"Take it into you mouth," he whispered, as if in pain. "Take it into your mouth and suck it. I need you to touch me there."

She did as she was told, opening her mouth and slowly sucking the head of his cock. He tasted hot and salty. Sweet. She could feel a rush of moisture building between her thighs — oh, she wanted him. One of his hands came up to grasp the back of her head firmly, pushing her down onto his length.

He wanted more from her.

She sucked him in further, careful to keep her teeth from grazing against him. She wasn't able to get him in all the way, and when he hit the back of her throat, she choked. Instantly his hand stopped pushing.

"You don't have to take more of me than you can handle," he whispered painfully. "Just take what you can…" His words broke as he moaned in pleasure.

She nodded, bobbing up and down on him as she did so. He gasped, and she realized just how much power this new position gave her.

He was hers now.

Moving slowly, she pulled up on the cock with one hand, mimicking the sucking motions of her mouth. Then she pushed back down. She repeated the movement, going more quickly this time. His hand clenched in her hair, and she did it again. Soon she was in a rhythm that seemed to be working for both of them. She could feel him growing harder in her mouth. More moisture leaked from him as well. Without thinking, she wrapped both arms around his hips and grasped the cheeks of his butt firmly in her fingers. She needed some leverage if she was going to do this right.

Her head moved back and forth, quicker and quicker. Each stroke brought him just a little closer to exploding. She could feel it in the way his muscles tensed, taste it in the seed he was already starting to leak into her mouth. His hand clenched her hair more tightly, the slight pain spurring her on.

Her mouth was starting to ache and her neck was growing tired. It should have been terribly uncomfortable for her to keep her pace, but it was as if she were no longer in charge of her own body. There was an ache building between her legs and in her breasts. She wanted his hands on them, to feel his rough fingers play with her nipples.

She wanted that hard cock inside her.

He gasped, all but whimpering with need. His hips started thrusting against her head, moving her faster and faster toward the explosion of his seed. He muttered something low under his breath, then both his hands were on her head, pulling her face into his cock with such force it should have been painful. All she could think about was how much she wanted him to thrust against her in another place. If he was too spent from this to fuck her afterward, she was going to die.

His cock was knocking at the back of her throat with each thrust now. She tried to time herself with it, and suddenly she was swallowing it, pulling him deep within her throat. He gasped and pulled her head more tightly against him. She swallowed again, feeling her throat muscles tighten around him. She couldn't breathe. Acting on instinct, she swallowed again and this time kept swallowing, massaging him with her muscles even as she started seeing spots from lack of oxygen. He gave a startled cry, and then he exploded into her. She could feel the hot spurts of come slither down her throat and felt light-headed. His fingers clutched her head so hard it hurt, and then he was slowly pulling out of her mouth.

She felt sore, almost raw. And so empty…

He slowly sank to the floor and pulled her close to his body. He was kissing her eyes, her nose, her mouth. He murmured soft words and rubbed the back of her head as she collapsed against his chest, gasping for air.

"I'm so sorry," he said, "So sorry, I didn't mean to hurt you, Beth. Oh, Bethie, I'm so sorry…"

It took her a moment to realize what he was saying.

"You didn't hurt me," she whispered, voice sounding rough even to her. "I startled myself there, but you didn't hurt me."

"You must be exhausted," he whispered, still cradling her. She nodded her head, realizing he was right. She *was* exhausted. But she was also far too restless and awake to sleep. The heaviness that had built up between her legs, in her breasts, was still there. She needed something to make it go away. She needed him inside her body.

Slowly, he stood and pulled her up with him. He led her to the bed he had made for them, gesturing to it vaguely.

"You need to rest," he said. "I won't bother you."

She looked him in the eye and started to unfasten the laces that held her dress closed across the front. He seemed startled, almost embarrassed.

"This is the only thing I have to wear," she whispered. "I don't want to sleep in it, too. Beside that, the fabric will bunch up as I sleep. I can't imagine I'd get much rest that way."

He watched in silence as she pulled the dress slowly down her shoulders, then stepped out of it. She was nearly naked now, only her shift separated her from his gaze. It was faded and thin from a thousand washings. She turned to face him, standing straight. Her nipples stood out, pink peaks clearly visible.

"I think we should go to bed now," she said softly.

Chapter Nine

ဢ

Jess had never felt so confused in his life. He'd all but raped this woman's mouth. Her lips were red and swollen from sucking him, even her voice rasped from the strain he'd put on her throat. Now she seemed to be inviting him to do more. Even though he had spent himself just moments earlier, his cock was already coming to attention.

He could bite her, she looked so ripe. How was he going to survive sleeping next to her?

Instead, he turned and strode to the door, flicking off the light. He pulled at his clothing as he felt his way back to the bed. She was already there, waiting for him. Still wearing the damn shift.

He lay down next to her, pulling a blanket over both of them. She turned away from him, facing the wall. He reached around her body and pulled her close. She snuggled up to him, tight little ass wiggling. If he wasn't careful he'd explode on the spot, he thought darkly.

He reached his hand up to her chest, allowing it to cup one of those full, ripe breasts he'd seen through her shift. It fit his hand perfectly as if she had been made specifically for his touch. He found the nipple with two of his fingers, squeezing it lightly. It was already hard, a little nub that cried out to be kissed.

"I'm going to take off your shift," he whispered. He felt her nod her head, and he rolled her toward him. He reached down beneath the blankets and found the hem of her garment, then slowly pulled it upward. His fingers brushed against bare flesh as he moved up her body. He could have sworn she shivered in response.

Then he had it up and over her head. Jess rolled her to her back and leaned down, mouth finding her breast in the darkness. He sucked the nipple in, tonguing it with satisfaction. It was tight and sweet, all his. He sucked it deeper and dropped a hand between her legs.

She was sopping wet.

A surge of triumph went through him. She wanted him, regardless of what had happened between them that day. He slipped his fingers between her folds, finding her clit. He let his fingers play it gently, and she quivered beneath him.

"Oh, Goddess," she whispered. "That feels so good, Jess."

Smiling against her breast, he rolled her clit again, then let two of his fingers sink into her hot, wet opening. He pushed them in as far as they would reach, wiggling them around before pulling back out again. He began to thrust into her with those fingers until she squirmed against his hand. Her fingers plucked at his shoulders and she whimpered in need.

"Do you want me to fuck you?" he asked finally, lifting his head from her breast. "Because if you do, I think you should ask me. I don't want to make any mistakes here."

"I want you to fuck me," she whispered. "Please, Jess, I *need* you to fuck me. Right now."

He shivered, then raised himself up over her body. He kneed her already spread legs further apart, then reached down to position himself at her opening. The moment felt unreal, as if he was stepping into one of his own dreams.

Slowly, steadily, he started pushing in. It was easier than he'd expected. She was so hot and wet that her cunt seemed to almost suck him in, pulling him down into her depths. He pushed until he could feel his balls against her body, then stayed there for a moment, quivering. She squeezed him a little, massaging him deep down inside, and he moaned.

Then he pushed himself to his knees and reached around to grasp her ankles. He pulled her legs up over his shoulders, moving her gently into position. He wanted to find her deepest spots, to impale her beneath him until she begged him for more. She whimpered.

Pulling out slowly, he started thrusting in and out with a steady rhythm. She twisted beneath him, but he ignored her movements, focusing only on maintaining his motion—in and out, in and out. Each stroke was torture. She was hot and wet and tight, but he was determined not to explode in her this time.

Not until she exploded around him.

He could feel his cock scraping against her clit with each outward stroke. He lifted himself a bit, bracing himself with her legs and leaning down into her. The change in position gave him new leverage. He was striking bottom now, bumping up against her cervix with every thrust. The little gasps she gave as he hit drove him wild.

He could feel the tension building between them—she was getting closer. Her breathing was ragged, and he could feel her muscles tightening around him. She whimpered again and then she was stiffened beneath him.

"Oh, Goddess," she whispered. "Oh, Goddess, this is too much. You have to make it end. Jess, you have to make this end or I'm going to die."

He laughed, then gasped as her muscles convulsed around him. She muttered something and arched her back. It felt like his cock was trapped in a vise, painful and incredible all at the same time. She squeezed him again and again, whimpering and thrashing her head. This was not a gentle pleasure, it seemed to be ripping her apart.

He wasn't able to control himself any longer. He pulled back, then slammed into her, pressing her body back down with his full weight. She screamed and he did it once more. He was going to come himself. He was ready for it, desperate to feel his own release. He slammed into her a third time, and to his triumph another orgasm hit her. She clutched him tightly and he exploded, shooting his seed into her body even as his hips bucked and trembled against hers.

Finally, when his head stopped spinning, he lowered her legs from his shoulders. She was limp, completely spent. He allowed himself to collapse on top of her body, remaining embedded in her flesh. Within seconds they were both asleep.

Chapter Ten

ဢ

Bethany sat alone in the small room she now shared with Jess.

Two cycles.

It had been two full cycles since he'd brought her there, and she still had no idea what was happening to the other women. She'd asked, of course. But Jess seemed reluctant to answer. It hardly seemed like a good sign.

For her part, she refused to tell him what had really happened to her father. Even though she had decided to confess to the murder before the revolt, she found herself strangely reluctant to take responsibility now. She was even less inclined to tell him the truth about Moriah. She had no idea what the future held for the woman. Regardless, a charge of murder wouldn't help. She knew how quickly the women could turn on their own. Jess had refused to let her return to the barracks because he was afraid that the women there might hurt her if they got the chance. They were convinced that she had had a part in the revolt. As much as she hated to admit it, it was probably a wise choice. The hatred in their eyes had been undeniable.

Of course, she wasn't completely alone. Jess spent every night with her. He spent time with her during the day, too. At least he did when he could. He and his fellow former slaves seemed to be extremely busy. Jess was tight-lipped about that, too. In fact, he hardly spoke to her at all. What he did do was touch her body again and again. There was something about him that seemed to take away her will. Time and again she promised herself she wouldn't consent to sex with him unless he gave her some answers, but as soon as he entered their room, she lost all thought of denying him. It would be denying herself, too.

It wasn't until the end of her second cycle in the room that she got her first glimpse of what the future might hold for her. There was a knock at the door, so she scrambled to her feet, calling out, "Jess?"

"It's Moriah. Will you let me in?"

Bethany unlocked her side of the door immediately. She could hear Moriah working the other lock from the other side at the same time. What must her friend think of all this? she wondered.

The door opened, and Moriah stepped in. It took all Bethany had not to burst into tears at the sight of her. She hadn't realized how alone and isolated she'd felt until that moment. They flew into each other's arms, only to jump apart when a man cleared his throat uncomfortably.

"I'll leave you two alone for a while," he said. "I'll be back in an hour or so."

"That sounds good," Moriah said, blushing. "I don't want to be away from the baby too long."

"What's been happening?" Bethany asked as soon as he was gone. "Who is he? Has he hurt you?"

"I don't even know where to begin," Moriah said softly, shaking her head. "Everything has changed. I can't even understand what's happening, and we're all having to make decisions."

"Decisions?"

Moriah gave a strange laugh, and shook her head again.

"Well, the station is destroyed, I think you already know that," she said. "The mining complex and greenhouse are intact, but the rest of it won't ever be livable again. The men are dead and now we had to figure out what to do with our lives."

Bethany stared at her blankly.

"I don't understand," she said finally. "Jess hasn't discussed this with me."

"I thought he might not have," Moriah replied softly. "He just whisked you away and we didn't know if you were even alive. They think you were in on the plot, that you betrayed us. Or at least, some of them do…" she added, voice trailing off. Moriah looked away from Bethany quickly.

"What about you?" Bethany asked tightly. "Do you think that?"

"I think that we would be dead by now if the elders had discovered your father's body," Moriah said softly. "And I think that my daughter and I have more hope for our future than we've ever had before. You did what you had to do."

"I didn't betray you," Bethany said tightly. "I didn't know about the escape. They used me, but I wasn't part of it. I wouldn't have done that."

"Not even after the way you've been treated?" Moriah asked softly.

"No," Bethany said. "Not even then."

An awkward silence fell between the two women. Finally, Moriah spoke.

"They're giving us a choice," she said. "The slaves are planning to leave, and they're going to send us away from here. They said that if they leave us here we'll die. We have to decide what we want to do."

"Have they hurt you?" Bethany asked again. "Have they, well, you know…?"

"No, nothing like that," Moriah said quickly. "Some of them have wanted to, but Logan won't let them. Not all of them are like that, Bethany. Some of them are actually quite nice."

"Have any of them been 'nice' to you?" Bethany asked. Moriah looked away.

"I see," Bethany said quietly. "Was that him, the man who brought you?"

"His name is Kresn," she replied softly. "And he hasn't tried to force me to do anything. But he has convinced me I have a choice about how I want to live. You see," she continued earnestly, "there are going to be four ships leaving here. One of them will take women and children to Karos, to the Temple. The Pilgrims there will help them. The slaves are even sending a load of ore with them to help pay for their expenses when they arrive."

"That seems awfully generous," Bethany said, confused. "Are you sure it isn't a trick?"

"What do they have to gain by tricking us?" Moriah said with a harsh laugh. "Our lives are already in their hands. We don't have any choice but to cooperate with them. They don't have to treat us this kindly."

"Maybe they want you to like them," Bethany replied. "Maybe this kindness is just a way to convince you to have sex with them."

"It's possible," Moriah said softly. "But I can tell you that in the last month I've been forced to have sex more than once by a 'decent' Pilgrim man. I like Kresn's approach better. So what if he's being nice to me so I'll sleep with him? It's better than being blackmailed."

"So you are sleeping with him?" Bethany asked.

"No," Moriah replied. A strange look came over her face, and she hesitated before continuing. "No, I'm not. He wants me to, but I don't think I'm ready for that. He hasn't tried to make me do anything I don't want to do. He's not like some of the others."

"Give him time," Bethany said darkly. "You can't trust men."

"I think I might give him some time," Moriah said, her face wistful. "We don't have to go to Karos. Some of us have decided we don't want to be Pilgrims any more."

"What do you mean?" Bethany asked, confused. "Of course we're Pilgrims. We were born that way. We can't just be something else!"

"We can now," Moriah said. A little smile tugged at the corners of her mouth and Bethany was struck by her beauty. She'd never realized how lovely Moriah was. She'd never seen her as anything but a frightened young woman she had to protect.

"I don't want to be a Pilgrim any more, Bethany. I want to be a free woman. Imagine it! I don't have to marry anyone. My daughter could grow up and do whatever she wants. I can even send her to school! I don't even really understand what that means, but it sounds like a wonderful thing. Did you know that she could even be a doctor? Like that man, Bragan? He's been examining all the women who will let him. He knows how to fix all kinds of things, Bethany. He made the shaking in Marta's hands go away. He even fixed that thing on Anna's neck! It's been causing her pain for three years, and now it's gone."

"He's an Imperially-trained physician," Bethany said quietly, trying to understand what Moriah was telling her. "He's also the one who took all the implants out of the slaves so they could revolt. I didn't know women could become doctors. Are you sure?"

"Oh, yes," Moriah said, face lighting up. "Yes, they can! I asked him about it. He's been letting me help him."

"So, where is this wonderful place that you might go?"

"It's part of something called the Saurellian Federation," Moriah replied in an excited voice. "Logan is a Saurellian, and he has a whole planet that belongs to his family, and we're all going to live there."

"Oh, really?" Bethany asked skeptically. "And you believe that? If Logan is so important, how did he end up a slave here? I think they're lying to you, Moriah."

"Maybe they are," Moriah said softly, looking away. "I know I want to believe them, but I understand they could be lying. I still don't want to go back to the way I was living before. For the first time in my life I have a chance to do something else. We've never had a choice before! How can I just go back to the way I was living before, knowing that I had a choice about it? I won't do that to my daughter."

"What if it's worse?" Bethany asked.

"It can't be that much worse," Moriah replied forcefully. "I was being raped by a man older than my father. He was already talking about a marriage alliance for my baby. I'm willing to take the chance."

"How many others are going with you?"

"About sixty, including children," Moriah said. "Logan says that when we get to his planet he'll help us. He'll help all of us."

"What about the slaves?" Bethany asked. "Do they believe Logan?"

"No, not all of them," Moriah said. "About thirty of them are taking their share of the ore and heading out on their own in the third ship. None of the women are going with them."

"What about the fourth ship?" Bethany asked, a tight knot forming in her stomach. "Who is going to be on that one?"

"That one is for you and Jess," Moriah said after a brief pause. "At least that's what Kresn tells me."

"We aren't going with the rest of you?"

"No," Moriah's replied. "Kresn says Jess hasn't told him where he's going. But he's taking you with him."

"I wish Jess would tell me what's going on," Bethany said quietly. "Does he know you're here?"

"No, I don't think so," Moriah said. "In fact, Kresn says he hasn't talked about you at all to any of the men, at least not that he knows of. That's why I asked him to bring me here. I didn't think it was fair that we're all getting a choice and you aren't. Kresn told me Jess hasn't let you out of this room since he brought you here."

"He's taken me out long enough to go to the fresher and clean myself up," Bethany said wryly. "Otherwise this place might have gotten a little fragrant by now."

Moriah blushed, then giggled.

"Well, I guess you're doing all right," she said. "So tell me…if you haven't been talking with Jess, what have you been doing?"

Now it was Bethany's turn to blush.

"That's what I thought," Moriah said. "For someone who's been locked away for two cycles you seem pretty happy. Although your hair looks awful," she added. Bethany started, then laughed.

"Yes, it does need to be trimmed," she said. "I don't have anything to trim it with, though. I'll have to ask Jess."

"How is he treating you? Is he good to you? Do you want me to talk to Logan or Kresn on your behalf?"

"I like Jess," Bethany said softly, shaking her head. "Or rather, I like touching Jess. I don't really know all that much about him, though. And I don't know where we'll be going after this. I guess I thought we'd be with the rest of the slaves. Now I don't know what to think."

"Maybe you should ask him?"

"I'm not sure I want to hear the answer," Bethany said slowly. "Things were so horrible. Now everything's changed so suddenly. In a strange way, these past two days have been pleasant, Moriah. No talking, no worries. I have no control over the situation and I can't do anything to change it. Instead, I've just been enjoying another person's body, and having him enjoy mine. I hate to think beyond that."

"Well, you'd better start thinking," Moriah said. "This isn't a dream. This is reality, and the choices you make over the next couple of cycles will determine where you live for the rest of your life. Don't forget that."

"I won't," Bethany said quietly. There was a knock on the door, and they looked at each other quickly. An hour hadn't gone by yet.

"Open the door," Kresn's voice came through, sounding strained. Bethany stood and quickly unlocked it.

"Jess is coming," Kresn said. "He found out I brought Moriah to see you and he's upset. We need to get going."

"If he's angry, I'll stay here with Bethany," Moriah said quickly. "I won't leave her to face him alone."

"No, it's all right," Bethany said. "If he was going to hurt me, he would have by now. You should go."

Kresn nodded, and reached out a hand for Moriah.

"Bethany's right," he said. "Jess isn't going to hurt her. I'm more worried about him hurting me," he added with a grin. "Let's go."

Moriah looked to Bethany one last time, then took Kresn's hand. Bethany noticed how gently he touched her, as if she were incredibly fragile and might break at any moment.

Jess never treated her that way.

Then the door was closed and she carefully locked it. She went back to the pallet and sat down to wait for him. It didn't take long. The door slid open and he entered the room. She was struck by his sheer size, just as she was every time she saw him. He was so much bigger than any man she'd ever met before.

"I hear you had a visitor," Jess said softly, his voice dangerously soft. A chill ran down her spine, but she refused to show how nervous he made her. She hadn't done anything wrong, she reminded herself. And neither had Moriah. She took a deep breath, steeling her courage.

"You know," she said, ignoring his comment, "you sleep with me every cycle. If I wanted to hurt or fight you I could have done it by now."

"I don't think you want to hurt me," he said.

"Then why do you keep me cooped up here?"

"For your own safety," he replied. "You can't go back in with the women, and I'm afraid to leave you alone with the men. You know that already."

"So if you're only keeping me here for my own safety," she said lightly, "then I don't understand why you would be upset that I have a visitor. I can only assume you don't want me to have any information about what's happening to the others."

"We've been over this before," Jess said, running a hand through his tousled black hair. He didn't look as angry as he had before. By asking him questions she'd managed to deflect him. Something to remember. "The women and children are fine because Logan and I are protecting them. I told you we'd take care of them."

"I have no reason to trust you," she said quietly. "You've already used me to betray my people. Doesn't that mean anything to you?"

"No," he said coolly. "They were men who held me captive. I saw them kill slaves who were helpless to defend themselves simply because they couldn't work any longer. It was only a matter of time before their actions led to my death, either directly or indirectly. As far as I'm concerned this was a matter of self-defense. It's not my fault that they refused to surrender. We didn't go into this intending it to be a fight to the death."

She nodded, and looked away. It amazed her that he could remain so calm over so many deaths. What kinds of things had he suffered to grow emotional calluses that strong?

"Moriah told me you're giving the women a choice over where they're going after this."

"Yes, we're giving them a choice," he said, coming to sit beside her. She inhaled and smelled his scent. Tangy, sweaty. Masculine. She felt a tightening in her nipples, and sighed, leaning her head back against the wall. Why was it that all she could think about when she was around him was sex? No wonder she hadn't gotten any information from him over the past two cycles. It was as if her body had been taken over by a complete stranger.

"Why?"

"Why?" he repeated, his mouth twisting in dark humor. "Maybe because we're all too familiar with what it feels like to not have choices. Have you considered that? Maybe we're human and have compassion for those around us. For a group of women who just lost all their menfolk, your people seem pretty happy. Quite of few have told us they don't want to go back to another Pilgrim settlement. More than I could have imagined, actually. "

"It isn't as if our lives here have been pleasant," Bethany said. "I suppose there were a few good marriages, though. Moriah had one before her husband died in an accident. What about me?"

"What about you?" he asked.

"Do I get that same choice?" she asked. "Moriah tells me that you won't be going with Logan and the others. You have some other plan. Do I get to pick where I'll end up in all of this?"

He stayed silent for a moment. One of his hands reached down and captured hers. He lifted it between them, playing with her fingers

"No," he said finally. "You'll be coming with me."

"What if I'd rather stay with Moriah and the other women?" she asked.

"The other women hate you," he said. "You wouldn't be safe with them."

"I'd be safe with the women who are happy to escape this place, the ones going with Logan," she said. "Moriah thinks that I helped with the revolt. She doesn't seem to care."

"It doesn't matter," he replied. "You'll be going with me. Accept it."

"I don't have a choice in this?"

"No, you don't," he replied. He turned to her, reaching out and cupping her chin in his fingers. He searched her face with those dark blue eyes and his expression grew intense, dangerous. She shivered.

"From the first time I saw you, I knew I was meant to have you," he said. "I wanted you more than I've ever wanted anyone or anything in my life. Now that we're together, I'm not going to let you go."

He leaned over and kissed her, his mouth taking hers roughly, as if to emphasize the point. For a brief moment she tried to fight against it. She wanted answers, not sex.

She was lying to herself.

She wanted sex all right. As soon as his lips touched hers, it was all she could do to keep herself from straining against him. Then his arms were coming around her, pulling her against him. He dragged her across his body until she clutched at his neck to keep from falling. His tongue thrust into her again and again. She could feel his cock prodding at her hip, searching blindly to get closer to her.

One of his hands came around the back of her head, fisting tightly into her hair. His head slanted across hers, his mouth plunging into her depths and taking as much as he could before rolling her over onto the pallet.

His weight came over her, crushing her down. His knees pushed between her legs, thrusting them apart as she bucked up at him, desperate to feel him within her body. He groaned in response as his fingers fumbled at his pants. She tried to reach down and help, but he captured her hands with his, holding her prisoner. He raised his head from hers, then spoke.

"You are mine. *Mine.* No one else gets to touch you, do you understand?"

She nodded, mesmerized.

He lifted his hips and thrust into her without preparation. She gasped at the sudden intrusion, but her body was hot and

Joanna Wylde

ready for him. He stretched her open, impaling her with his cock, and allowed his head to drop down toward hers.

"Mine," he whispered again, this time softly in her ear. "You are mine."

He punctuated the declaration with steady strokes into her.

"Who do you belong to?" he asked harshly when she didn't respond. He lifted his head, midnight eyes seeming to look down deep into her soul. "Who do you belong to?" he repeated, voice growing strained. She closed her eyes and shook her head, unwilling to answer him. He stopped his steady thrusting, and slowly pulled his cock partway out of her body. She whimpered, lifting her hips toward him. It wasn't enough.

"Who do you belong to?" he asked a third time. She kept shaking her head, and he pulled out of her completely. He transferred both of her hands to one of his, and reached down between them. His fingers found her clit, touching it lightly. She jumped, and he laughed without humor.

His fingers started a slow stroke up and down her clit, tweaking it as he moved back and forth. She whimpered in protest but he ignored her, focusing instead on his fingers' slow movements. Sparkles of sensation came to life at the center of her being. They started in her clit, spreading out in slow circles through her pelvis before skittering up her body to her nipples. The opening between her legs felt so empty. The space he had once stretched to the point of pain cried out for him now. Desire wound its way through her and she twisted with need. A part of her felt angry, betrayed. Why was her own body doing this to her? It wasn't right that he should be able to control her responses so easily.

"Who do you belong to?" he asked once more, fingers slowing in their exploration of her crevices. She shook her head, whimpering. She wasn't going to give in to him, not like this. He thought he owned her, she reminded herself. He couldn't own her. She wasn't going to allow it. His fingers stabbed into her again and she gasped. One finger, two, three fingers entered her body, his thumb still moving restlessly across her clit. She twisted and he laughed again.

"I think you belong to me now," he said softly. "I think you know it, too. You don't like it, but you can't control yourself. You're mine."

She didn't bother to shake her head in denial this time. It was taking every bit of her strength not to break down and beg him for release. She kept remembering how he felt inside of her, how he would stretch her open, moving slowly at first before going faster and faster. She would feel her muscles start to shiver and trembled, and his cock would swell inside her body. Jess pulled his fingers out of her body abruptly, and the illusion was broken.

"Please," she whispered, beyond fighting. "Please…"

"Who do you belong to?" he asked a final time, and she broke down.

"I belong to you," she said. "Please, I need you inside of me."

He positioned the head of his cock against her entrance, pressed in lightly then stopped.

"I want to hear it again."

"I belong to you," she said again, tears of frustration running down her face. "I belong to you, dammit. Now fuck me before I die."

He laughed again, the sound low and dark. Then he shoved the entire length of his cock into her with one smooth motion. Her frayed nerves exploded and she bucked against him. All the tension that had built up in her body tightened in on that one moment and she flew into oblivion. She could hear him panting in her ears as he thrust into her body toward his own pleasure, but it was as if she were in a universe all her own. She simply lay there, basking in the pleasure and surreal brilliance of her orgasm.

She really *did* belong to him, she mused, still caught in a sense of unreality. Her body certainly didn't have any doubts. She couldn't imagine anything better than this. Nothing could be more perfect. He released her hands, bracing both palms on the pallet beside her head. His upper body rose, allowing him to slam into her more fully. She raised her legs and clenched them tightly around his back, holding him deep within her body as his orgasm hit. He gasped, shuddering. She could feel him pulsating within her and she smiled as the hot seed hit her cervix.

He belonged to her, too, she thought with satisfaction. He needed her just as much as she needed him. He collapsed against her, breaking her train of thought, and she wrapped her arms around him. They lay there together for several minutes, panting. No wonder it was so hard for her to think when he was around, she thought wryly. Every time they touched, they exploded.

After several moments he lifted himself from her body and stood. He turned away as he tucked himself into his pants, erecting an invisible wall between them with his silence. It was far too early for sleep. He would be leaving her now. He always did after moments like this. They had to talk.

"Jess, wait," she said.

"What?" he asked, turning back to her. He suddenly seemed so cold, so distant. She sat up and pulled her skirt over her naked flesh. She felt embarrassed, almost dirty.

"We need to talk about what's going to happen to us," she said softly. "I want to know what your plans are. I want to know what's going to happen to me."

"I'll take care of you," he said tightly. "You don't need to worry about anything else."

"I'd still like to know where we're going. Moriah tells me you're taking the fourth ship. You aren't going with Logan?"

"No," he said tightly. He turned, making it clear the conversation was over. She sat back against the wall, pulling up her knees and wrapping her arms around them. She felt utterly alone. Against her will, she felt tears building up in her eyes and she wiped them away quickly. Without thinking she sniffed, and he turned back to her.

"Oh, shit," he muttered, coming back to sit next to her. He pulled her into his arms and she allowed the tears to flow. For the first time in months—years—she allowed herself to let go, to feel all the frustration and hurt she'd pushed back so many times. It felt good to just let him hold her, to feel his arms around her and collapse against his chest.

He stroked her hair until she stopped crying, and kept stroking it while she hiccupped for a few minutes. Then he reached down and lifted her face with one finger, kissing her softly on the lips. It was a sweet kiss, undemanding and comforting, and the kindness of it almost made her start crying again.

He finished his kiss and pulled away from her. She looked into his eyes, and was suddenly struck again by how much he resembled Logan. Without thinking, she asked, "Are you brothers?"

"What?"

"Are you and Logan brothers?" she repeated. "You look so much alike, I can't help but wonder."

"No," he said after a long pause, his face troubled. "Why were you thinking about Logan while I was kissing you?"

"I wasn't thinking about Logan," she said, feeling herself smile. It felt good to smile, she realized. "But you do look like him. Are you related? I don't know anything about you."

'No, we're not," he said finally. "I've been a slave all my life. I was created and raised in on an Imperial slave farm. Logan is Saurellian. The Saurellians are at war with the Empire."

"What are we?" she asked. "I mean, here in this asteroid field? Are we Imperial or Saurellian?"

153

"We're Saurellian right now," he said slowly. "Or at least we were when I was sold to your father. But we had only been under Saurellian control for a short time. Who knows what we are now?"

"Which would you rather we be?" she asked. "I mean, what would be better?"

"I don't know," he said slowly, tucking her into the crook of his arm. She snuggled up to him, allowing herself to simply enjoy his touch for once. "I don't suppose it matters to me all that much. I doubt either of them will care very much about a small slave revolt on a Pilgrim mining station. They have more important things to worry about."

"So where are we going?" she asked again softly. "If we're going together, don't you think I should know?"

He sighed, then nodded.

"I suppose so," he said softly. "I'm not used to telling other people my plans."

"Well, I'm not used to having plans," she replied lightly. "But a lot of things have changed."

"We're going to find my sister," Jess said after a pause. "Her name is Calla, and she's a slave at Discovery Station. She's owned by a Pilgrim woman named Jenner. I can't leave her behind."

"I didn't know you had a sister," Bethany said. "I guess I don't really know all that much about you."

"No, you don't," he replied, giving her a gentle kiss on the top of her head. He pulled her tighter and his voice grew distant. "You know nothing about me at all."

Part III

The Journey

Chapter Eleven

❧

Jess gazed through the ship's view-screen at the massive space station where he had lived for most of his life. *Discovery Station.* The name was so promising, implied so much hope for the future. In reality it was a cesspit. There was no promise here, just load after load of ore from the asteroid belt being processed into the raw materials for an empire. *Or maybe a federation,* Jess thought with wry humor. It hardly mattered who was in charge of the station. All he cared about was getting his sister and returning for Bragan.

They'd been forced to leave the doctor behind. He had removed the slave implants from most of the men successfully, but even with all his training, ten of the men had died. No one had been even close to being capable of removing Bragan's implant. The irony of the situation was hardly lost on Jess. When he and Bethany had set out for Discovery Station nearly two months before, he had promised Bragan that he would return with a doctor to rescue him. Jess had every intention of keeping that promise. He figured they would be able to shave about twenty days off their return trip if he could trade the ore freighter they were traveling in now for something smaller and faster. It seemed likely that they'd be able to. There was always a demand on Discovery for freighters. In addition, the ore they carried was worth a small fortune. It should be more than enough to cover their needs.

The ship shuddered beneath him as he turned away from the viewing portal. They were docked at one of the ore processing centers while their cargo was unloaded. He'd already negotiated a decent price, although he hadn't been able to glean much information. The sale had been made long-distance. The refining plant itself was completely automated. It would take them another twenty-six hours to unload all the cargo, and then he and Bethany would go to the main station. The thought of it made his stomach hurt.

If he wasn't very, very careful, she might be able to get away from him there.

He walked back toward the small cabin they had made their own for the past two months. She had already packed what few things they had into a small rucksack. Now she was in the fresher, cleaning up. He could hear her singing a little song, her voice slightly out of tune. She was always singing like that. He'd asked her once if they were Pilgrim songs, and she'd given an embarrassed laugh. She'd made them up all by herself. He'd found himself humming them off and on as time went by. Just one more thing about Bethany that fascinated him.

Another shudder shook the ship, filling Jess with a sense of desperation. The past two months had been like some kind of wonderful dream. They'd been living for the moment, some days not even bothering to get out of bed. Now it was all ending. He needed to be close to her.

Quickly, he pulled off his shirt and pants, kicking them to one side of the bed, then let himself into the fresher unit. There she was, standing in the sonic shower unit with both arms stretched above her body. Her eyes were closed as she relaxed in the gentle waves that cleaned her body. *She was so beautiful,* he thought. High, firm breasts. A softly curving back, each muscle clearly defined by years of hard work. His cock leapt to attention, and he stepped in with her. She gave a little startled gasp, then turned toward him, wrapping her arms around his neck.

Without speaking, they kissed. His erection, trapped between them, throbbed with need. He could feel one of her legs rubbing up and down the backs of his, and then he reached down to cup her butt firmly. He lifted her body, bracing it against the shower wall. She wrapped both legs around his waist, and they writhed together, skin stimulating skin in a way that seemed almost electric.

It was perfect.

He rubbed his cock against her belly again, enjoying the slow torture of being so close without penetration. He wanted to dive into her body with his but at the same time, he also wanted to simply savor the moment, allowing himself to be close to her.

If she managed to escape, this could be the last time he held her like this. The thought was intolerable. He was filled with a sudden need to mark her, to claim her as his. He wanted her to know with every fiber of her being who she belonged to. She was his. He would die before he allowed another man to touch her.

He pulled back with his hips, then thrust forward into her. She gasped, clutching him tightly, and he thrust again.

"Jess," she moaned. Her voice was needy, almost painful with desire. He grunted, and pushed into her again. He could feel his cock bumping up against her cervix, feel her body shuddering in response. He knew by now that nothing sent her over the edge faster than such deep, hard penetration. He would make her scream before he was done. The ship rocked again, and they bumped against the wall of the shower. As he slipped out of her, she laughed.

"Let's go into the bedroom," she whispered. "This could get dangerous."

He nodded, and stepped out of the shower while still supporting her body. He carried her into the bedroom and lowered her to the bed slowly, kissing her as he did. He followed her body down, but before he could come back into her, she pushed up, rolling him to one side.

"It's my turn," she said with a laugh. "You don't always have to be in charge, Jess."

"Yes, I do," he said, unwilling to joke. She scrambled away from him, sitting up on her knees and crossing her arms in front of her chest. Her face turned serious.

"You don't," she said quietly. "You can't expect me to be your prisoner forever, you know. Have you considered that maybe we need to form a partnership, here? If you can't trust me even a little bit, we're not going to get very far."

"I trust you," he said tightly. "Don't I sleep next to you every night? You could strangle me. You could do all kinds of things to me."

"I know," she said. "You trust me not to kill you. But you don't seem to be able to trust me to think for myself. Not even in bed. You never give up control, do you?"

"I've spent most of my life without control," he said. "I'm not going to go back to living that other way ever again. You can forget that."

"I don't want to control your life," she replied, shaking her head. "But I would like to share control of our relationship. I thought you didn't believe in slavery."

"I don't," he said in frustration. He hated it when she talked like this. She just didn't understand how important it was to him that they stay together. Just the thought of her leaving him was enough to make him sick. And he had no reason to believe she would stay of her own free will. If he were in her situation, he would try to escape.

The feeling that he was being a hypocrite washed over him for the hundredth time, but he ruthlessly pushed the feeling of guilt back. He had been through enough already. He wasn't going to give her up. Not now, not ever.

She rolled off the bed, then reached over to pull on a dress.

"What are you doing?" he asked roughly.

"I'm getting dressed," she replied in a cool voice.

"What about finishing what we started in the fresher?" he asked, as a tight knot started growing in his chest.

"What about it?" she asked. "I was under the impression we were having consensual sex. But that kind of thing involves two partners, not a man and his receptacle. If you want to finish it, you'll have to rape me."

She stood facing him, hands clenched tightly on both hips. The knot in his chest grew heavier. He was losing her already.

"You won't have sex with me?"

"I'll have sex with my lover," she said. "You're my captor. I suppose you have the option of raping me."

He stared at her, utterly confused. How had she managed to turn this into rape? His cock was throbbing, but it was nothing to the pain inside of his heart. They had fucked a hundred times but he'd never felt low and dirty before now. Somehow she'd tied him up neatly in a little knot and made him feel like a criminal. How had she done it?

"I'm going to go look through the viewing port," she said, turning and walking about of the room. Jess felt naked and foolish. He had to find some clothing, had to find a way to regain control of the situation.

He had never felt so alone in his life.

* * * * *

Jess' hand gripped her arm tightly as they stepped through the airlock several hours later. He had warned her not to say a thing when they entered the space station. He seemed to be afraid she was going to try and escape. Of course, she didn't know that for sure, as they had hardly spoken since their abortive session in the shower. Not that he needed to worry.

It was all she could do to put one foot ahead of the next.

Never in her life had she seen anything like the Discovery Station port. She couldn't have even imagined something like it existed. There were hundreds of people all around them, each dressed differently. They were all sizes and colors, although most seemed to be essentially human. The women were the most amazing. All her life she had been taught that females should be modest, obedient, but these women walked and talked like men. They even wore tight, form-fitting clothing that showed off their every movement.

Some of them wore hardly any clothing at all.

She watched in wide-eyed amazement as one, wearing only bits of feathers attached to some kind of string and draped around her breasts and waist, walked up to Jess and kissed him deeply on the mouth.

"Why don't you park the wife and come visit with me?" she asked him seductively. Bethany stiffened, terrified by her suggestion. What was going on here? To Bethany's horror, Jess simply laughed.

"I have other business to take care of," he said. "Maybe another time."

"Any time for you," she said. "Just ask for Mary. You can always find me if you ask."

"I'll keep that in mind," he said, laughing. Bethany fumed.

He tugged at her arm, pulling her to the center of the massive corridor.

"There's a transit tube here," he said. "We'll take it to the center of the station. I've reserved a room for us there. Then I need to take care of some business."

"Are you going to sell the ship?" she asked, wondering what other kinds of business he had in mind. Would he be going back to see Mary once he got rid of her?

"Yes," he replied. He pulled her through the crowd, and she soon forgot to be angry.

Trying to see everything around her while keeping up with him was nearly impossible. She watched with wide eyes as the crowd swirled around them, unable to imagine why he was afraid she'd run away from him in this place. She was simply terrified that they'd get separated.

He pulled her on to a small platform, and then a pod-like vehicle was pulling up next to them. The door opened, and a rush of people came out. Jess pulled her inside, gesturing for her to sit down on a plast-crete molded bench. The doors slid shut, and the pod started moving at an incredible speed. She closed her eyes, feeling dizzy.

"All the ships have to dock on the station's outer concourses," he said. "If we tried to walk the entire way, we could spend the next ten hours trying to get there. In fact, we're lucky to have gotten a docking place at all. Sometimes ships are placed in a holding pattern and you have to ride a shuttle in."

She nodded, pretending to understand him. She was trying to figure out just how big Discovery Station really was. The entire mining station she'd grown up on could have easily fit in this corridor alone.

They had only traveled a few minutes when the pod came to a stop. Jess tugged her arm and they stood. The doors slid open, and a rush of people came at them. She cowered back, but he held her firmly and pushed forward through the crowd. They stepped out of the pod, and suddenly they were in a broad cavern of a place. At first she thought it was simply the largest room she'd ever seen. Then she realized that above her was open space and her heart started racing instinctively. How could they possibly be safe in a place like this? What was holding the air in?

"Don't worry," Jess said, as he seemed to read her mind. "This dome is made out of the same material that protects the Emperor's sky palace on Tyre. We're perfectly safe."

"Oh," She replied, unsure of what to say. She certainly didn't feel safe, no matter what he said. For all she knew, he was making it up, just to calm her down. "How do you know that?"

"I *did* grow up here," he said, pulling her through the crowd. It was hard to hear him through all the noise. There was music and advertising everywhere and she could feel a dull throbbing starting in her head. If they didn't get somewhere quieter soon, she was going to go crazy, she thought desperately. *Someplace quiet and with a ceiling,* she thought.

"In here," Jess said. He pointed to a door with a sign above it that she couldn't understand.

What's that?"

"It's a hostel," he said. "I'm going to drop you off at the room and then go out to take care of my business."

"Is your sister here?" she asked, trying to focus on what he was saying. "Are you going to find her?"

"Yes," he said. "She's here, but I'll go and get her later. Right now I want to pick up some things for us, and I have an appointment with a broker to discuss the ship."

"Aren't you afraid that someone will recognize you?"

"No," he said. "The population of the station changes pretty quickly. Even if someone did see me, they have no way of knowing why I'm here."

"Don't you think they might find it kind of strange that you're back here after being shipped off to the mines?" she asked. He frowned, and she realized all her questions were starting to annoy him.

"Let me worry about that," he said tightly. "All you need to do is wait for me to take care of everything. We'll be getting a new ship soon, and then we'll go back for Bragan. You'll like Calla. She's a great girl, a real sweetheart."

He pulled her through the entryway and back down a hall lined with doors.

"I've gotten a room for us already," he said. "You'll just need to wait for me," he added, opening one of the doors.

She looked around the room. It was small, but very nice. In fact, she found the close quarters somewhat comforting after all that open space. Like home. Then something strange caught her attention. There was some kind of covering on the floor. Unable to control herself, she pulled away from him and dropped to her knees. She had to touch it. It was so soft... How would anyone be able to keep such a useless and decadent thing clean? It was crazy.

"What is this?" she asked softly. Jess started laughing and she blushed.

"It's called carpet," he said. "It's very common, at least in places not owned by Pilgrims."

"I've never been anywhere that wasn't owned by Pilgrims," she said with a shaky laugh. He smiled.

"I think you'll like it here a lot more than any Pilgrim station," he said. "Come here."

He stood near the bed, reaching one hand out to her in invitation. She stood and slowly walked toward him. They still hadn't resolved their earlier fight, but she found herself wanting his touch regardless. Discovery Station was so new and strange. It was exciting, but a small part of her was frightened, too. There were so many things she'd never seen before, never dreamed could exist. Everyone around her seemed to simply take them for granted. How would she ever fit in to a place like this? Compared to them, she was a cultural mutant.

Then Jess' arms closed around her. Things didn't seem as frightening. She was safe. He would take care of her. He rubbed his hands up and down her arms, kissing the top of her head softly.

"It's going to be all right," he whispered. "We just have to take care of a few more things and then we can start building a new life for ourselves. You have to trust me, Bethany. I know what's right for us."

He kissed the top of her head again, then pushed her gently away. He reached down, taking her hands into his. At first she smiled at him. Then she noticed that his grip on her had grown tight.

"I need to go and see about our new ship," he said. "While I'm gone, I'm going to lock you in the fresher."

"Oh, no," she said, heart sinking. "Jess, you can't leave me locked up in this strange place. It's not right."

"I'm sorry," he said. "But I don't have a choice. I can't risk having you run off."

"And just where do you think that I would go?" she asked sarcastically. "I don't exactly know anyone here. What do you think I'm planning to do?"

"I won't risk it," he said, no longer meeting her gaze. She could tell from his tone that the subject was closed. Still holding her hands firmly in his grasp, he walked her toward the fresher.

"Don't bother trying to make a lot of noise," he said as he locked her in. "The room has been sound-proofed. We're close enough to the spaceport that sound baffles are required in all the rooms."

"Just who do you think I'd be trying to attract?" she asked. "Jess, I don't know anyone here. I don't even know how to read half the signs we passed on the way in. They're in another language. Why do you think I'm so bound and determined to run off?"

He didn't reply. Instead, he pushed her into the small room and shut the door. She sat on the floor, feeling as if she were caught in some kind of bizarre time loop. No matter what she said to him, he still didn't trust her. He treated her well ninety percent of the time, yet he still wasn't secure enough to leave her alone.

She didn't *want* to leave him.

She liked him, touching him made her happy. She'd been angry with him at first, but she wasn't a fool. The slave revolt had given her new hope and the chance for happiness. Happiness with him. Even if that weren't enough reason to stay with him, she had her fear. This new world he was showing her was frightening. She didn't understand how it worked, didn't understand how she would be able to survive here without some kind of help. She liked the idea of building a life with him, although she had no idea how they were going to do such a thing if he wouldn't talk to her about it. They couldn't go on like this indefinitely, she already knew that. They would drive each other crazy, end up strangling each other. This was no way to live.

She sat there and waited for him for several hours. Finally she fell asleep, only to be awakened by the sound of the door opening. He was back. Within seconds he opened the fresher door. He stood tall over her in the door, reaching one hand down to help her to her feet, his face grim. She shivered.

He looked completely different. Instead of wearing the monochrome, drab coveralls that all Pilgrim men wore, he was in a sleek black suit. Well tailored, it clung to his body, emphasizing his broad shoulders and muscular chest. It was severe and simple, yet far more elegant than anything she had ever seen before. He was incredibly handsome, almost unreal. *What if he left me?* she wondered, feeling faint and suddenly self-conscious. Her hair was ragged, her hands were rough. What would a man like this see in her, especially when there were so many women on the station who seemed more than eager for his attention? Women who wore feathers, like Mary. Exotic women.

"I brought you some things," he said, unaware of her troubled thoughts as he pulled her to her feet. He turned and walked over to the bed. She stood and followed him on shaky legs. There were several packages, all brightly colored.

"What are they?" she asked.

"Clothing," he said. "I bought you some new things. Go ahead and open them."

She touched one of the boxes hesitantly, then pulled it open. The fabric inside was soft, far softer than anything she'd ever felt.

"That's called Fella sheen," Jess said. "It's only woven on Fella, from the cocoons of tiny creatures that live in the trees there. It's very lightweight, but incredibly durable. I thought it might make a nice change for you. Why don't you try it on?"

She held it up, amazed to see the small puddle of fabric expand into a full-length dress. But not a dress like anything she'd ever worn before. There were slits up the sides. She pulled out another piece of cloth and discovered a matching pair of pants. Just how was a woman supposed to wear something like this?

"Many of the women here wear jumpsuits like mine," he said quietly. "But I thought you might be more comfortable in something like this. You wear the dress over the pants, but when you walk, your legs are still covered. It's a very popular style."

"Why can't I just wear my own clothes?" she asked nervously. So many things were changing so quickly, she hardly knew what to think about this. Was he ashamed of the way she looked? She raised a hand to her hair, fingering the rough ends self-consciously. She'd done her best to even them up after he'd cut part of it off during the revolt, but it was still uneven.

"Because I've sold the ship," he said. "We're not Pilgrims anymore, we're tourists. We need to look the part. I've got new identities for us, too."

"New identities?" she asked. "I don't think I understand."

"You can buy anything on Discovery Station for the right price," Jess said lightly. He turned from her, walking across the room to sit down in a chair. "We've already got the paperwork. We'll go in tomorrow for the surgery."

"Surgery?" she asked, feeling the blood drain from her face.

"I need surgery to change my finger and retinal prints," Jess said, smiling. "Don't worry, it won't take long. The DNA patch is just an injection. They'll test you, too, to see if you're in any databases. I'm betting you won't need any surgery. I doubt the Pilgrims bothered to register you with anyone."

"That's a relief," she said, shivering.

"I'll get Calla tonight," Jess added. "She'll need the surgery, too. I did some checking around. Jenner, the bitch who used to own me and who still owns Calla, seems to have left the station, and the Saurellians have commandeered her business. I'm hoping this will make rescuing Calla easier."

"If it's so easy to get a slave away from here, why didn't you escape a long time ago?" Bethany asked worriedly. "I don't understand."

"There are two reasons I didn't escape before," Jess said, his face growing shadowed. "Calla was too afraid, for one. And I didn't have any money. Between selling the ore and selling the ship I've got plenty now. More than I'd ever dreamed."

"Didn't you have to buy a new ship, though?"

"Yes, but it was relatively cheap compared to the freighter," Jess said. "Everyone here is looking for big ships. Getting something small was easy enough."

"I see," she said, not understanding him at all. Things were moving too quickly for her.

"Aren't you going to put on the dress?" he asked after a brief pause. "I thought I might take you out for dinner."

"Out for dinner?" she asked. What was he talking about?

"Yes, out," he replied, laughing. "They have businesses here called restaurants, where they provide food for a price. This way we don't have to worry about cooking."

"This is a wonderful place," she said, eyes growing wide. "Is there anything that they don't do for you here?"

"As long as you have money, you'll get whatever you want," Jess replied with a smile. "Anything."

Chapter Twelve

∞

Jess had certainly been right about that, Bethany thought, her head swimming. She had just finished her third glass of something he called wine. It had taken her a while to figure out it was alcoholic, because it didn't have the harsh bite that *bakrah* did. This stuff was definitely going to her head. She swayed in her seat, reaching out with one finger to wipe the last of the sauce off her plate. It was rich and meaty, and so spicy that it made her ears burn. She could actually feel the hot blood rushing through them, and giggled. Jess shot her a look across the table, and she stuck her tongue out at him. He needed to relax more, she thought, taking another deep drink of the wine.

It was the best meal she'd ever had, even though Jess wasn't letting her eat as much as she wanted. He kept insisting she was going to make herself sick. At that moment she hardly cared. Getting sick would be a small price to pay for food as good as this.

They sat in a small, dimly lit restaurant. All around them were other couples, laughing and talking softly. They all seemed happy, as if they were having a wonderful time. Music played in the background, creating a low, pulsing noise that made Bethany feel like swaying in her seat. There was something about this place that was amazing, and so relaxing she didn't even feel strange about the crazy clothing she wore any longer. Jess had been right, most of the other women were wearing jumpsuits. She might not be fully covered by the clinging fabric, but she was far more covered than the women around her.

Their waiter brought them a small bowl of something cold and sweet. There were two spoons in it, and Bethany gave a squeal of delight as she tasted it. It was the best thing she'd ever eaten. She could hear Jess laughing at her, but she didn't care. She just ate spoonful after sweet spoonful, letting each melt in her mouth and moaning with pleasure. When they were done, she stuck her finger in, scooping out the last traces.

Jess stood, and reached out to take her arm.

"I think we should head back to the hostel," he said, dark blue eyes glowing. She shivered, enjoying the way he looked at her. He was dark, intense, and his eyes burned with lust. He wanted her and it made her feel powerful. This incredible man, the one all the women were looking at, wanted her. The slave revolt really was the best thing that had ever happened in her life.

Together they walked out of the restaurant into the spaceport's main thoroughfare. Even though it was late in the cycle, the place was filled with men and women laughing and drinking. Several men looked at her in ways that made her blush, and more than one woman smiled an invitation at Jess. She craned her head, wondering if that Mary was around anywhere. She was so busy looking that she stumbled, although Jess caught her easily enough. She blinked, surprised by how unsteady she felt. Just walking was confusing. Which way was their hostel, anyway?

She lurched away from Jess as something caught her eye. There was a woman in the air above one of the doorways, writhing naked with some kind of creature wrapped around her. What was it? Bethany stopped, cocking her head and staring in wonder. Jess tugged at her arm, but she refused to move. What was that thing? And what was the woman doing with it?

Jess turned back, and laughed when he saw what she was looking at.

"How does that woman just hang up in the air like that?" Bethany whispered, completely confused.

"It's a hologram," Jess said. "It's just a projection. The woman is actually inside on a stage. Or it may just be a recording."

"What is she doing?"

"That's a little harder to explain..." Jess said, a grin playing around the corners of his mouth. "It's a sex show. Entertainment. People pay money to see others performing sexual acts."

"I've never heard of anything that looks like that," she replied. Someone jostled her, and she bumped against Jess. Mmm... He smelled good. She reached her arms around him and pulled him close.

"Have you ever seen one of these sex shows?" she asked. She could feel his muscles tighten beneath her fingers, and his cock hardened against her body. His eyes grew smoky and his expression softened.

"Yes, I have been to a few of them," he said.

"Can we go?" she asked. The look on his face made her laugh. He was clearly startled by her request.

"I don't know that it's a good idea, at least not tonight," he said finally. "I'm going after Calla soon, and I don't think this is the best way to get ready for that particular task."

She pulled at his arm, trying to get him to follow her into the show, but he stood firm.

"Bethany, we really need to go back to our room," he said. She studied him, trying to gauge if she had even a chance of changing his mind, but his expression remained the same. *It wasn't going to happen,* she thought mournfully.

They walked back toward the hostel slowly, Jess holding her hand, and she soon forgot her disappointment. The port was amazing, filled with hundreds, thousands, of people. Some of them spoke languages she couldn't understand, and all of a sudden a thought hit her.

"What language do I speak?" she asked. "I never realized that there was more than one. Is this a Pilgrim language?"

Jess started laughing.

"No, this is Basic," he said. "As far as I know, Pilgrims don't have their own language."

"What is Basic?" she asked. "Is it the Imperial language?"

"Well, it's the trade language," he said. "On many worlds, it's the primary language, and certainly the primary language on most space stations like this one. Almost everyone speaks Basic, although most people speak their own language, too."

"Do you speak more than one language?" she asked suddenly.

"Sort of," he said. "I speak Basic and I also know slave sign."

"What's slave sign?"

"It's a method of communication between slaves," he said. "It allows us to talk with each other without being overheard. At least much of the time."

"Do all slaves know it?"

"No," he said quietly. "Generally only Imperial slaves. Men and women raised on slave farms, like myself. Sometimes those who are enslaved later in life learn, but not always."

"You were raised on a slave farm?" she asked. "What is that?"

"You have a lot of questions tonight," he said. "I'll tell you about the slave farm some other time. I think we should try to enjoy ourselves now. I have work to do later."

"What are you doing later?" she asked, her mind reeling. It was hard keeping things straight when you drank wine, she thought.

He burst out laughing. "You don't listen very well, do you?"

"No," she said pertly. She grinned at him, and he leaned over to kiss her on the mouth. The touch sent a tingle of sensation coursing through her and she leaned against him. He held her close and they stood there, frozen in time for a moment, before someone in the crowed jostled them.

"This is such an amazing place," she said suddenly. "I didn't realize that so many people could be all together like this at once. I can hardly believe it's real."

"It's real all right," he said. "And very interesting, but I think I'd like to go back to the hostel now."

"Oh really?" she asked archly, rubbing against him. She could feel his arousal rising, and reveled in it. "Did you have any specific activity in mind for when we get there?"

"Many things," he said, kissing her softly.

The touch of his lips against hers made her shiver, and she sighed. How wonderful it felt to be with him here, on this night, in this place. Who would have thought such a thing was possible?

Pulling her gently by the hands, Jess started moving towards the pod-shaped vehicle that would carry them across the port to their hostel. She allowed herself to simply enjoy the moment, the rough feeling of his hand in hers, the warmth of his body. It was so good to be with him, to not be worried about anything for once.

To not be afraid.

That's what it was, she realized. For the first time in her life she wasn't afraid. She was safe with Jess. Somehow she knew that, deep within herself. She knew it beyond a doubt. Jess would always protect her.

The shuttle pulled up before them and they stepped in. She allowed herself to settle beside him as he wrapped his arm around her shoulders. She was tired, just a bit sleepy, so she let her eyes close and simply luxuriated in the feel of him next to her. She could smell him. He was clean, but that slightly tangy, almost spicy scent she had come to associate with him was still there. It seemed as if there was a halo of energy surrounding them, walling them in and allowing them to build their own special little world. She imagined herself as a green, flickering flame. His energy was a red flame, strong and shot through with streaks of black and orange. Her green should have paled next to him, but instead lived within it, sheltered by the stronger energy of his body.

So perfect, as if they were created for each other.

She nodded, drowsily imagining their flames burning together, until the pod came to a stop. Then he was pulling her to her feet, and they stumbled out into the wide corridor. There were fewer people around them now. It was a good place to be, she thought. Going home. Not that the hostel was really their home. Maybe the new ship would feel like a home, she thought suddenly.

"How much did the new ship cost?" she asked suddenly curious. "How much money do we have left over? Will it be enough?"

"Oh, it will be enough," Jess said quietly. "Between selling the ore and the ore carrier, we have more than enough to start a new life for ourselves. More than enough for Calla and Bragan, too."

They were at their hostel now, all closed up for the night. Next to the door was a security box. Jess pulled a small card out of his pocket and stuck it in a slot in the door. It swished open, and he guided her through the door and down the silent hall to their room. Then he opened that door, and they walked inside. Bethany tripped lightly once more and Jess caught her.

He pulled her into his arms, and she went to him with a sigh. *What was it about this man that gave her such pleasure?* she wondered She wrapped her arms around his body, feeling the muscles under his skin tensing as her fingers danced across them.

"Kiss me," she demanded, tilting her head up toward him.

Jess looked down at her, taken for a moment by the strange mix of her commanding tone with the soft blurring of her gaze. She was a little drunk from the wine, and more relaxed with him than he could ever remember her being.

How had he managed to find this woman? His life was suddenly all but perfect. He had Bethany, a ship, a future. Soon he would have his sister back, too, and together they would rescue Bragan. After that, who knew what wonderful things might happen. For the first time in his life he had a future, and the Goddess had even been gracious enough to give him someone to share it with. It was nothing short of a miracle.

Filled with a sense of wonder, he allowed his lips to take hers, marveling at their soft texture. He kissed her, lips closed, for several minutes. The soft warmth of her mouth against his was amazing—beautiful and exciting all at once. He could feel the blood rushing between his legs, feel his cock rising with anticipation. Soon he would slide that hard part of himself into her body, and the delicious warmth and wetness of her would close around him. The friction of her folds would carry him to new heights, and the squeezing of her muscles would draw a climax out of him more stunning than any other he had experienced before meeting her.

How had he even imagined those earlier fleeting encounters to be true sex? They were nothing compared to this, simply the release of tension, a bodily function completed. This was so much more.

She pressed closer to him, and he could feel the soft mounds of her breasts against his chest. Her nipples slowly hardened as his own responded. She shifted her legs against his restlessly, and then her tongue stole out of her mouth, burning a path along his lips. He opened for her and their tongues met playfully. One of her hands stole down between them, cupping his erection lightly, and he shuddered.

He reached down and cupped both hands around her buttocks, lifting her easily into the air. She gasped, the motion pulling her head from his. Her hands clutched his shoulders for balance, and her legs wrapped tightly around his waist.

He carried her across the room to their bed. It was larger and far more comfortable than that on the ore hauler, almost decadent in comparison.

Jess had been dreaming about taking her on a bed like this one since the first time he'd seen it. Now he carried her toward it, wishing their clothes were already gone and that he could thrust into her immediately.

Bethany seemed to be feeling the same way. She rubbed her clit against the hard ridge of his cock through their clothing, straining at him for more stimulation. He laughed, and leaned over to settle her gently on the bed. She kept her hold on him, pulling him down with her. The move caught him off guard, and he fell down over her. She pulled him, rolling him across the bed until she was on top of him, leaning down against his chest and kissing him deeply. It took him off guard, although not in a bad way. He was simply amazed, and not for the first time, that the shy, quiet woman he had first met on the mining station had turned out to be so fiery. Even when he had first taken her from her people, she had seemed meek enough. He knew better now. She would be a formidable opponent if she ever turned on him.

The thought cooled him momentarily, then was gone as she kissed him again, pulling on his shirt. She wanted him naked, now. Her actions were clear. He wasn't about to fight with her.

He reached down to the hem of her dress, pulling it up and over her head. It was hard at first, their arms kept tangling together as they tugged at the clothing. Then she slithered out of the silky pants she wore under the dress and he raised his hips to lower his own pants. The cool air hit his cock, but did nothing to dampen his arousal. He wanted to feel that slick warmth close over him. He would never get enough of her. Never.

Now she was naked, with the warmth of her soft skin fluttering against his body in so many places he felt like he was dying. How could a man survive something like this, night after night? His heart was pounding, every nerve in his body singing. He could feel the pressure in his loins, building and growing impossibly stronger as she pushed against his erection.

Then she moved to straddle him, and he could feel her heat. It was a tangible presence, all but touching him even though his aching cock was still inches from her opening. She lowered her body over his slowly and deliberately, her fingers catching and stopping his hand when he tried to pull her down more quickly. It was tortuous and beautiful all at once. He was going to die.

She sheathed him. For one glorious moment he was content, held within her pulsing body as she squeezed slowly and steadily. Their heartbeats seemed to meld, as if they shared a physical connection so strong that they truly were one creature at that moment. Then she squeezed him again, and he was filled with the need to move, to thrust into her deeply, repeating himself until she screamed and spasmed around him. But she wasn't playing along.

Bethany raised her body and laughed as his hips pulled back from hers, pressing down into the bed. He needed more friction, more movement. It wasn't enough to simply experience this teasing slowness. He had to feel more, had to have her flesh rubbing back and forth against his. Time to take control.

Without warning, he sat up and flipped her over beneath him. She squealed in protest, but he ignored her, grimly thrusting in and out of her. She was slick with need for him, and her grunts as he started pounding into her were more than enough evidence that she was enjoying it every bit as much as he. He wanted to go harder, deeper. He wanted to plant his seed in her. The thought of it turned his vision red, and he closed his eyes, focusing every bit of his energy on thrusting into her again and again.

She was panting and gasping now and he knew her orgasm must be close. The thought of her beneath him, helpless, surged through him like the sweetest of wines. He could taste her need, thrust into her to emphasize that only he could provide her with this. The thought of her approaching another man flitted through his head. *No.* He wouldn't let himself think of that. She was his, all his, and he was marking her.

She would never forget who she belonged to.

He thrust deeper, feeling the bed sway beneath them as they moved. She whimpered something at him, her voice needy. He couldn't understand what she was saying. The blood was pounding too hard in his ears and slowing down was not an option. Each thrust brought him that much closer to the achingly beautiful conclusion they both needed. He had to go harder, faster. He had to hold on and not give in to the desire to explode. They were going to come together, or not at all. He wouldn't give her a choice about that.

A sudden, sharp pain broke through his thoughts, and he realized that she had scratched his back. Her fingernails tore through his skin, each one clawing a trail of fire through him. It helped him focus. He reached down to pull her hips more firmly under his and she gave a little scream.

Time to finish it.

He pulled one hand free and pressed his thumb against her clit, rubbing it back and forth as he breached her. She gasped, and a fine sheen of perspiration broke out across her face. He could feel her muscles stiffening, could see her pulling air deep into her chest. It was only a matter of seconds now. He gave one last mighty thrust, working her clit with his thumb, and watched her face intently. Her head flung back as she came with a scream. Her internal muscles gripped him tightly, and he gasped. He wanted to watch her, take her pleasure into himself, but it was too late. His own orgasm was upon him, his body had taken over and was making the decisions now. He could feel the pressure and tension explode out his cock as waves of pleasure shot through his body, radiating out from his pelvis. It was spectacular, better than he could have dreamed.

Was every time with her going to be like this? A new high, a new kind of sexual ecstasy? If so, he may very well die with the next few weeks, he thought wryly. One man's body was not designed for this kind of stress…

* * * * *

Jess stole through the corridors of the station, taking care to attract as little notice as possible. It wasn't hard as it was the middle of the sleep cycle and this was a quiet area.

It was amazing to him how things had changed, and yet stayed the same. He had lived in these halls all of his life, yet everything was different now. Their Saurellian overlords had been active during their brief tenure. The port was still wild and full, but there seemed to be more order in the rest of the station. There were certainly more guardsmen. There were also more public receptacles for trash, and much less graffiti.

The Saurellians, apparently, preferred their space stations to be clean.

Another major difference was the public notices calling on station residents to register to vote. He had no idea what they would be voting on. He couldn't even imagine doing so. Never, in his entire life, had there been a vote on the station about anything. Strangely enough, the few businesses owned by Pilgrims appeared to be shut down. Was Jenner's disappearance connected, he wondered?

He was near the hostel where he had grown up now, and it was hard to remember caution. He felt far too comfortable here, yet was far more dangerous for him outside the port. There, the population was transient. Now he found himself among people who might very well recognize him and report him as an escaped slave. Under Imperial rule that would have resulted in his death. The Goddess alone knew what the Saurellians might do to him.

If anything happened, Bethany would be all right, he reminded himself. He had registered her as owner of their new ship. The hostel owner had instructions to check on her if Jess didn't return. She'd be all right. There was more than enough money for her to survive.

He'd come too far to be caught now, though. He was going to free Calla and get out of this hellhole once and for all.

Finally, he reached his goal—the long, narrow passageway. There was a vent at the end that would lead to the storeroom in Jenner's hostel. He and Calla had discovered the secret route as children. They'd always assumed that Jenner had created it in a bout of paranoia, something common enough among Pilgrims. After all, they tended to hoard supplies and tried to always have at least one escape route. Now he would use it to steal Calla right out from under the noses of her masters.

Moving quietly, he opened the vent and started crawling down the shaft. Every inch of it felt familiar to him. He'd used it a thousand times to sneak out of the hostel. As a child, he would go down to the port and follow the traders around, copying their speech and asking questions about foreign worlds. He could have escaped long ago, if Calla hadn't been so afraid.

As a young man, he had discovered the joys to be found among the women of the port. He was handsome and strong—even the women of the most expensive pleasure houses had welcomed him to their beds. More than one had offered to buy him his freedom.

Once again, he had stayed because of Calla. His stomach turned as he realized how foolish they had been. Calla had been fearful, terrified that they would be caught and killed. He realized now that death was far from the worst fate a slave could suffer.

Moving through the passage, he counted down the vents until he reached the one that opened on the hostel. With a flash of triumph, he discovered it was still loose. The vent cover was supposed to be firmly welded directly to the station, making it impossible for a man without sophisticated tools to open it. The welds on this one had been broken for decades, but he had been half afraid the Saurellians would have noticed and fixed it.

Keeping quiet, he pushed the grill open and lowered it to the floor. He slithered out of the vent into the room. *Dank and dusty as ever*, he thought with satisfaction. Nobody was coming in and out of here regularly.

He crept across the floor and listened carefully at the door. Outside was silence. Unless things had changed significantly, everyone would have been asleep for hours. Calla would be in the kitchen, her pallet laid out with those of the other women. For the first time he realized Calla might not be the only slave who wanted to leave. His gut twisted. It would endanger them all if he brought too many back with him to the ship, but he didn't have a choice. If his fellow slaves wanted to leave, he would help them.

It was the only right thing to do.

Walking down the hall, he looked carefully at each door, trying to determine if anyone was awake. Jenner's office was open, although there was no light inside. He'd never seen it left open like that before. She really was gone. It was hard to imagine in some ways. Jenner had always seemed like a force of nature to him, immovable and certainly unstoppable. Yet she had left for the first time in years. Was it really a business trip, or had the Saurellians frightened her that much?

He kept moving until he reached the kitchen. Fortunately, Calla always slept closest to the door because she had to go to the fresher at least once every night. He'd teased her about it mercilessly as a teenager. He eased the door open, eyes searching the dimly lit room. Things were different, he realized. Most of his life there had been four or five women who slept here, all slaves. Now there was only one. Calla? No, whoever this was, she was smaller than Calla.

Her body was completely covered by the blanket, a nicer one than he'd remembered having when he'd lived with Jenner. What had happened, where was everyone? And how was he going to find his sister?

He would have to wake the woman up and ask. It was likely that he knew her. He doubted that Jenner would have bought another slave so quickly. The old bitch was notoriously tight with her cash. He walked carefully over to the sleeping woman and knelt silently beside her. Her hair was a soft gold, familiar to him it. It was Hari, the kitchen girl. They had been slaves together for more than a decade. She would never betray him, he thought in relief.

He touched her shoulder softly, shaking her and whispering her name.

"Hari, wake up," he said. She muttered something, and tried to roll over. He had to hold in a laugh. Some things never changed. Hari had always been the last one up in the morning, and grumpy for hours afterwards.

"Wake up," he repeated, and she opened her eyes.

"What is it?" she asked sleepily, brushing her hair out of her eyes. "I'm sleeping. Jess, is that you?"

She sat bolt upright, looking at him with wide eyes.

"Yes," he replied, unable to keep from smiling at her. She seemed so young. They were nearly the same age, but now he felt like he was centuries older. Life had been so easy here, he thought longingly. He hadn't known what suffering was...

"What are you doing here? We all thought you would be dead by now!" She gasped, flinging herself into his arms. "Oh, I can't believe this. We have to go tell the others that you're alive."

"*Shhhh,*" he said. "No, we have to be quiet. I can't be caught here."

"No, everything has changed!" she said. "Oh, Jess, you're safe here now. Jenner's gone."

"I know," he said. "But that hardly makes us safe, Hari."

"Oh, no, it does!" she said. "We're free now, Jess! All of us! The Saurellians wanted to keep using the hostel but they didn't want to manage it, so they turned it over to us and we're running it for them now. It's wonderful."

He shook his head, unable to understand what she was saying. The Saurellians had freed Jenner's slaves?

"Where's Calla?" he asked. Her face changed abruptly, and she looked away.

"I think we should wake Karin up," she said suddenly, referring to the head cook. Jess narrowed his eyes.

"No, I want to hear where Calla is," he said, gripping her shoulders firmly. She tried to turn away from him, and he shook her shoulders roughly. She whimpered. "Where is Calla?"

"Jess, she's dead," Hari said quietly. Jess suddenly felt dizzy, and shook his head.

"What did you say?" he demanded.

"She's dead, Jess," Hari whispered miserably. "It happened right after Jenner sold you to the miners. She disappeared that night, and a few weeks later they found her tracking implant in the recycling plant."

Jess shook his head, unwilling to believe what she was telling him. Calla couldn't be dead. She was a sister, his other half. He had overcome incredible odds to rescue her. What Hari was telling him was impossible. He refused to accept it.

"Jess, I'm so sorry," Hari said miserably. "We never did figure out what happened. We thought maybe she tried to escape, and got picked up by somebody down at the port. You know what can happen to a woman alone down there."

Jess tried not to listen to her, but reality was sinking in against his will. He was all too aware of what could happen to a woman alone. Or even a man alone, if he didn't know what he was about. There were certain areas of the port where predators lurked. They were the very same kinds of places that might attract a young woman trying to escape her owner, he thought desperately.

It wasn't uncommon to find bodies in the station's recycling pits, either. Or rather, parts of bodies. Her tracking implant was probably the only part of Calla that still existed, he thought numbly. Why hadn't he forced her to go with him, to escape while they had a chance? He could have saved her, if only he'd been stronger!

He knew it was a question he would ask himself for the rest of his life.

"I have to go," he said abruptly, unwilling to look at Hari. She had been part of his life here. That life was all over now. All over except for one thing. He still owed Mistress Jenner, wherever she was, a visit.

* * * * *

Bethany had long since given up trying to sleep on the floor in the fresher. He had left her several blankets and a pillow, but all she could think about was Jess, creeping through the station. He was going to find his sister, but what if someone stopped him? Would they realize he was an escapee? What would happen to him, and what would happen to her? There was a cold ball of icy blue fire in her belly. No matter how many times she told herself everything was going to be fine, she couldn't bring herself to believe it.

Something was going to go terribly wrong. She just knew it.

She had no way of measuring the time, but it seemed like hours had passed before she heard noises in the outer room. She listened carefully. One set of footsteps, and no feminine voice. If it was Jess, he didn't have Calla with him. Or maybe someone else had gotten into their room?

A moment later the fresher door opened. She stared up at the man in the doorway, unable to see his face in the darkness.

"Jess, is that you?" she asked softly.

"Yes," he replied, his voice sounding harsh. Something was terribly wrong. There was no other explanation.

"Where is Calla?" she asked, afraid to hear the answer. He turned away from the fresher and walked back toward the bed. She stood shakily and followed him.

"Calla is dead," he said harshly. "I don't want you to mention her name again."

"But what—" she started to ask, but he cut her off.

"Be quiet," he said coldly. "We'll leave in the morning. You'd better get some sleep."

"What about you?" she asked.

"I don't need any sleep," he said tightly. "I need to think."

"All right," she whispered. She crossed the room and slid into the bed, watching him as closely as she could in the darkness. He took a seat in a chair, leaning it back against the wall and putting his feet up. Silence stretched between them, a tangible thing that seemed unbearably painful to her. He was so alone and every part of her ached to comfort him, to pull him into her arms and soothe his pain.

He wasn't going to allow that, she knew already. He didn't want to admit how much he was hurting. In the darkness, she could hear his breathing. It grew rough, as if he were running, and then it caught. He cleared this throat noisily, turning his head away from her.

He was crying, she realized. Crying for his sister.

Her heart ached, but she kept still. He would never want anyone to witness such weakness. Not for one moment could he concede that he was anything less than hard and tough, a man who could handle any obstacle. If only he understood that he didn't need to be alone, she thought sadly.

Of course, he couldn't even figure out that he didn't need to lock her up to keep her, she thought with dark humor. Yet she couldn't imagine leaving him. He had become everything to her, and he didn't even realize it.

* * * * *

Bethany had just fallen asleep when the entire room shuddered, rolling her halfway across the bed. Loud sirens filled the air, and an emergency light started strobing.

"What's going on?" she gasped, sitting up in the bed. It was the most horrifying racket she'd ever heard. The light wasn't helping. Everything seemed surreal, jerky.

Jess was already on his feet, moving toward her and pulling her into his arms.

"There's been a hull breach," he said, voice strained. He ran his hands over her body, checking her for injuries. "The station is under attack."

Chapter Thirteen

೫

The words "hull breach" struck a fear into her heart. A child of the mining belt, she knew that nothing was more dangerous that a breach. Within seconds, all the air on a station could be sucked out into the cold night of the vacuum. They were going to die. She shivered, and he stroked her hair.

"Don't worry," he said, his voice soothing. "It's going to be all right. We're safe in here. As soon as we were hit, every door on this station locked tight. We've got plenty of back-up air sources, and we'll be fine."

"Who do you think did it?" she whispered. "Why would they attack the station?"

"I don't know, I suppose it could be the Empire," Jess said. "But don't worry—this station is far too valuable for them to destroy it. And the Saurellians have it well defended. We're going to be fine."

She started to ask him something else, but she was cut off as a cool, smooth woman's voice came over the intercom into their room.

"Can I have your attention, please," the voice said. "This is the Discovery Station Emergency Protocol System. Discovery Station had been attacked by a small ship and a minor hull breach has occurred. The breach is located in Sector 8, levels 2-4. Please remain calm as station personnel repair this breach. Further instructions will follow as needed."

The voice stopped, although the lights continued to flash.

"Has this ever happened before?" she asked quietly, settling against him. Her heart was still pounding rapidly, and so was his. Yet she could feel the quiet strength in his arms, the warmth of his body, and her initial panic was dying down.

"Sure," he said. "I can think of two or three times that this happened as I was growing up. It must not be anything too serious or they would have given specialized evacuation instructions to the people in those sectors. The breach is small, and it's in a storage area. With any luck nobody was hurt."

"What could have caused it?" she asked.

"Well, a small ship could have crashed into the station. Or perhaps a missile of some kind, although if it were an attack, I'd think that they would notify us."

The voice crackled into the room again.

"May I have your attention, please," it said. "The hull breach has been sealed and the state of emergency has been downgraded to a state of alert. The station is now secure. The Station Commander has directed all civilian personnel to remain in their quarters until further notice. If there is a medical emergency, please contact your sector captain for assistance. A listing of sector captains is available on all public and private information terminals by pressing zero. I repeat, all civilian personnel are to remain in their quarters until further notice."

The light stopped flashing, and silence filled the room. For a moment, Bethany couldn't help but wonder if the entire thing had been some sort of surreal dream.

"That's strange," Jess said. "There must be something more than an accident going on. Something suspicious, but less than a full attack. Let's turn on the news channel. Computer, please turn on vid screen."

The screen embedded in the wall across the room flickered to life, and sound filled the room. A woman with a calm face and perfectly coifed hair smiled out at them from the screen.

"The station commander assures us that the attack was insignificant, and was not orchestrated by Imperial forces," she said. "According to station sources, the hull breach was sealed quickly according to emergency protocol. The effected areas have been evacuated, and repair crews are already moving into place. We do not yet have an estimation of the damages or an anticipated time of repair. There is also no estimate of casualties, although the affected area was not heavily populated. "

She stopped speaking for a moment and cocked her head.

"This just in," she continued. "Station Command has just informed us that ore processing plant number 15, located in the third sector, has been destroyed. The ore processing plant is one of the smaller plants servicing Discovery Station and was unmanned. Command informs us that they suspect sabotage, although they have not clarified whether they believe it to be sabotage from within the station, or if the saboteurs are at large within the system."

"It takes a lot of firepower to destroy an ore processing plant," Jess remarked coolly. "This could make things more difficult. They're going to be looking very closely at everyone who goes in and out of this station. We may have to lay low for a while."

"What about Bragan?" she asked softly. "He's waiting for us."

"Well, he'll just have to wait another week," Jess replied. "It won't do him any good if we're arrested and never make it back to him."

"And the doctor?" she asked. "Do you think he'll still be willing to go after an attack like this? We can't rescue Bragan without him."

"I never asked the doctor if he was willing to go with us," Jess said.

"You're planning to kidnap the doctor?" she asked. "That's crazy!"

"No more crazy than planning a revolt on a mining colony," he replied. "I won't hurt him, and he'll be paid for his time. It's a better deal than Bragan ever got. Any of the slaves, for that matter."

She stayed silent, unsure of how to respond. On the one hand he was right, but on the other... It was just one more crime. How many crimes would they have to commit before they were free? She didn't like thinking about it.

She pulled away from him, laying back down onto the bed and trying to think. The vid screen still flickered in the darkness, but he had turned down the volume. She closed her eyes, willing herself to sleep. Sleeping would be so much better than having to think at this point.

Jess lay down beside her, wrapping one arm around her possessively. For one moment she thought he wanted to have sex but he simply held her. Perhaps he needed comforting, she thought. She certainly did. She snuggled back into his arms, grateful for the warmth. She would worry about everything else tomorrow.

* * * * *

Jess lay awake in the darkness, holding Bethany and thinking. He could tell when she finally dropped off to sleep as her breathing grew slow and steady. The tension in her arms and back also disappeared, and she made a soft snuffling noise as she burrowed into his side.

Nothing was going according to his plan.

How could he have gotten this close to freeing himself and Calla, only to find out she was dead and they were caught in the middle of an attack on Discovery Station? How good were the new identities he had purchased for them? With a sinking feeling, he realized they wouldn't find out until they tried to use them. After an attack like this one, the Saurellians wouldn't be inclined to treat them kindly if they were caught with false documents.

Then there was Bragan, patiently waiting for their return. The poor man was alone in that Goddess-forsaken place. Completely isolated, how long would the man last? Even if he survived physically, how would he hold up mentally? And what if some other group of Pilgrims arrived to find their station destroyed before he could get back.

What would the bastards do to Bragan? He shuddered at the thought.

Bethany was counting on him, too. She had no idea how to take care of herself in the larger world. She had no skills, no education. He had to admit that, in many ways, his life as a slave on the station had been far better than hers as a woman in the mining belt. He owed it to her to make a better life for both of them. He also owed something to Calla. Revenge. Calla was dead because she'd tried to escape, tried to find him. It had happened the same day Jenner had sold him to the miners. Bitch. She had a lot to answer for, and he would see that she paid. First he would rescue Bragan, and then he would find Jenner.

After that? He and Bethany would be free. Truly free. They would find some place far away and build a new life together.

She twisted in his arms, nestling her head into the crook of his arm.

She deserved so much more than she'd gotten out of life. He would give her everything she deserved and more, he vowed. Just as soon as he avenged his sister.

* * * * *

Bethany awoke to find Jess sprawled across her. On the vid screen there was a diagram of the entire mining system, with an arrow pointing at an area almost directly opposite Discovery Station.

"Computer, raise volume," she said softly. The newscaster's voice came into the room.

"The destroyed outpost is in orbit on the far side of the mining belt," she was saying. "Apparently Saurellian officials have known of its destruction for several days, although that information did not become public until early this morning."

Bethany shook Jess awake. He raised his head, blinking.

"Jess, they're talking about Bethesda Station," she said. "Or at least I think they are."

His gaze turned alert, and his eyes moved to the vid screen.

"For all of you waking up," the newscaster said. "I would like to repeat the morning's news. Following last night's attack, Saurellian officials have announced that a mining station belonging to a small religious sect, calling themselves Pilgrims of the Apocalypse, has been destroyed. The explosion encompassed more than 500,000 square miles of space. Discovery Station Commander Ivankov has also notified us that station officials received a message this morning from a group identifying themselves as Pilgrims. The group is claiming responsibility for this morning's attack on the Discovery Station, apparently in retaliation for the destruction of their mining outpost. The commander will be addressing all station residents in approximately one standard hour to discuss the situation."

"Jess, what they are talking about?" she whispered quietly. "Why would somebody destroy the mining outpost? Who could do something like that?"

"Well, as far as I know, only the Saurellians or the Empire has that kind of fire power," he said softly. "I can't imagine why they'd target the outpost, though. There was nothing left there..."

"Bragan was left there. Do you think he's dead?"

Jess took a deep breath, then replied, "Yes, he has to be. There's no way he could have survived something like that, and we were his only hope of rescue."

Bethany shook her head. So much destruction.

"Poor Bragan," she said softly. "He'd been through so much already. It's not fair."

"Life isn't fair," Jess said curtly, rolling out of bed. "I'm going to take a shower before the station commander does his address."

Bethany nodded, watching him stalk into the fresher. Then she leaned back against the pillows, eyes moving to the vid screen. The newscaster was now presenting an overview of Pilgrim beliefs.

"The Pilgrims of the Apocalypse have existed in small pockets for more than 1,000 years," the woman was saying. "Very little is known about this obscure and secretive cult. Until recently, they have been largely located within the Empire, and are headquartered on the planet Karos. Their founder, known as the Celestial Pilgrim, was a young Imperial nobleman who gave up his rank and status, retreating to a cave in the mountains above his ancestral home. Nearly ten years later, all but forgotten, he re-emerged and announced that he was the new incarnation of truth and reality. He invited all those present to follow him into the realms of enlightenment, and the Pilgrim movement was born.

"The Basic tenets of the Pilgrim religion are obscure, although rumors abound. Only elders and a handpicked group of priests are given access to the full range of writings and instructions left behind by the Celestial Pilgrim. The rest of those born into the cult are trained to be obedient pawns, working blindly to fulfill the goals of the group."

Well, that was certainly accurate, Bethany thought darkly. She had never been privy to the secrets of the religion that governed her life. Of course, neither had her father. She gave a wry smile as she thought of what they had all been taught. *Only that which is needed is known. Do not question the Pilgrim's needs, strive to meet them.*

As far she knew, nobody in the mining outpost had known what they were truly working toward. All they knew was that the Pilgrim had asked them to work for him, and they must obey.

"While the Pilgrims have been the victims of some persecution under the Empire," the newscaster said in the background, "nearly 200 years ago they reached an agreement with then-sitting Emperor, Nahn'vet VIII, on taxation and religious freedom. Since that time, they have operated largely independently within the Empire, although always respectful of Imperial law. They do not participate in any type of local government, and have been excused from fighting in the Imperial army. They are not known to exist within the Federation."

Jess came back out of the fresher.

"What are they talking about?" he asked.

"Pilgrim culture," she said. "Did you realize that they know more about the Pilgrims than I do?"

"Are you sure they're right?" he asked. "That doesn't make sense to me."

"I think being a Pilgrim doesn't make much sense," she said darkly.

"I can't argue with that," he said, rubbing a towel against his hair.

"I love how the showers here have water," she said quietly. "I've never seen anything like it."

"It's actually pretty common," he said, voice muffled by the towel. "The only places that don't have water are some of the long-haul cargo ships. Even those usually have both, though."

"Oh," she said, feeling foolish. There was so much about this outside world that she had no understanding of. It was hard at times. He turned away from her, and suddenly she felt very alone.

"Jess, would you like to come back to bed?" she asked softly. She didn't like this distance between them. It needed healing.

"No," he said tightly.

"There's nothing else we can do," she said. "We're stuck in here. Maybe it will help."

He shook his head and she sighed heavily.

Throwing off the covers, she went into the fresher herself. Might as well take advantage of the shower if there was nothing else to do.

The hot water sluiced over her, washing away some of her fears. Just standing here, allowing this water to run down her body, seemed so decadent. Dangerous, even. There was so much more to life than she'd ever realized.

It was good.

She turned her face into the stream and closed her eyes. Despite everything—the suffering, the loss, the pain—life was good. Even if she died within the next hour, she had had this one perfect moment in the shower. The absurdity of her thoughts hit her, and she laughed out loud. The sound echoed off the walls of the shower, and she laughed again with sheer pleasure.

The door opened abruptly.

"Bethany, are you all right in here?" Jess asked, his voice tense.

"I'm wonderful, Jess," she said, laughing again. "You have no idea how wonderful this shower is."

"Bethany, what's going on?" he asked, stepping into the room. She could hear the concern in his voice, and realized that she must sound crazy to him.

Fair enough.

"I'm happy, Jess," she said, pushing open the door to the fresher. She smiled at him invitingly, lifting her arms and slicking back her wet hair. She could feel her breasts lifting, her nipples hardening as the cool air hit them. The look on his face was priceless.

"I'm happy despite everything that is wrong right now, because I'm alive and I'm in a shower and all the odds were against success. Would you like to join me?"

He shook his head slowly, and she laughed again. She reached up and cupped her breasts, kneading them softly with her fingers.

"Are you sure?" she asked archly.

He grunted, then shrugged out of the pants he must have pulled on after she left the room. He stepped into the small booth with her, reaching both arms down to her butt and pulling her up hard against him. His mouth took hers, harsh and demanding. She wrapped her arms around his neck and sunk into his kiss with a sigh of relief.

They were connecting with each other again.

He was hard against her, and she wiggled, enjoying the feel of him as he grew more eager for her touch. Bethany felt as if the Goddess were inside her, feminine energy and power pumping through her veins as her tongue darted out, meeting his in a dance as old as time. He groaned, and then kissed her even more deeply. He pressed her against the wall of the shower, his pelvis pumping against her even as he sought entry to her body.

She lifted herself, and he thrust deep inside her. He hit her cervix and she gasped. It always amazed her that they fit together so well. He was massive, yet her body seemed to have been created for his touch. Nothing they did could be anything less than perfect.

He pulled out of her and then thrust back inside, seeming to go deeper and deeper with every motion. Tension built within her. She was aware of the slippery surface of the shower wall behind her in a vague way, and that the hot water still slid over them, yet he never lost his grasp. A sudden thought caught him. What would it be like if they could do thing this together in a tub full of water? Before she could think any further on her new idea, he thrust against her again, this time at a slightly different angle. She could hardly breathe because now his entire length was rubbing against her clit. The arousal that had been slowly dancing along her nerve ending grew suddenly urgent. She couldn't breathe and she could hardly hold on to him. Everything in her body seemed to be wrapped up in him. He was her ground, her base, the source of her energy. She needed to take him into her fully, to become one with him.

She tried to urge him to move more quickly, grasping at his neck and shoulders as hard as she could, but the water kept her from gripping him like she needed to. Instinct cried out for her to clutch him tight, to bind him to her as her mate. Without thinking, she opened her mouth against his shoulder and bit deeply. He moaned, and she felt something salty filling her mouth. Blood.

He was pounding into her now, each thrust grinding her clitoris against her pelvic bone. The tension was tight within her, and she squeezed him, desperately seeking something more. More pressure, more of his hardness. She had to be filled.

Then it slammed over her. She felt the waves of heat moving through her body, and she screamed out in a mixture of triumph and joy. He followed her a moment later, hips pulsing as hot waves of his seed shot deep into her body. She collapsed against his shoulder and his grip on her softened.

They stood there in the shower, breathing heavily, for several minutes. He leaned down and kissed her wet face softly. She started to say something, but she was cut off by a low-pitched buzzing noise.

"May I have your attention please," a voice said coolly and calmly from a small speaker in the corner of the shower. Bethany started, then realized it was yet another emergency system announcement. "Discovery Station Commander Ivankov will be addressing all station residents in two minutes. Please proceed to your vid screen for this important and mandatory presentation."

Jess reached behind himself, fumbling to turn the shower off.

She relaxed her grip on his shoulders, expecting him to set her down, but he lifted her away and strode out of the fresher. He carried her all the across their room to the bed, where he sat down, still holding her close. They were dripping all over the bedding, but he didn't seem to care. Instead, he simply pulled her against him, then grabbed a blanket to cover them both.

Within seconds, the vid screen flickered to life, and a man who looked strikingly like Jess came into view.

"Who are these guys?" she asked. "Why do they all look like you?"

"They're Saurellians," Jess replied. "And they don't look like me. At least not to anyone besides you."

"Are you sure?" she asked, doubting him. "I thought you looked an awful lot like Logan."

"You're crazy," Jess said, kissing her on top of her head. "I'm a slave, I wasn't even born on the same side of the quadrant as these guys."

She pursed her lips, wondering how he could miss the resemblance. Sure, he and the man on the vid screen looked different. The man was wearing a military haircut, and his eyes were a different color. But that was just a matter of dress and grooming. Their bone structure was strikingly similar, although Jess was far paler than the man...

"As I'm sure you are aware, the station was attacked early this morning. We have determined that this attack was planned and executed by members of the Pilgrims of the Apocalypse, apparently in response to activity that has taken place on the far side of the asteroid belt.

"Several days ago, our sensors detected an extremely large explosion centered in this region. We have yet to determine who was behind this explosion, but we have assured ourselves that Imperial interference is highly unlikely. Not only have our scouts failed to detect any sign of Imperial spacecraft in the area, we have received assurances from the Imperial capital that they were not involved in this incident. Given the fact that such an attack would cause the Emperor a great deal embarrassment, combined with a complete lack of any understandable motive for such an attack, we find no reason to believe they were involved with events within this system.

"What is clear is that this fringe group holds the Saurellian government responsible for the destruction of a large area they inhabited. I can assure you that our government had no reason to attack, and until now had very little interest in the Pilgrims on any level. Now that they have attacked our facility, this has changed."

He paused, and Bethany shivered, snuggling further into Jess' arms.

"I wonder how many Pilgrim mining camps were destroyed," she whispered.

"I wonder *how* they were destroyed," he replied, his voice sober. "It takes a hell of a lot of firepower to pull something like that off."

"The majority of those involved with the attack on Discovery Station are dead," the station commander continued, his face stern. "The attack on the station proper appears to have been a suicide attack. The ore processing plant is a different story because timed explosive devices were placed there. We have also discovered that every known inhabitant of the station who was affiliated with the Pilgrim group evacuated several days ago. We can only assume that plans for such an attack were in place even before the destruction on the far side of the asteroid belt. Presumably, the explosives that caused the destruction there were meant to be used against Discovery Station itself."

He paused for a moment to allow his words to sink in. Jess caught his breath.

"There are more than a million people living on this station," he said quietly.

"I can't believe that!" she replied. "How would my people have pulled off something like that? I'm sure I would have heard something about it. How could you keep a plan like that completely secret? And why would they want to kill all these people?"

"As a result of this attack, the Saurellian Federation feels that it has no choice but to consider the Pilgrims of the Apocalypse a dangerous and unwelcome group. If there are any Pilgrims lefts on the station, they are encouraged to turn themselves in to Saurellian authorities within the next cycle. They will be granted amnesty, and the opportunity to return to Imperial space or build a new life for themselves outside the Pilgrim movement. Those Pilgrims who do not choose to take advantage of this one-time amnesty can expect to be arrested on sight once this twenty-four hour offer of immunity expires. We have already put plans into place that will allow us to more closely scrutinize everyone entering or leaving the station. If you're one of them, we will find you," he concluded, his voice ringing with controlled menace. She shivered.

"How are we going to get off the station?" she asked quietly. "They'll know that we arrived here on a Pilgrim transport ship. Maybe we should give ourselves up."

"No," he said. "For one thing, we have no idea that they're telling the truth about how they'll treat Pilgrims who turn themselves in. For all we know the poor bastards will be shot for their trouble. It's the sensible thing to do with saboteurs, and the Saurellians are no fools. They're capable of all kinds of things."

"So what are we going to do?"

"We'll brazen it out," he said coolly. "For one, nobody really knows who that ore ship belonged to. It was registered as a derelict in station records. I simply claimed to have salvaged it before selling it. From there the trail is even harder to follow. I accepted payment for it in cash—"

"Cash? Isn't that kind of dangerous?" she asked. "How did you know the seller wouldn't just hit you over the head and take the money back?"

"Because I sold it in the Exchange hall," he said. "It's policed by the smuggler's guild. There's no safer place on Discovery Station, trust me. You make one mistake in there and you'll never be seen again. I also bought the new ship there. It's completely clean, brought in a few weeks ago by a traveling Saurellian soldier reporting for duty. He sold it because he didn't need it any more."

"That still won't explain how we got here," she said anxiously. "Won't they find it strange that we appeared on the station out of nowhere and purchased a ship?"

"I've got that covered too," he said, running one hand through her hair absently. "Our new identities belonged to a couple who arrived here on a freighter about two months back. They came to a rather unfortunate end, but their deaths had never been documented. I checked the records myself, before I bought their identities."

She looked at him in horror.

"Were they killed for their identities?" she whispered. "Did they kill them just for us?"

"No," he said. "Not that I'm denying things like that occasionally happen here, but that wasn't the case at all. According to the information broker, they were killed during a botched robbery, and I don't get the impression he was lying to me. It happened weeks before we arrived."

"Oh," she said, still not feeling much better. In some ways, the world outside the mining belt wasn't much safer than what she'd left behind, she thought grimly. He pulled her close and kissed her forehead softly.

"Don't worry about it," he said. "Their death had nothing to do with us. We're going to use their names to make a new life for ourselves. That can't hurt them."

"I guess so," she said, still feeling uneasy. "So, now what? Now that we don't have to go after Bragan, does that mean we're finally free to do whatever we want?"

She deliberately didn't mention Calla. He'd been so distant when he first came back to the room, she didn't want him to turn into himself like that again.

"Not quite yet," he said softly, He reached up with one hand and stroked her hair softly. "I still have one more thing to do. Then we'll be free."

"What's that?"

"I need to find Mistress Jenner," he said.

"The woman who used to own you?" she asked. "Isn't she gone? I thought you told me she was a Pilgrim."

"She is a Pilgrim, and she is gone," he said. "She's also the reason that Calla is dead. If she hadn't sold me into the mining belt, then Calla wouldn't have tried to escape. She wouldn't have been killed. Instead, we'd both be free by now. The Saurellians freed all the slaves at Jenner's hostel when she left."

Bethany bit her lip, unsure of what to say. If he hadn't been sold into the mining belt, she never would have met him. She'd still be there. Or rather, what was left of her would still be there… She — and everyone else — would have been killed in the explosion. She didn't point that out, though. Instead, she held him, wishing she had some way of showing him how much she cared, how much she wished she could take his hurt into herself and heal him.

"I think I know where I can find her," he said softly. "Or at least a place to start looking. We're going to have to move quickly because the Saurellians are going to be looking for her, too. I don't want them to find the bitch before I do."

"You know, if you gave the Saurellians whatever information you have," she said softly, "they'll probably reward you and catch her themselves. You can have your revenge that way. You already said they'd probably kill any Pilgrims they caught."

"I want to find her," he said, voice cold. He stiffened in her arms. "I want to find her myself and look her right in the eyes while I kill her. I want her to know why she's dying and who's responsible."

She shivered at his tone. It was as if the tender, caring Jess she'd come to love had disappeared. In his place was a grim and frightening man she hardly recognized, a man who scared her.

"How long do you think it will take you to find her?" she asked.

"I have no idea," he said. "But I can promise you this. I won't give up until I have."

* * * * *

Leaving the station wasn't a problem, just as he'd said. After waiting a week for things to calm down, they'd simply filed their paperwork with the station controller and hired a runabout to take them out to the ship. Bethany held her breath until they started slowly pulling by the station's main defenses, amazed that it had been so easy to sneak in and out. No wonder the Pilgrims had been able to attack. The station all but had a revolving door instead of an airlock. She shivered, and hoped that they would find a way to tighten up security before there was another disaster.

"You can never really control a place like this," Jess told her as they pulled away. "There are too many people coming and going, and none of them want their actions examined too closely. If the Saurellians crack down too hard, they'll lose half their commerce. It was the same way when the Empire held the station."

She had nodded, pretending to understand. Sometimes her own ignorance of the outside world frightened her. Jess fell silent, focusing instead on watching the sleek little ship's control board. He wasn't piloting himself, but he seemed to be trying to learn, she realized. It must be unsettling for him to rely solely on the auto-pilot computer. He'd watched the control board on the ore transport, too.

"Is this ship easier to fly than the transport?" she asked after a while.

"Well, it's designed to be relatively simple," he said softly. "But I still think it will take me a long time to figure it out.

There are tutorials, but I doubt I'd be able to do much for us in a pinch."

"A pinch?" she asked. "What do you mean by that?"

"Well, there are all kinds of things that could go wrong," he said. "If we got caught in the middle of a battle, or more likely if we ran into smugglers..." His voice trailed off.

She stifled a little whimper. It had never occurred to here that there might be predators out in space.

"Are we ever going to find a safe place?" she asked softly. He looked at her with surprise written across his handsome face.

"Of course we are," he said. "There are all kinds of wonderful places out there. We just have to decide which one is right for us. Then we'll sell this ship and build a new life for ourselves. We'll be able to do whatever we want."

"After we kill Jenner," she qualified, her voice soft.

"Of course," he said. He leaned toward her, taking her hands in his and looking into her eyes intently. "I know that it's hard for you to understand, but I have to do this. This woman is responsible for destroying my life and killing my sister."

"Jess, has it ever occurred to you that she's just one cog in an entire system that killed your sister?" she asked softly. "You've told me that you were created on an Imperial slave farm, that you were born into slavery. Is it really Jenner's fault that she happened to be the one who bought you?"

"You have no idea what you're talking about," he said abruptly. Something inside her sparked at his condescending tone.

"You're right," she snapped back. "I have no idea what it means to have lived my entire life under someone else's control. I have no idea what it means to work your fingers to the bone and get kicked for your efforts. And of course, I've never had to fear for my life."

The stunned look on his face was priceless, and without thought she burst into bitter laughter. He frowned as she stood and walked out of the cockpit, shaking her head. Men. They were all so arrogant. How dare he think she wasn't capable of understanding his anger? She just didn't see the purpose in chasing one Pilgrim woman—however cruel—around the quadrant when they had been given a chance to start over with their lives. It wasn't going to bring Calla back.

She stalked down the corridor toward the suite of comfortable rooms that formed the bulk of the small ship's living space. She'd noticed a console in there earlier. Perhaps the ship had a library. She needed a distraction.

* * * * *

Jess gazed after her as she left, utterly confused. How had he become the bad guy? How had a conversation about his suffering ended with him feeling like such an ass?

Of course she knew what suffering was about, he thought angrily. How could she doubt that he understood what kind of pain she had experienced? But her suffering was over and the men who had hurt her were dead. She had her vengeance; it was easy for her to move on.

He couldn't just let Jenner get away with what she had done to destroy him and Calla. She had sold him to the miners deliberately, he knew that. She'd wanted him dead. He knew too many of her dirty little secrets. Sooner or later he would have embarrassed her. Still, he'd thought there was more time.

He shook his head. No point in wishing he could go back. Calla was dead. Jenner had to pay. It was simple enough, so why didn't Bethany understand? Damn woman.

He sat there for several more minutes, trying to concentrate on following the control board as the auto-pilot propelled them to the edges of the system. Once they were good and clear, it would initiate a jump through hyperspace. Not for the first time, he marveled at the technology that made travel across the vast reaches of space possible.

But the computer couldn't hold his attention forever, and his thoughts kept turning back to Bethany. She had been so upset when she left. He hated seeing her that way. He loved it when her face turned to his with a smile. She had a special way of looking at him that made him feel as if everything in the world was just right. When he came into a room she was always happy to see him. She would jump up and run over to him, giving him kisses interspersed with a thousand questions about some new aspect of life outside the asteroid belt.

None of that life had been in her face when she'd left him. He shook his head and sighed, leaning back in his chair. He needed to go and talk to her.

Leaving the auto-pilot to its mysterious tasks, he walked slowly down the corridor toward their living quarters. For a small ship, it was extremely comfortable. Three sleeping chambers, a sizeable fresher, living area and galley. There was even a small exercise room. Even more amazing to him was that they owned this lovely little vessel. Between the ore shipment and selling the freighter itself, they had done quite well financially. He realized he probably had more money at his disposal than Jenner did. It was a comforting thought. He entered the living area. Bethany was sitting in the living area before the main data terminal. She had to have heard him walk in, but she ignored him. He came to stand behind her, studying what she was doing. She seemed to be scrolling through a history text written in Basic.

"I didn't know whether you could read or not," he said.

She spoke curtly. "While the Pilgrim educational system is not particularly good, we do learn to read," she said.

Damn, he'd said the wrong thing. Now she was even more offended.

"We also took basic arithmetic and computer programming," she said quieter. "It's fairly difficult to live on a mining station filled with complex equipment like recyclers and our hydroponics gardens without a little bit of education. Of course, I'm sure it's not up to your standards."

"I didn't mean to sound so insulting," he said, bringing his hands up to rest them lightly against her shoulders. She didn't respond, so he started to slowly knead. The muscles were tight beneath his touch. She wasn't going to make this easy.

"I'm also sorry about our discussion in the cockpit," he said. "It was wrong of me to belittle what you've been through. We're both survivors of slavery, just different kinds."

"I'm glad you realize that," she said. He continued kneading her shoulders, feeling some of the tension leave her body. Against his will, he could feel himself growing aroused. The smell of her hair wafted up toward him, and he inhaled deeply. A second later he wished he hadn't. His pants were suddenly too tight and he shifted uncomfortably. She seemed to be completely unaware of his arousal, continuing to scroll through the text before her. The silence between them lengthened, and he shifted again.

"Will you accept my apology?" he said finally. She shrugged her shoulders, and something in him snapped. He needed her forgiveness. He swiveled her chair around and knelt before her. Then he took each of her hands in his and looked directly into her face. She stared back, eyes questioning and a little surprised.

"I'm truly sorry," he said softly. She nodded her head at him, and he smiled. Then leaning forward, he kissed her gently on the lips.

It was a sweet kiss, almost passionless at first. At least on her part. His entire body clamored for him to pull her down, to jump on her and take her. He fought the urge, knowing it would be a terrible mistake. He wanted whatever happened between them next to come from her. He wanted her to acknowledge what he said, to let him know she understood his meaning deep down inside.

He held back a surge of triumph as she leaned forward into the kiss, deepening it slightly. It was still soft, and both of their mouths were still closed. But she was responding, nuzzling at his mouth just as he was nuzzling at hers.

They stayed that way for several minutes, and then he ended the kiss. He leaned his head against her chest, reaching both arms around her slender form to pull her close. She was soft, warm. His. He still wanted her, but that initial physical urgency had disappeared in a rush of emotion. He didn't want to simply roll her beneath him, to take her body with his.

He wanted to be close to her. Bethany. Close to whatever it was about her that had scared him so much a moment earlier when she hadn't wanted to talk to him.

Holding her made everything feel right again.

He could feel her fingers in his hair, stroking gently down, and then she kissed the top of his head. She shivered, then pulled him tightly against her body. He could feel her shaking, and pulled away to see what was wrong.

She was crying.

A feeling of helplessness washed over him, and he tucked himself against her, stroking her back in what he hoped was a comforting way.

"I'm so sorry," he whispered. "I'm so sorry I hurt you. Please stop crying, Bethany. I won't do it again, I promise."

"That's not why I'm crying," she replied, her voice breaking. "I'm scared, Jess. What will we do if this Jenner woman finds out you're following her? What if she's with other Pilgrims? They might hurt you."

"I won't let them hurt me," he said.

"No?" she asked. "You think you're so powerful? It's a risk and you know it. Don't you understand? We're free, Jess. We have money. We have time. There's nobody in the whole damn universe who knows or cares where we're going. Why are we following this woman when we could be making a life for ourselves?"

"Because I have to," he said, still holding her. "I have to do this, for my sister and for myself."

"You aren't even sure where to find her," she said quietly. "There are a thousand places she could be, a million places. We could look for her the rest of our lives and never find her. Do you really think your sister would want you to waste your freedom on some stupid quest for revenge?"

He stayed silent, trying not to think of what Calla would say. Calla would agree with Bethany, he knew it in his heart.

But Calla and Bethany were women. They needed protection from the harsh things of life, couldn't possibly understand why he had to find Jenner, to kill her. Every time Bethany sniffled, pain ripped through him. He hated this, hate the fact that she was suffering. He had to get her to stop crying or he would end up crazy.

So he lifted his head again, this time taking her mouth in a kiss that was completely different from that he'd given her before. This was a kiss meant to seduce. He nibbled at her lips, ignoring the salty taste of her tears, and she opened before him.

He pulled her entire body forward on the chair so that her breasts were pressing against his chest and her legs wrapped around him. He dug his fingers into her hair, holding her still for his touch, and as his tongue delved into her mouth, she whimpered. She shifted against him and his cock leapt to attention. There was nothing new in that. It seemed like he'd had a full erection since the first time he'd seen her. No matter how much they made love, it was never enough.

He pulled his mouth away, ignoring her little sigh of disappointment as the kiss ended. His lips fell to her neck. There he traced the lines of her throat with one hand, each light touch followed by a kiss. He was filled with the realization of how special she was to him, how much his happiness was intricately and inevitably wound up in hers. He didn't have any way to tell her his feelings with words, though. He had to let his touch speak. He could only hope she would understand.

She whispered something as he kissed the hollow at the bottom of her throat, but he ignored it. If she was telling him to stop, he didn't want to hear it. He had to show her how much she meant to him, that they were made for each other.

She sighed and leaned back in the chair, allowing her arms to fall to one side. He took advantage of the change by gently opening the front of her blouse. It was soft, silky. So different from anything she'd worn on the Pilgrim station that he'd been concerned at first that she wouldn't like it.

She had loved it, just as she loved all the new clothing he brought her. She treated each item like an exquisite gift, though they were clothing any other woman would take for granted. She took nothing for granted, he thought. It was just one more thing he loved about Bethany. She was so very alive.

He kissed down the opening of her shirt, enjoying the feel of her breasts rising on either side of his face. He moved down along the curve of one, dropping light kisses on it and nosing the underside of the swell with infinite gentleness. She gasped, and he smiled. He did the same to the other side, taking care not to touch her nipples. Indeed, fabric clung to them, twin points keeping the silky fabric from falling away to either side. He sat back for a minute, just enjoying the sight of her. She was spread before him wantonly, her face filled with nothing more than sheer pleasure in the moment.

He reached up with both hands, cupping her breast lightly through the fabric, allowing it to slide back and forth across her nipples until she shivered. The tight tips pressed against his fingers, and she arched her back in the chair.

"Jess…"

He smiled, then pushed the cloth aside. Her breasts were so lovely. Not too large, but full and round, gentle mounds topped with red nipples that cried out for some kind of attention from him. He wouldn't leave them wanting, he vowed.

Leaning forward, he took one of them into his mouth, sucking it deeply. She gasped, and raised one had to cup his head. He ignored her, moving back slowly until her nipple was free. She whimpered a protest, but before she could do more, he started on the other nipple. Back and forth he went, sucking deeply one time, flicking lightly with his tongue the next. She was whimpering more and more, her lower body twisting in the chair. The time had come to move to the next level, he thought with satisfaction. Soon she would be screaming for him.

Careful not to break the sensual spell that had come over them, he trailed one finger down across her stomach, pausing only briefly at her navel, then slid it beneath the loose waistband of the silky pants that matched her top. She had loved this particular outfit immediately, he remembered with a smile. It was sensual and modern, but also similar to what she had worn most her life. The pants were full, almost as full as a skirt, and they flowed around her as she walked like a bright river. She had laughed at herself when she'd first seen herself wearing them in a mirror, but she looked beautiful.

The ache in his cock grew stronger as a damp spot appeared between her legs. She wanted him almost as much as he wanted her, he thought in satisfaction. For one second he was tempted to simply rip the pants off and pull her down.

No.

This was about giving her pleasure, showing her how much she meant to him, he reminded himself. Beside that, she would be upset if he ripped the pants, he thought with a grin. No matter that a thousand other women owned pants just like them, they were precious to her.

Instead, he allowed his fingers to reach down past the elastic, pulling it lower as he went. There it was, the forest of dark brown curls that marked her most private place. He touched her there, fingers growing damp as her moisture washed over him. There was her clit, a tiny piece of flesh that had the power to give so much pleasure that the world was hardly big enough to contain it. He rubbed one finger against it, feeling the slick flesh glide smoothly over the rough skin of his finger. Above him, she shivered. Oh, she liked that all right.

He rubbed it again, this time pressing still lower between her legs, finding the folds of her labia and nudging them apart. Instinctively, her legs parted for him, giving him greater access.

He dropped his head to her stomach, kissing it softly and trailing his tongue into the small indentation that marked its center. He slid his fingers into her body, resting his cheek against her stomach for a moment as the sheer need to be inside her nearly overwhelmed him. He froze, willing his unruly cock to behave. This was about her, not him.

When he felt like he was back in command of his own senses, he slid the finger in again, allowing a second digit to join it. Tenderly, he rubbed back and forth, moving in and out of her body with great care, as if she were some rare and precious porcelain he was afraid of breaking. The image brought a smile to his face. She was rare and precious, but she wouldn't break. Not easily, he knew that for certain. How many women could have survived what she had, and with such courage?

He kissed her again, and then he trailed more kisses down her belly. He pulled his hand out from her pants, allowing the waistband to slide back up, then kissed down over the soft fabric. She shivered, and then he was at the spot between her legs where his fingers had teased her just seconds earlier. He pressed forward with his tongue, clearly outlining her clitoris through the silk, and she gasped.

"Jess, you're going to kill me," she whispered.

He didn't reply, stiffening his tongue and centering it on her clit instead. She twisted against him so he brought both hands up to her hips to steady her. He wasn't going to let anything interfere with her pleasure, not now. Not when she was so close.

Inhaling her scent deeply, he set back to work on her clit. At first the fabric between them seemed a barrier, but as it grew wetter, it provided a delicious friction between them. Every tiny, perfect strand of silk massaged her clit as he moved. She bucked against him, silently begging him for more.

He renewed his efforts, determined to bring her to orgasm with only his tongue. He stabbed her with it again and again until her hands gripped the back of his head, pulling him closer to her body. She was shaking and gasping, she had to be close. Now to bring her over the edge.

Without warning, he let go of her hips and reached down under her legs. He pulled her lower body forward off the chair, slinging her legs over his shoulders and grinding her clit into his face. She gave out a low moan as he sucked her clit, still encased in the fabric, deeply into his mouth. Her hips heaved against him violently. He sucked again, working her with his tongue and rubbing his nose against her mound. She twisted, then exploded in his arms with a guttural cry

He could feel the orgasm in her legs as they stiffened and clenched his head. He could feel it in the moisture that flooded his mouth, too, so much that it easily saturated the silk and filled his mouth. He continued sucking her, more gently now, as the waves of pleasure washed over her and she slowly relaxed. Then he eased her legs back over his shoulders and lowered her to the chair.

Putting his arms back around her waist, he cuddled against her, enjoying the rushing of her blood and the pounding of her heart beneath his ear. It was a beautiful thing to hold his woman, he thought to himself. A beautiful thing indeed.

After a few moments she leaned forward, kissing him gently on the head.

"Thank you," she whispered.

Without pausing to think, he spoke. "Bethany, I love you," he said. "I don't want to fight with you, I only want to be with you and share pleasure with you."

She grew still.

"I love you, too, Jess," she said quietly. "I've loved you for a long time, I think."

"Thank you," he whispered. He took a deep breath, then lifted her up and carried her into the bedroom. Her arms wrapped around his neck and she cuddled into him. He loved it when she held him like that. It made him feel so strong, as if she depended on him for everything.

As if she would never leave him.

He lay her down on the bed, following her down and kissing her long and slow. This time it would be for both of them. He dropped his hand between her legs, and she whimpered. She bucked against him, pushing his lower body back. He pulled his hips away, confused at first. Comprehension dawned as she used the extra space to slither out of her pants. Then she wrapped both legs up and around his waist.

He tore his lips free of hers, and they both gasped for air.

"Jess, let me this time," she said. He nodded, and together they rolled to the center of the bed. Now Bethany was on top of him, straddling him. He reached up and slid the fabric off her shoulders. Her breasts heaved as she drew her breath in. Her face was soft, then a little smile stole across it. A wicked gleam came into her eyes and without warning her fingers dug into his side, tickling him viciously.

He howled, bucking against her body in protest. She simply laughed, and tickled him harder. They wrestled together, fighting for control, and finally she wound up beneath him again. She grinned up at him unrepentantly.

"Why did you do that?" he demanded. She laughed breathlessly.

"Because you were looking just a little bit too smug for your own good."

He shook his head, then leaned down to kiss her. Again she started tickling him, and this time managed to buck him off. He fell to one side, completely surprised by her second attack. She jumped up, kneeling on the bed and laughing at his startled look. Caught in the moment, he laughed back, unable to control himself. She was so adorable. Bethany was his woman—naked, completely free of guile.

He started crawling slowly toward her, and she inched backward.

"Think you can catch me?" she asked archly.

"Oh, I know I can catch you," he replied with a grin. "The only question I have is what I'm going to do with you once I have you. I think you need to be punished."

Her grin faltered. For a moment her lower lip trembled, then she whispered in a frightened voice, "Jess, please don't hurt me."

Stunned, he stopped and stared in dawning horror.

"Bethany, I would never hurt you," he said softly. She looked deep into his eyes, holding him with her gaze. He didn't even see the pillow until it hit him in the face, knocking him to one side.

"Gotcha," she shrieked, breaking into new peals of laughter. He growled and scrambled after her. Now she would *really* pay.

He caught her from behind, just as she reached the edge of the bed. He pulled her naked body back against his, shuddering as she came into contact with his aroused cock. Time to show her who was in charge, he thought.

Reaching between them, he loosened his pants and shoved them down. Then he thrust into her wet opening and they both moaned.

"Damn, Jess," she muttered. "You don't do it half way, do you?"

"Nope," he replied. "This is what you get for tricking me like that."

"I guess I've been very bad," she said lightly. She wiggled her butt against him, and he groaned. "You'd better punish me."

"Witch."

She gave a bright, tinkling laugh and deliberately squeezed him deep inside.

Gripping her waist tightly, he started moving back and forth, roughly delving deep into her body with each motion.

She was hot and slick for him, pushing back against him in a rocking motion that took his breath away. He tried to reach down between them, to touch her clit, but he couldn't quite make it. Fortunately she didn't seem to care or notice. Even as he felt a fine sheen of sweat coat his body, he could see the flesh of her back starting to shine. Every part of him seemed centered on the point where they connected. Her flesh enclosed him time and again, squeezing him until he felt like screaming. The need to let loose in her, to allow his seed to shoot out, was almost painful in its intensity. But he wasn't ready yet. He didn't want to come until she did. This was for both of them, he reminded himself.

She grunted now, little pants of sound that escaped her mouth every time their bodies slapped together. Their movements grew jerkier, every motion a struggle toward that pinnacle that awaited them. Jess gritted his teeth, holding back the release. Not yet.

Her groans turned into whimpers, then every muscle in her body clenched, including those surrounding his cock. She gave a high-pitched wail, and he lost control. Seed exploded out of him into her body. His fingers clutched her so tightly he knew there would be bruises later. He closed his eyes, threw back his head, and allowed the waves of orgasm to engulf both of them.

Chapter Fourteen
Berengaria Space Port, Three Months Later

છ૭

Bethany looked at Jess in disgust.

"I can't believe you're doing this," she said. "I have never given you any reason to believe I intend to leave you. For love of the Goddess, I don't even know how to survive on my own. Can't you just trust me for once?"

They were sitting in the living area, having reached their sixth destination. It was a small planet, but one where Jess knew Jenner had friends. Or at least business partners. He'd decided from the first that they'd start with known associates and go from there.

Jess turned his head, refusing to look at her.

"I can't be out there looking for Jenner and worrying about you at the same time," he said, pulling on a boot with quick and rough motions. "This is a strange port, and a dangerous one. If I know you're safe, I'll be safe."

"I'll be safe as long as I stay on the ship, right?" she asked tartly. "But you don't trust me to stay on the ship by myself."

He didn't reply. Instead, he stood and pulled on a jacket made of dark leather he'd purchased in the last port. His hair was pulled back with another strip of the same leather, tied neatly at his nape. It was quite long now, reaching nearly half way down his back. She watched him thoughtfully, realizing he hadn't cut it since his escape from the mining camp. Was that on purpose or was it part of a disguise? He slipped a knife—the same one he'd used to cut her hair with that fateful day of the rebellion—into a scabbard in his boot and stood. She shivered and hugged herself. He looked quietly menacing, a different man from the Jess who shared her bed and laughed with her.

"You'll be fine here while I'm gone," he said. "There's plenty of food and we're hooked into the planetary 'net. There's enough credit on deposit with the port for you to order anything you need."

"Except my freedom."

"Except that," he said. "But don't worry, if something happens to me they'll come to check on you in three days. I've already made the arrangements."

"Thanks," she said tightly.

"I suppose a kiss goodbye is out of the question?" he asked.

"Good guess," she said, turning away from him.

Bethany fumed as he strode out of the ship. Once again, she was locked into their living quarters. Once again he had chosen not to trust her, despite the fact that she had done nothing to betray that trust. She hadn't even considered leaving him, yet he insisted on locking her in like a wayward child.

She stood and walked over to the data terminal, idly flicking on the port information channel. It looked like a horrible place, she thought. Certainly not the kind of place that would tempt anyone bent on escape. Berengaria had only been settled for two centuries, and the air was not yet breathable. The entire population lived in a series of domes, venturing outside only long enough to tend the machinery that ran a string of chemical plants. Some day, in another two or three hundred years, the entire planet would be suitable for farming. Billions of people would have food to eat because of the work being done in this port. But for now, it was still a hellhole.

She flicked through several more information channels, then took a deep breath. She was feeling sick to her stomach again. Lately it seemed like she was sick all the time, although she'd tried to hide it from Jess. She knew he would worry about her, but she was fine. It was just a little stomach trouble.

Standing carefully, she made her way into the fresher and knelt before the waste unit. Within seconds it came. A flood of vomit rushed out of her, sickening her further with its smell. Usually it stopped with that, but this time it was worse. Her stomach heaved again and again, and resentment for Jess' lack of trust built in her. The stress of being locked up every time they came into port was probably responsible for her illness.

Two hours later she wasn't so sure. She had never felt so sick in her life. She had long run out of anything to vomit, yet the heaves kept coming. Shaking and weak, she stood up and stumbled out into the main room. Time to consult the auto-doc. This was ridiculous.

The complex machine was located in a closet-sized storage area between two of the bedrooms. Neither of them had used it, although Jess had pointed it out to her not long after they first came onto the ship. Fortunately, it was designed to be simple to operate. There were a series of instructions with pictures detailing how to turn it on. She followed them and was rewarded when the unit blinked to life and a cool voice asked, "How may I help you?"

"I'm feeling sick," she said. "I've been vomiting."

"Please disrobe and seat yourself in the unit for an examination," the voice replied. A panel slid open, revealing a reclining chair/bed. She slid out of her clothing and climbed into it carefully, feeling somewhat intimidated.

As soon as she was seated, the voice spoke again.

"I will now close the panel door and begin the examination," the voice said. "Please lie back and relax. I will need to take several tissue samples. A sleeve will now enclose your right arm, facilitating this."

Before she had time to protest, her arm was wrapped in a metal sleeve. The lights dimmed, and soothing music started to play. She hardly noticed as the panel slid shut, enclosing her fully within the unit.

Her seat reclined back and she noticed a tangy scent in the air. Then she was drifting to sleep. Her last thought was a vague hope that Jess wouldn't come back while she was still in here. He'd probably think she ran away…

* * * * *

Bethany yawned and stretched. Strange, her bed didn't feel like it usually did. There was music playing, too.

"Please remain in the examination chair until you are fully awake," a smooth, emotionless voice said. Her eyes popped open as she tried to remember where she was. In the auto-doc. She shifted, and felt slight discomfort in several places. What had the damned thing done to her while she was out?

"I have your examination results," the auto-doc said. "All system functions appear to be normal and within regular parameters. Fetal system functions are normal as well."

"Fetal?" she asked, growing suddenly still. "Are you saying I'm pregnant?"

"Pregnancy is confirmed," the machine replied. "Fetus age is estimated at six weeks."

"How is that possible?" she asked. The machine hummed for a second, then spoke again.

"Please refine question."

"How is it that I am pregnant?"

"Pregnancy appears to be the result of sexual intercourse, although further examination would be required to rule out artificial insemination," the machine responded. She burst out laughing.

"I know how people get pregnant," she said after a moment, wiping her eyes. She felt light-headed, out of breath. She raised one hand to her stomach, trying to feel something. Everything was just as it always was. She frowned, trying to remember her last menstrual period. When had it been?

"I had been under the impression that I was infertile," she said finally.

"Nothing in my tests indicates that you have ever been infertile," the auto-doc replied emotionlessly. "The diagnosis was incorrect."

The diagnosis was incorrect. But how? So many years she and Avram had lived together. He'd had children with his previous wives so why not her?

She sighed, realizing she would probably never have an answer to that question. Moving creakily, she rolled out of the chair and stepped out of the auto-doc.

Pulling on her clothing, everything seemed unreal. She was going to have a baby. Jess' baby. It was so amazing, so beautiful that she felt like crying. She drifted out into the main room, wanting to tell him. Wanting to tell someone, anyone, about the miracle taking place in her belly.

Unfortunately, she was still completely alone.

Unable to contain herself, she wrapped both arms around her body and whooped, squeezing herself tightly. If only he was here. They would hold each other, talk about the child. Would it be a boy or a girl, she wondered? Would it look like him? She rubbed her stomach again, mind filling with possibilities. This was so much better than anything she could have imagined. They would have a child together. Perhaps more than one. Neither of them had ever had a real family, but they would make one now.

This chasing of Jenner had to end, though. They needed to find a place to live, a way to support themselves. He kept insisting that they had plenty of money, but she wasn't so sure. It couldn't last forever. Beside that, it was one thing to traipse halfway across known space in search of vengeance with only themselves to think of. It was quite another to drag a child around like that. They didn't even have the kinds of supplies they would need for a baby. She wanted a home of some sort, a real home. And a real doctor, she thought darkly. There was no way she wanted that talking closet to examine her baby, let alone deliver it.

She and Jess were going to have a talk when he got back. He needed to choose. He'd get either his revenge or her, not both. She had to get firm with him because it wasn't just about the two of them any more.

* * * * *

Jess stalked across the port, bitter anger seeping from every pore of his body. She had been here. Just days earlier she'd left. He'd been so close to her that he could still smell her foul, unwashed body with every breath he took. Bitch.

At least he had a good lead, though. There was no way she'd get away from him this time. She was headed to Jezra, and from there to Karos, the Pilgrim homeworld. He had to catch her before she left Jezra, though. Karos crawled with Pilgrims, and the last thing he wanted to do was surround himself with more of those foul snakes.

He caught a shuttle out to the pad where the ship was docked. It had taken him less than a day to track down his information. Hopefully Bethany wasn't going to be too angry with him, although he wasn't betting on it. He could understand her feelings. Of all people, he knew what it felt like to lose one's freedom. He hated being contained, subject to the will of another. But the thought of her leaving him made his heart clench. She told him she wouldn't do it. She assured him again and again, but he couldn't bring himself to trust her completely. He wanted to, but he couldn't quite do it. If he was wrong, the penalty was simply too high.

The transport latched on to the ship's airlock, and a moment later he stepped inside. There was a slight whooshing noise as it cycled shut, and then he entered the main corridor. It only took a few strides to reach the locked living quarters and open the door. She jumped up, her face glowing and excited. He paused, confused and immediately suspicious. Why was she so happy to see him? Usually she was spitting mad after he'd locked her up.

"Jess," she called, running up to him. She grabbed both of his hands with hers, and squeezed them. "I have wonderful news, Jess. We're going to have a baby. I'm pregnant."

He froze, completely shocked. Her lovely green eyes, bright with hope and excitement, looked up at him expectantly, and the meaning of her words filtered through his consciousness. They were going to have a baby.

He pulled her close, kissing her. She was laughing, and to his shock he realized moisture was collecting in his eyes. Then he pulled her up into his arms and swung her around, whooping. A baby. A little piece of him and Bethany.

She shrieked with laughter and pounded against him until he set her down, and they leaned against each other breathlessly.

"How long?" he asked.

"The auto-doc says I'm six weeks along," she said. "That gives us plenty of time to find a place to live."

He nodded, mind moving quickly.

"It will only take a few more weeks to track down Jenner," he said. "I've already been thinking about where we should…" His voice trailed off as he realized she had stiffened in his arms.

"Jess, you have to give this up," she said softly.

"What do you mean?"

"You have to give up this hunt you're on," she said. Her eyes searched his anxiously. "We're going to have a child, Jess. Taking care of that child has to be our primary responsibility."

Some of the joy faded as he realized what she was saying.

"Bethany, I know where Jenner is," he said. "She's on her way to Jezra. She only left a few days ago. All we have to do is go there and get her. Then we'll be free."

"We're free already," she said, shaking her head. "If we keep chasing after her, who knows how much longer it will take."

"Two weeks," he repeated. "All we need is two more weeks."

"You thought she would be here," Bethany countered. "You swore to me that she would be here, that we'd be finished with this by now. You have no way of knowing whether she'll be there or not, do you?"

"If she's not there then she'll be on Karos."

"Karos?" Bethany exclaimed, her tone rising in distress. "That's half way across the Empire. I've been studying, you know. I know where things are. It's also the Pilgrim homeworld. You'll have no way of getting to her there. You'll stick out and they'll catch you immediately. There is no way I'll allow you to take me to Karos"

"You don't allow me to do anything," he said, his emotions twisting and turning so quickly he could hardly keep up. "I'm the one in charge. You do what I say."

She stood back from him, both hands planted on her hips.

"Are you prepared to be a father to this child?" she asked. "Because if you are, then you have no business following some damn stupid quest for revenge. You'll get yourself killed, and then where will we be? Where will *your child* be?"

He shook his head, forcibly restraining himself from reaching out and shaking her. She just didn't understand. He had to find Jenner. He had to make her pay for what she'd done to him, to Calla. If he didn't, she would haunt him forever.

"I see you're more interested in getting your revenge than taking care of your family," Bethany said quietly, her face bleak. She turned and walked away from him. He strode after her, grabbing her arm. She stiffened, glaring at him until he let her go.

"I would prefer to sleep in one of the other rooms tonight," she said. "I've been feeling sick, and I think we'd both be more comfortable that way."

She was lying, she just wanted to get away from him. He opened his mouth to disagree with her, then closed it slowly.

She was right. It was better to take a little time and let their emotions cool off. They could discuss things again in the morning. He had too much to think about right now, and the last thing he wanted to do was say something he'd regret.

Nodding abruptly, he turned away from her. She disappeared into one of the rooms, and he wandered over to the kitchen to grab some food. His thoughts moved at a thousand miles per second. There was a baby growing in her belly, his baby. They were going to be a family.

His frustration fled before the thought, and a silly grin came across his face. Grabbing a meat roll, he wandered into his room and flopped down on the bed.

He was going to be a daddy. Life was good.

* * * * *

Bethany sat and brushed her hair. Again and again she pulled the brush through the brown locks, the childhood ritual comforting in its familiarity. It was much shorter now, a remnant of what she'd once had. She smiled wryly, remembering how afraid she'd been when Jess had whipped out that enormous knife and cut her free with it. She knew now he would never deliberately hurt her, at least not physically. She'd thought he was going to kill her back then, but what he'd done instead was far more devious. He'd made her fall in love with him and now he was ripping her heart out.

She had been patient with his quest. She didn't like chasing Jenner, but she liked being with Jess. She understood he had his demons to lay to rest. But it wasn't just about her anymore—it was about their baby. After the first euphoria of discovery had worn off earlier that afternoon, she'd given her situation a lot of thought. She knew how determined Jess was to find and kill Jenner. She also knew that she and her child wouldn't be safe on such a quest, especially if that quest led them to Karos. She'd given him his chance to accept the baby and give up his hatred, but he had thrown in back in her face.

She was going to have to leave him.

A traitorous part of her mind whispered at her to stay, to give him another chance. After all, he might be right. Jenner might be at the next port they visited. Or she might not be there. Then what? They would go on to Karos, the root of all Pilgrim activity. Just the thought of it made her shiver in horror. He was almost sure to be captured there, and if he were captured, she would be, too. She would probably live. They would see value in a pregnant woman. But there was no way she'd risk such a life for her child, not after she'd seen what the other options were. She was going to have her baby in freedom. Her baby wouldn't grow up to be a Pilgrim no matter what she had to do, no matter how painful it might be.

Standing, she pulled her hair back out of the way and fastened it carefully. She stood, stretched, and took a minute to breath deeply, calming herself for the task ahead. She already had what she needed hidden in one of the drawers. It only took a second to get it out and slide it into her pocket.

She opened the door and stepped into the main room. As she suspected, he had already gone to bed. He had to be tired after his hunt, he always was. That, combined with the sedative she'd dribbled over his dinner, would be enough to weaken him. She took another deep breath and forced a calm smile on to her face. Time to face him.

She opened the door to the suite they usually shared. A small, dim light glowed against one of the walls. He had fixed it there for her, she remembered painfully. One night she'd tried to go to the fresher and tripped. He hadn't mentioned it beyond checking to see if she was all right, but the next night the little light had been glowing. He was so thoughtful of her needs. How was it that he could be oblivious to the fact that his woman and child needed him now?

She shook her head, pushing the thoughts away. Time to focus on her task.

He was lying in bed, apparently asleep, but as she approached his eyes cracked open.

"Bethany?" he asked. He reached out one arm for her, struggling to sit up. Her heart clenched again.

"Yes, it's me," she said softly, coming to sit next to him. He tried to sit up again but couldn't.

"Sorry, I'm just so tired," he whispered, voice trailing off. "I don't know why I feel this way."

"Don't worry," she said. "It's all going to be fine." she leaned over and kissed him on the lips. Then, before she could change her mind, she slipped the air-syringe the auto-doc had prepared to her specifications earlier and pressed it against his upper arm. Confusion registered in his gaze as it pierced his skin, but the drug was fast acting. Within seconds he was completely out.

To her disgust, she could feel tears welling up in her traitorous eyes. She didn't want to leave him like this. She didn't want to leave him at all. You don't have a choice, she reminded herself. It's not about you any more, it's about the baby.

Quickly, she left the room and retrieved the small bag she'd packed earlier. She'd put her time at the data terminal to good use. She already knew the time and place of departure for the Grandal, a freighter bound deep into Saurellian territory. It would be slow but safe. Jess had never bothered hiding his stash of credit vouchers from her, so money was no issue. She pawed through the pile of vouchers, trying to decide how much she should take. She wanted to leave him plenty to continue his quest, but at the same time she had to be sure there was enough money for her and the baby. Finally she simply scooped half into her bag, hoping it would be enough. She didn't really know how much things cost anyway, she realized. She had so much to learn it was frightening at times.

Stepping through the door of the living area into the main corridor, she made her way quickly to the cockpit. This was the hard part—she'd seen him call out on the radio several times, but she wasn't even quite sure how to turn the thing on. She fiddled with several dials and knobs before a soft voice spoke.

"This is the ship's computer. May I be of assistance?"

She jumped, then laughed nervously. How silly she was. The computer would call a transport for her.

"I need a transport to the Grandal," she said. "Can you arrange that?"

"Certainly," the computer said. It fell silent, although several lights on the flickering display flashed. "Transportation has been arranged. Please go to the airlock and I will inform you when transportation arrives."

"Thank you," she said, running one hand over her hair nervously. It was so strange to be leaving the ship without Jess. She just hoped she was able to take care of herself.

Don't be a ninny, she thought firmly. Of course she would be able to take care of herself. She didn't have a choice, the baby needed her.

She left the cockpit and walked down to the airlock. The wait seemed to last forever. Was something wrong? She kept looking nervously toward the door to the living quarters, a part of her expecting Jess to burst out any minute. That was ridiculous, of course. He would be asleep for at least twenty-four hours. The auto-doc had assured her of it.

A green light lit up over the hatch, and the computer spoke to her again.

"Ground transportation has arrived," it said. "Please proceed into the airlock."

The door slid open. Taking a deep breath, she stepped through it.

Chapter Fifteen
Two Months Later

෨

Bethany stretched wearily, and pulled the last of her possessions out of the small storage locker she'd been assigned after booking passage on the Grandal. It was a good thing she hadn't brought much with her, she thought wryly. She looked at her bunk, one of twenty in the cramped room, and sighed in relief. After two months of travel she was finally going to be getting off the decrepit old freighter that had taken her away from Jess. She'd had no idea space travel could be that slow and uncomfortable.

Just thinking of his name was enough to make tears well up in her eyes. It disgusted her, this weakness that seemed to come with pregnancy. Not only was she desperately lonely for Jess, she was an emotional wreck. According to what she'd read, such emotional upheaval was normal during pregnancy, but that didn't make it any easier. Not by a long shot.

She went down to the holding area, mingling with a mixed group of fellow passengers and ship's crew. None of them spoke with each other. The crew kept to themselves, and the passengers were all there for the same reason. They'd been desperate to get away from Berengaria and didn't have enough money to travel like civilized beings. She suspected that more than a few of them might even be on the run. It wasn't a situation that led naturally to friendly feelings.

They stood silently, waiting for the next shuttle to the surface of Vlaxon, a small, agricultural planet that was next on the Grandal's slow run of borderline worlds. The population wasn't huge, but she hoped it was large enough for a woman to lose herself in. According to one of her fellow passengers, there was often seasonal work available in the fields. Having never been out in the open on a planet before, she wasn't sure how she felt about that. Would the sky be frightening to her? Or would it be exciting, a time of new discovery? Either way, she had to have a job, had to find a way to feed her child. If she had fears, she'd get over them, she thought grimly.

The light over the airlock turned green, and the doors leading into the shuttle opened. They all stood back as a group of planetary officials came out. One of them, a tall woman with bright red hair in a gray uniform, spoke.

"May I have your attention," she called out. "Before we allow you to enter the shuttle and descend to the surface, we will need to see your paperwork. There will be a more extensive interview down below before you can leave the area of the spaceport. Please form a single line starting here."

She drew a line on the floor with her shoe, and they obediently lined up.

Bethany shuffled into place with the rest of them, suddenly anxious that her new identity wouldn't hold up. The woman hardly bothered to glance at it when her turn came, waving her through quickly enough. Bethany entered the shuttle and found a seat. It was good to be leaving the freighter, she told herself. Deep down inside, she was terrified.

When the shuttle was full, the doors closed and they pulled away from the ship. There were no windows, but the pull of gravity as they came into the atmosphere told its own story. The shuttle was moving very quickly, indeed.

Ten minutes later they were on the ground, and she stood. Time to see her new home.

Disappointingly enough, she didn't walk out of the shuttle into a wide, open vista of sky. Instead she found herself in a corridor, constructed of the same metal that could be found in a thousand ships. Everything looked the same as it did on the space station.

She followed the crowd of people down the hallway. The closer they got to the end, the louder the noise grew. The sounds of the port were starting to envelop them. A hundred merchants all vied for attention at the same time. Advertisements, holographic and flat screen, flashed out at her from the walls and ceilings. She could feel a headache growing behind her eyes—it was all too much. Agricultural planet or not, this port was just as noisy as the one on Discovery Station.

The end of the corridor was upon her. Her companions of the last two weeks moved quickly, dispersing in different directions, never to be seen again. Everything seemed a bit unreal. She stood, trying to decide which direction to go, when someone grabbed her arm.

"Hello Bethany," Jess said quietly. She stiffened, turning to look at him. What was he doing here? How had he found her?

"I'm glad I caught up to you," he said, his voice a menacing whisper. She looked into his beloved face and her heart froze. He was angry, terribly angry. Far angrier than she' ever seen before, which was saying a lot.

"Jess, what you are doing here?" she whispered, swaying with shock. He smiled at her, baring his teeth like some kind of feral animal.

"I'm here to pick up something that belongs to me," he said. "Something that was misplaced."

She shivered and he laughed. The noise had nothing to do with amusement.

"Don't look so afraid," he said. "I'm not going to hurt you. I was a fool to trust you before. I won't make that mistake again. Come with me."

He turned, pulling her along behind him as if she weighed nothing. She tried to pull back and he stopped abruptly, dragging her close to his body.

"You will follow me and you will keep quiet," he said with cold menace. "If you do anything to draw attention to us, I swear to you you'll regret it. Do I make myself clear?" she nodded, eyes wide. He had made himself *very* clear.

They moved through the concourse, surrounded by the sights and smells of a thousand worlds. She didn't bother to look around. It was all too confusing and frightening. Just imagining how and why Jess was here made her head hurt. He turned down another corridor, similar to the one she'd arrived on but much smaller. They reached the end and joined a short line of people. Jess pulled her close to his body, wrapping one arm tightly around her waist. His leaned in to her ear and whispered, "Behave."

She nodded, but he didn't reply. Instead he kept his head lowered to hers, inhaling deeply as if drinking in her scent. She could feel his warmth around her, feel the strength of his arms flexing through his shirt. Desire for him flickered to life, dancing along her nerves, and she gritted her teeth.

It wasn't enough that he caught her, she thought in disgust. Her traitorous body had to want him, too. It wasn't fair.

They entered the shuttle and took a place toward the back. A small console on the back of the seat before them lit up, and Jess leaned over, punching information into it.

"This will take us back to our ship," he said. "The trip will take a while because they'll be going to several other ships first. I don't want to hear a word out of you while we're here."

She nodded, sitting back in the seat and waiting. A tone buzzed, indicating it was time for launch. She braced herself as the gravity pressed her back in her seat, swallowing nervously. It hadn't taken her long to decide that she didn't like this particular part of traveling.

The trip was slow and grueling. Tension grew between them with every stop. By the time they reached the ship, she was almost grateful for an excuse to move. Anything was better than sitting with him in this horrible silence.

The people around them seemed oblivious to their private battle. What would happen if she called out to them for help, she wondered? Would they care? What would she say?

If she told the truth, Jess might be charged with kidnapping, assuming that was a crime here. She couldn't allow that to happen, she thought quickly. She wanted to protect him.

"We're the next stop," he said finally. A few minutes later the transport gave a small shudder, and they locked on to a dock. Jess stood, waiting for her to go ahead of him. She did so, keeping her eyes down. She didn't want to look around, didn't want to watch the people around her as she blushed in humiliation.

They walked out into a small docking station. It was little more than a waiting area, with long corridors leading off in several directions.

"The ship is out at the end of concourse seven," Jess said, taking her arm. His grip was firm, as if he expected her to run. Not likely, she thought. There was nothing here, nowhere to go. They walked quickly down the corridor, passing several airlocks. Finally he stopped in front of one, inserting a small card into the command box. Seconds later the door whisked open. He pulled her in after him, and then they entered the ship.

"Living quarters," he grated out, nodding his head abruptly to indicate where he wanted her to go. She ducked her head and did as he said. He had changed things, she realized as soon as she stepped inside. The furniture had been moved to accommodate something new, an enclosure made out of translucent bars running from floor to ceiling.

A cage. Right in the main room.

"Where did that come from?" she asked, shocked into stopping, He pushed her forward, one hand against her back.

"You aren't seriously expecting me to go in there," she asked. "You can't!"

"Only when I can't be here to watch you," he said, his voice completely void of emotion.

"That's horrible," she said, feeling suddenly panicky. "You can't expect me to do that. I won't."

"You don't have a choice," he said. "Sit down." He gestured to the couch. She turned on him, and for a moment she considered attacking him, biting him, anything to get away. His gaze was cold and steady, his muscular arms flexed. He seemed to read her mind.

"Don't try it," he said. "You'll regret it."

She turned and walked over to the couch, trying to compose herself. She wasn't going to get out of this one. Her luck was finally up, she realized. Whatever softness she had seen in Jess before appeared to be gone.

"How did you find me?"

"Well, you left several clues," he said in a sarcastic tone. "Among other things, you used the ship's computer to call for transport, and asked it to take you to the Grandal. That, and it was the only ship leaving the planet at that time."

"And your ship was faster," she said, filled with understanding. How could she have been so stupid? Catching her had been child's play for him, she thought in disgust. "Why did you come after me, Jess?"

For the first time, some of that cold anger left his face. He looked a little surprised.

"What did you think I would do?" he asked.

"I thought you would go after Jenner. By chasing me here you may have lost track of her."

"I'll find her eventually," he replied coldly. "But I couldn't just let you go traipsing off. You have no survival skills. You'd end up dead or enslaved at this rate."

She lifted her chin defiantly.

"I don't think you're giving me enough credit,' she said. "I didn't just take off without a plan, you know. I did my research.

I certainly had enough time trapped alone on the ship to do it," she added bitterly.

"And just what was this brilliant plan?" he asked, sneering. "And what about my child? How did *he* factor into your thinking? Or were you going to get rid of him?"

"I would never do that!" she gasped, one hand rising to cover her stomach protectively. "What kind of monster do you think I am?"

"The kind who would stab a man with a hypodermic while he's sleeping," he said.

"I did what I had to do to escape," she countered. "You of all people should understand that. You've had a bit of experience doing it yourself."

He didn't reply, instead pinning her with a dark, steady look that made her want to drop her eyes. She forced herself to meet his gaze. She wasn't ashamed of what she'd done.

"Why did you do it?" he asked finally. "I thought you were happy with me. You told me you loved me. Was all that a lie to get me to let down my guard?"

She stood and paced across then room, filled with sudden anger. She forced herself to take several deep breaths, trying to regain her calm before replying to him.

"You are such an ass," she finally said, her voice controlled and tight with suppressed emotion. "I am pregnant. We are going to have a child. Do you understand what that means?"

"It means we're going to have a child," he said, voice smooth. "I thought you were happy about that. You certainly *seemed* happy enough when you first told me about it."

"I am happy about it," she said, shaking her head in disgust. "As far as I'm concerned it's a miracle. I never thought I would be lucky enough to have a child. But you don't seem to be prepared to give us a fresh start. I don't want to go through this pregnancy as your prisoner. I don't want to go through this traipsing around looking for some old Pilgrim woman who hurt you and your sister. You have to let this go. We have a life to build together. It isn't just about us any more. It's about the baby. He or she deserves more than this! Can't you understand that?"

He stayed quiet for a moment, then spoke.

"Jenner would be dead by now if you hadn't run away," he said. "This would all be a moot point."

"Jenner is not the problem," she said coldly, infusing every bit of the anger and hurt she'd felt into her voice. "You are. You won't let me off the ship. You don't even tell me what world we're on half the time. You have this quest that obsesses you, and it takes up all your time and energy. *That* is my problem. I don't care about Jenner. Don't you realize that even if you do kill her, Calla will still be dead?"

He stood, arms folded in front of him. She let her eyes feast on his beloved form, pleading with him silently to understand, to take her into his arms and tell her that he was ready to move on with his life. That they could be a family.

Instead, he turned away and strode out the door. As he left, he spoke.

"Get yourself strapped in," he said. "We're leaving."

"Where are we going?" she asked, terrified of the answer.

"To Karos."

She shuddered and collapsed into a chair. They'd come so far, and now they were heading right back into a nest of Pilgrims. *The* nest of Pilgrims.

Jess was going to get all of them killed before he was finished

* * * * *

The truce between them was ugly.

Unlike before, she was no longer willing to pretend that everything might turn out all right, to tell herself that once he found Jenner, it would be over. They had arrived at Karos, the very planet where the Celestial Pilgrim had been born and first started sharing his message more than a thousand years earlier.

The worst possible place she could imagine for her child to be born.

They had traveled a long way to get here, out of Saurellian space and half way across the Empire. All based on a rumor that Jenner had been headed this way. How many more rumors would there be? Even if this were their last stop, would it be because Jenner was dead, or because they'd been caught? She had no illusions that the Pilgrims of Karos would show them any mercy.

A wall of ice now stood between them. They still slept together at night, still had sex. Intellectually they were in such different places that they couldn't communicate, but at night their bodies spoke for them in a dance of love and frustrated concern. Sometimes he fell asleep with his hand placed wide over her belly, as if trying to send some kind of message to the tiny baby growing inside. Would that baby live to meet its father?

Now they were in orbit above Karos, and he was ready to put his carefully crafted plan into action. He would claim to be a messenger from the mining belt, a merchant who had once done business with Jenner. He was passing through on business and was bringing her some money he owed her. It was a plausible enough scheme, according to Jess. He knew the man in question, knew that Jenner had often invested in his trading expeditions. Jess insisted that the man was honorable enough to pay her if given the opportunity, so he doubted that Jenner would suspect anything.

She wanted to scream at him, to force him to give up this foolishness. It was hopeless. Instead, she sat on the couch and watched as he sent a message to the surface from the vid terminal. With any luck, the promise of money would get Jenner's attention. Then he turned to her, his face softening.

"Bethany, I know you have trouble accepting this, but this will be over soon."

She shook her head, unwilling to go through the same argument again. He sighed, then ran a hand through his hair. They both knew what would happen next. He would wait for Jenner's response, then track her down on the planet's surface. While he was risking his life in search of vengeance, Bethany would be forced to wait for him on the ship. Caged. Of course, it was probably comfortable enough in there, and she knew that he had programmed the ship's computer to release her if he didn't come back for some reason.

That certainly didn't make it any more tolerable, though.

She would sit there, confined like an animal, waiting for him. Every moment would be an eternity. Would he return? Once he walked through the door another question would arise. Would he have found Jenner? Would their quest finally be over?

She wasn't even sure they'd be free if he *did* find Jenner. Sometimes it seemed like a part of him was broken. She wondered if he he'd somehow convinced himself that he needed to follow Calla to the grave. He seemed to think that everything would be all right if he could just find Jenner, but she wasn't that naive. Even if he found her, if he killed her with his bare hands, it still wouldn't bring back his sister. What would he do when he realized that?

He came over and sat down next to her, pulling her over into his lap. She went willingly. Even after spending months with him, the smell of his body and the touch of his skin against hers was enough to make her weak with desire.

She reached up with one hand, allowing her fingers to comb through his hair. The soft strands slid between her fingers, a sensual trailing that stimulated nerves she didn't even know existed. She had never realized how erogenous that small bit of webbing right at the base of her fingers could be...

"Bethany, I don't want to fight with you any more," Jess said as he pulled her head against his chest. He tilted his head down, kissing the top of her head tenderly. She crumbled.

"I don't want to fight either," she said. "I just want to be with you. Safe, where we don't have to worry all the time."

"You don't have to worry now," he said. "I'm going to take care of you."

There was no point in talking to him, she thought. He simply didn't understand how vulnerable he was—all three of them were—as long as he continued along this path. So instead of replying, she snuggled up to him, not wanting what might be her last memory of him to be unhappy. As usual, his body reacted to hers. She could feel a distinctive bulge growing along her hip. Things might be a little easier, she thought wryly if his body didn't call to hers like it did. Even when she was angry with him she still craved his touch.

She twisted and turned around, straddling him on the small couch. Her head was on a level with his as she leaned over and kissed him.

She meant it to be a soft kiss, a gentle touching to bring them together slowly. But when her lips came into contact with his mouth, all she could think about was how soon he would leaving her and whether he would return. Pilgrims didn't take kindly to spies.

The need and longing she felt washed over her and she took action. Without pausing to think, she grabbed his head with both hands and crushed his mouth between them, taking his lips roughly, almost angrily. He was hers, dammit, and he didn't even seem to realize it. She needed to show him, she thought suddenly. She needed to mark herself on his body, his spirit, the same way he had marked her. She wasn't his passive vessel. She was his lover, his partner, and he needed to acknowledge that.

The force of her anger surprised her, as did the force of her arousal. She wanted to suck him into her body, squeeze him and take him as he had taken her so many times. When he was down on that planet looking for Jenner he would be remembering Bethany. He responded in kind, his lips fighting with hers for domination. His arms wrapped around her, pulling her against his body so tightly it was hard to breathe. She pulled her head back, unwilling to give up control. His lips chased hers and she nipped him with her teeth. She bit again, harder this time, and he squawked in surprise and outrage.

"Why did you do that?" he asked. She smiled at him, baring her teeth, then licked her lips deliberately.

"You think you're the one in control here," she said. "But you aren't, Jess. This partnership goes both ways. In bed and out of it."

He shook his head and opened his mouth to speak. Her mouth covered his again, tugging and sucking until he moaned his surrender. It was like pouring rocket fuel on coals. She wanted him more than she'd ever anything before in her life. Her nipples were hard, twin points of fire between their bodies, and the feeling of his cock pushing up at her urgently was almost more than she could take.

Reaching down between their bodies, she pushed up the loose skirt she wore and pulled at her undergarment. The damn thing wouldn't slide down her hips with her legs splayed, she realized. She was going to have to get up.

His hand fumbled against hers as he ripped open his pants, then his erection bobbed up between them. She rubbed against it sensuously, the sweet torture of the fabric between them more pain than pleasure.

She lifted herself to pull off the wretched garment that separated them, but his hands found her waist beneath the skirt and held her. They came around the front of her undergarment, and she felt a tug. A ripping sound filled the air, and she was free.

Immediately she slid down, taking him into her body to the hilt. He filled her so much that she shrieked in shock. She was ready for him, but it still came as a surprise to take him so quickly. Delicate membranes stretched, every breath brought new tensions and pressures from within. She moved tentatively and was rewarded by his groan. This was affecting him every bit as much as it was affecting her, she thought with satisfaction. He was hers for the taking.

She opened her eyes to find him staring at her. Everything was suddenly surreal. Here she sat, impaled upon a man she hadn't even known six months before. She was pregnant and he would soon be in danger. Her entire world had changed. Suddenly she felt like crying. It was all so much to deal with, more than she had ever dreamed possible. The sexual drive to possess him, the need to take his body and make it hers that had filled her mere moments earlier, was gone. In its place was a desire for comfort, for the tenderness and understanding she knew he was capable of giving with his body. She let herself fall forward against him, wrapping both arms around his neck and squeezing him tightly from within.

"Jess, please don't leave me," she whispered in his ear. "Please don't make me and the baby wait for you, wondering if you're still alive."

To her shame, she felt tears welling up. She hated crying, hated showing weakness. She had learned early on that to cry was to give your opponent an edge, something her father and her husband had never failed to take advantage of.

Jess was different, though. She felt him stiffen as her mood changed, then his arms wrapped around her and held her close. He seemed unsure of what to do next, but he was trying to comfort her. The simple fact that he cared enough to try made her cry even harder. She was sobbing now, and with every convulsion of tears she squeezed him within. His body was tense beneath hers but she didn't care. All she wanted to do was let out the hurt, the grief over everything that had happened, and the fear she felt whenever she thought of him leaving her to hunt Jenner one more time.

They stayed that was for a long time. Finally her tears slowed, and she realized that he was murmuring quietly to her. It was a soothing noise, as if he were comforting a child. She lifted her head, looking at him through tear-blurred eyes, and snuffled.

"I guess this wasn't really what I had in mind when I jumped you," she said wryly, feeling herself flush. He smiled at her with so much tenderness, her heart clenched.

"Well, I'm good for more than just sex," he replied. He reached up to grasp a strand of her hair, smoothing it back behind one of her ears. "Although the timing could have been better," he added, grimacing and shifting slightly. With a start she realized he was still embedded deep within her. Her eyes widened, and she blushed.

"Sorry, I forgot what we were doing before," she said. He laughed.

"Bethany, sweetheart, that's not the kind of thing a man likes to hear from his woman," he replied lightly. She blushed harder and shook her head.

"Thank you for understanding," she whispered, and laid her head back down against his shoulder. He laughed again, and this time she could hear the deep, rich chuckle course through his body. She squeezed him experimentally with her pelvic muscles. His laugh stopped abruptly, and his hips thrust up at her. She responded in kind, wiggling herself on his engorged flesh. The breath came out of his body in a startled *whoomph.* He grabbed her and abruptly twisted. Seconds later her body was under his, lying flat on the couch. Instinctively she wrapped her legs around his waist.

He started thrusting in and out of her with all the energy that had gripped them earlier. She grunted, pulling him into her, wishing there were some way she could keep him there. Why couldn't they just stay like this? Why did he have to go to the surface? He thrust into her again, this time rubbing against her clit. She shuddered, and other thoughts disappeared. How did he manage to do this to her time after time?

Every stroke brought her a little bit closer to satisfaction. She could smell him, see his strong muscles flexing with each thrust. His entire body was tense and tight. Beads of sweat built up on his forehead. She closed her eyes, focusing all her attention inward. The tension was almost unbearable—as if she were filled with a thousand tiny strings, each pulled tight and centered where he pushed inexorably into her. Each thrust brought him deeper, every motion wound the strings tighter. She was going crazy.

Then it hit Bethany, the most powerful orgasm she'd ever had. It ripped through her body, sending her into convulsions as her nails dug into his shoulders. He shuddered, then groaned as he came with her. Through the explosion of sensation, she felt his hot seed spurting into her. Again and again his hips bucked against her, until finally he collapsed. They lay there panting for several minutes before a chime caught their attention.

"It's a message from the surface," he said, rolling off her. Still naked, he strode across the room to the vid terminal, pressing a button. She watched in silence as he scrolled through the message. Then he spoke.

"It's Jenner," he said. "She's on the surface, and she wants her money."

Chapter Sixteen
Karos, Home of the Celestial Pilgrim

৪১

Here she was, stuck sitting in a cage on a ship on Karos, Bethany thought in disgust. The father of her child was responsible for putting her in that cage, and now he was heading out to kill a woman. There was a good chance she'd never see him again, a good chance that before long Pilgrim guards would come looking for *her*. And when they found her she would be an easy target. He insisted that wasn't going to happen. Of course, he insisted a lot of things, she thought uneasily. She'd believe they were safe when she saw it, and not one moment earlier.

It wasn't fair, she thought, settling down into the chair he'd thoughtfully placed in the cage. All she got to do was sit and wait, while someone else determined her fate. Again.

She reached down to her stomach, laying both hands flat across it. She was still amazed that there was actually a tiny being growing in there. It seemed so unreal to her, even though her body had already started to change in many ways. Her stomach was still almost flat, but there was a difference. It was as if the muscles had relaxed, making way for the new life to come. Her breasts had gotten larger, too. They had been sore at first, but she was getting used to the feeling. She murmured softly, rubbing her stomach and thinking of the child. Was it a little boy? Jess seemed to think so. She would prefer a girl, though. A daughter who would grown up strong and proud. A little girl who would choose her own destiny. A young woman who might never marry at all. Instead she might become a teacher, or a doctor. Like Bragan.

A sudden chill ran through her, and she whispered the dead man's name. Would Jess still be alive in the morning? If he was, would he still be whole? What if he found Jenner and killed her… Would vengeance give him the satisfaction he was looking for? Or would it leave him empty.

Would he still be the same man when he came back?

Visions of his dead and mangled body filled her mind. Without thinking, she slid out of the chair and knelt on the floor. She closed her eyes and clenched her hands tightly together, silently calling on the Goddess to watch over him and bring him back to her. At first it seemed to help, but then a small voice whispered in her mind's ear. Why would the Goddess care about one man's fate, especially a man bent on vengeance? Was she even listening?

She whispered another prayer. Tears of desperation welled up out of her eyes and started running down her face. She wiped them away with one hand and opened her heart to the Goddess once more.

The Goddess was silent.

* * * * *

Jess sat in the darkness, idly cleaning his fingernails with a long, wicked blade. It had taken him so long to find Jenner that he could hardly believe he'd gotten to her so easily. She'd replied to his message, going so far as to invite him to the hostel where she was staying. Now she was his. She would be coming up to her room soon, and when she did, she would see the face of justice. His face.

Calla is dead.

Hari's words had played through his mind a thousand times since that night on Discovery Station. Calla's implant had been found in the station's recycling pit, her body disposed of like so much trash. He should have been able to take care of her. He would have, too, if that bitch hadn't deliberately sold him into slavery in the mining belt. She'd wanted him dead, but she hadn't been willing to simply throw away her investment. No, she'd sold him into what she thought was certain death. She'd tried to kill him, and she'd succeeded in killing his sister.

Now it was time for Jenner to die.

He could hear the stairs outside creak as she heaved her massive form up to her room. It wasn't as nice as her apartment on Discovery Station, but she was lucky to have made it to Karos at all. Of course, her luck was about to change, he thought with grim humor. She'd survived the Saurellians' manhunt for Pilgrims, but she wouldn't survive him.

The door opened, and the light from the hallway outlined her form. She sighed heavily, then turned to switch on the light and close the door. His blaster was already raised by the time she caught sight of him.

"Hello, *Mistress* Jenner," he said tightly, savoring the moment. "I think you should sit down on the bed."

Jenner did as she was told, her snake's eyes wide with fright.

"I'd like to draw this out," Jess said, feeling almost playful now that he finally had her in his grasp. "I've dreamed about this day for years, you know. All those nights you made me come to you when I was younger? You're going to pay for them now."

Jenner gave a little moan of fear, and he almost felt pity for her. Almost. Then he thought about Calla's lifeless corpse and the pity disappeared.

"Unfortunately," he continued. "I have other business. We'll make this quick."

He tossed her a bottle of pills, a lethal concoction specially prepared by the ship's auto-doc. They would kill her, but the medicine itself was common enough. It certainly wouldn't raise eyebrows if anyone examined it.

"I've already written a little note goodbye for all your friends," he said thoughtfully. "About how you're so filled with guilt you can't bear to live any longer. I'm prepared to give you a choice. Either take the pills, or I'll use the knife."

"You wouldn't dare," Jenner whispered, but she was wrong and she knew it. He could see it in her eyes.

"Oh, I would enjoy it," he murmured with dark satisfaction. "Which way do you want to go?"

"I'll take the pills," she said finally. "I suppose you want to watch?"

"I've seen you stuff your face a million times while those around you were hungry," he replied coldly. "This time I plan to enjoy the sight."

He stood over her with the blaster as she took the pills, watching carefully to make sure that she swallowed all of them. There was enough in the bottle to kill her ten times over, but he wasn't going to take any chances.

After an hour, he rose to check her pulse. Nothing. Jenner was dead. He waited for the triumph to wash over him, but her death left him feeling hollow. Everything left him feeling hollow, he thought, feeling suddenly exhausted. Everything except for Bethany. She was all he had left.

He went over to the window and opened it silently before crawling out on to the roof. Karos was surprisingly backward, and security was poor. Hardly what he would have suspected from a planet that was home to the Celestial Pilgrim. The man must not have been quite as "celestial" as the Pilgrims liked to believe, he thought. It had been ridiculously easy to break in to the hostel and find Jenner. Escaping was just as easy. Within seconds, he blended into the darkness of the streets.

His ship was parked at the edge of the primitive landing field. The small town where Jenner had taken refuge was too insignificant to have a true spaceport. He hadn't even had to register a flight path with the planetary controllers. Checking carefully to make sure no one had followed him, he palmed the airlock open and stepped in. It took all of two seconds to reach the door that opened on to the living area.

His eyes flew to her cell in the corner. Bethany was sitting on her chair, watching him with a shadowed face.

He walked across the small room, pulling out the key to open her cage. She stood with dignity, watching his movements.

"Is it done, then?" she asked.

"Yes," he said tightly. He didn't want to discuss Jenner with her.

"And did it make you feel good to kill her?" she asked in a mocking tone. "Is Calla alive again? Have you stopped being a runaway slave?"

Jess glared at her.

"Please," he said, running a hand through his dark, curly hair. "Please don't. I just need to hold you tonight. Will you let me?"

She stared at him, as if trying to judge his sincerity. The look on his face must have convinced her, because she dropped her militant stance and came over to him. She wrapped her arms around him, pressing her body against his. It was like coming home, and Jess felt himself harden in response. She was the only person who could make him feel anymore.

"Let's go to bed," she whispered. "We're both tired. We'll think of what to do tomorrow. Tonight let's just be together."

"All right," he said, dropping a kiss on her head. Then she stepped away from him and held out her hand. Taking it, he let her lead him into the bedroom.

* * * * *

Bethany lay back in the bed, one arm thrown over her eyes. She was filled with the sweet, almost liquid lassitude that came after a night of making love. Jess had been fierce with her last night, almost as if he believed that if he only touched her in enough ways, it would make the events of the previous months disappear. She knew better, though. Nothing was going to make his memories go away. Only time could heal his pain.

He'd been like a lost child when he'd returned to the ship. At first she'd felt a sense of relief so profound that she'd wanted to cry. She had been so certain they'd catch him. She'd been told stories of Karos her entire life. It was supposed to be a glorious planet, millions of people united in the dreams and idea of the Celestial Pilgrim, all working together to complete his masterful plan.

Instead, it was a backward, rural place filled with subsistence farmers. There was only one real spaceport on the whole planet, located near the central temple. The thousands of Pilgrim guardsmen she'd expected didn't exist. Jess hadn't encountered anyone who even seemed to question his presence, let alone cadres of religious zealots.

Karos was just a pathetic, sad little place filled with pathetic and sad people.

After their first, frantic love-making session, he'd left her just long enough to lift the ship into orbit. Then he was back at her side, sliding into the bed and taking her into his arms. He'd been slow that time, exploring every spot and crevice on her body, slowly stroking her with his lips and hands until she'd cried out, begging for relief. He'd stop, then, right as she was on the peak of ecstasy, only to start again. Finally he'd taken her, pushing them both to a level they'd never felt before. Her throat was still sore from the cries she'd given. They'd both slipped into sleep, exhausted physically and emotionally.

Now as she lay in bed, she wondered what she would say to him when she got up. Jenner was dead and the quest was over. This was the time where they were supposed to take their child and find some place to settle in peace. But vengeance hadn't given him the peace he'd sought.

Last night he'd screamed in his sleep, alternately calling out for Calla and swearing imprecations against Jenner. When she'd tried to wake him, he'd turned on her, pinning her to the mattress. She'd called out his name and he woke up, confused and horrified at his actions. Then he left her and went to sleep on the couch. She missed his warmth immediately, the comfort of his touch and the sound of his breath. But a small part of her had also been relieved. The hate in his eyes as he'd pinned her down was terrifying. How could a man with such hate in his heart become a father?

A sound at the door caught her attention, and she shifted her arm. He was there, watching her. His face was grim, his eyes dull.

"You need to get up," he said quietly. "We have to talk."

She nodded her head and crawled out of the bed. He watched, seemingly unaffected by her nudity, as she pulled a robe on and moved toward him. He stepped aside as she approached the door, gesturing toward the couch in the living area. Feeling heavy, she sat down. He pulled a chair up before her, turning it backward and straddling it.

"We have to decide what we're going to do now," he said quietly. "You and the baby need a place to live."

"What about you?" she asked. "Don't you need a place to live, too?"

"Yes," he said dispassionately. "I've done some research, and found about four different places that might work out. I've printed out descriptions for you to look over. One of them is the planet Logan is from. He told me that I would have a place with him, if he was successful in his return."

"Do you have any idea if he was successful?" she asked.

Jess shook his head, then replied. "No, but Logan said he'd leave word for me at Dalaron Station if he had a place for us. It's located just inside Saurellian space, a way-station for anyone traveling through the Federation. We'll know for sure before we have to make our final decision," he replied. "It sounds like a good enough place. Mid-sized and well-established without being over-populated. If we don't like it we can always move on."

"How far is it?"

"It's a long way," he replied. "It's in the Saurellian Federation proper, not just under their control. It's actually on the far side of Saurellian space."

"I can see some real advantages in that," she said slowly. "You don't have to worry about being caught by the Imperials, and I doubt there are any Pilgrims there."

"No Pilgrims," he said, his eyes showing life for the first time. "It's probably a good, safe place."

"Then it sounds good to me," she replied, leaning forward. He remained silent as she cupped both hands around his face and kissed him. It was a slow, soft kiss, almost chaste. She wanted to show him how much she loved him, how much she and the baby needed him in their lives. He didn't respond, although his eyes were filled with an almost infinite sadness as she pulled away. What was going through his head?

He stood, and reached down with one hand to help her up.

"I'll go plot the course," he said. "We should be ready to start accelerating for our leap into hyperspace in an hour or so."

With that, he turned from her and walked out of the room. She sighed, and some of his sadness washed over her. She shook off the emotion deliberately.

Somehow she had to find a way to connect with him again, she told herself. He was living in the past, filled with regrets. It wasn't going to work like this. Her child deserved a father, not a ghost.

Chapter Seventeen

ଛ

No matter what she did, Bethany simply couldn't get through to Jess. He was kind to her, and very considerate of her physical needs, but there was always something missing when he looked at her. There was no sparkle in him, only sorrow. Not that he would dream of discussing his pain with her. No. Jess was too strong for that. Or at least he was pretending to be.

They were approaching Dalaron Station. As soon as they arrived, she would finally know where her future lay. If Jess had a message from Logan then they already had a home waiting for them. If not, there were several other planets which seemed to hold promise as possible destinations. Either way, they would be making a decision about where to go soon. It couldn't come fast enough for her. It had taken nearly three weeks to travel the distance from Karos, deep within Imperial territory, to Dalaron Station. Every day the baby moved within her. Her stomach formed a gentle mound, and every instinct within her cried out for the stability of a home.

Now they approached the station, Jess carefully maneuvering the ship into the docking area. She sat beside him in the cockpit, watching his fingers fly across the controls. It was still amazing to her how much he had managed to teach himself about flying. The computer helped him, of course, providing him with simulated runs and technical manuals. He'd had thousands of hours to practice while they were traveling. She'd been doing a bit of studying of her own, and had discovered that he was very close to being qualified for a pilot's license. No matter where they decided to go, he would never have trouble finding work. Pilots were always needed, even more now that the Empire and the Saurellian Federation had called a truce. Interstellar commerce was starting to flow again, after years of war.

They entered the docking cradle with a gentle nudge, and then her stomach gave several flip-flops as Jess turned off the ship's artificial gravity, tapping into the station's generators instead. It only took a brief second for the station's gravity to kick in, but it seemed like an eternity to her. Against her will, she leaned over and vomited suddenly into the sturdy plastic bag she'd taken to carrying with her everywhere. Her morning sickness had started to settle down several weeks ago, but the shift in gravity was just too much for her.

Jess was by her side instantly, pulling her hair back and supporting her head as her breakfast came back up. He made soothing noises, and she could feel tears building up in her eyes. She loved their baby fiercely, but she hated this feeling of helplessness that came over her whenever she was sick. She didn't like the fact that she wasn't in control of her own body, either physically or emotionally.

She gasped for air, slowly regaining her composure as the heaves faded. Jess eased the sack from her grasp, then handed her a small square of fabric to wipe her mouth with. He'd taken to carrying them with him at all times since she'd started getting sick. Just one more tiny thing he did to make her life easier.

She'd trade all of those little things if he would just talk to her, though. She knew he loved her because it showed in his actions. Why couldn't he trust her with his feelings?

He sat back on the floor of the cockpit, pulling her into his lap and cuddling her.

"Feeling better?" he asked after a while.

"Yes," she managed to whisper.

"I was going to offer to take you out for dinner on the station," he said after a brief pause. "I guess that might not be such a good idea, under the circumstances."

She managed to give a faint laugh, then shook her head.

"Let's not give up just yet," she said, trying to find some humor in the situation. "Who knows how I'll feel in a few hours? These things come and go, you know."

He chuckled in response, but she could tell his heart wasn't in it. She looked up into his face and saw his eyes were distant. He was once again focused on his own thoughts. Unable to control herself, she spoke.

"What are you thinking, Jess?"

"Nothing," he responded slowly. He closed his eyes and leaned back against the bulkhead. She rolled her eyes, disgusted.

"You're obviously thinking something," she said, trying to keep herself from sounding too upset. "What is it? Are you worried about whether Logan has sent you a message?"

His voice was distant when he replied.

"It doesn't matter if Logan has sent for us or not," he said. "Either way, we'll find a good place for the baby. There's plenty of money. Everything is going to be just fine."

It was the same kind of platitude he'd been giving her for weeks, she thought, anger mounting.

"I'm not a child, you know," she said sharply. "I think we should discuss these things. I don't need you to take care of me."

"Oh really?" he asked, nodding toward the pan of vomit. "It sure seems like you need me to take care of you."

She pulled away from him, rising to her knees to confront him.

"I don't need anyone to take care of me," she said in a firm voice. "I accept your help while I'm sick because it makes my life easier. If a person has a partner, they can share some of the responsibilities. But choosing to have a partner and needing a caretaker are two very different things, Jess. Don't make any mistakes about that. I can handle myself."

"You don't know anything about the world out there," he replied, his voice tight. "You wouldn't last a day without me, and you know it."

"That's ridiculous," she snapped back. "I did manage to get all the way to Vlaxon by myself. And if you hadn't come after me, I would have found a job and supported myself."

"Is that right?" he asked.

"Yes, it is right," she replied. "I'm not the same ignorant woman you kidnapped off the asteroid, Jess. I've seen more ports that most people do in a lifetime by now, and I've had plenty of time to study while you've been preoccupied with your stupid little hunt for Jenner. I've been keeping my eyes open, learning things. I may not have much experience, but I am not stupid. I'm ready to take care of myself."

The passion of her outburst was a little startling, even to Bethany, and she took a deep breath after she stopped talking. Her words seemed to have an impact on him. He'd certainly shut up. He looked at her, an unreadable expression on his face, then he abruptly pushed himself to his feet.

"You've made your point," he said, not reaching down to help her up as he usually would. "You don't need me. You are a strong woman and you're more than capable of caring for yourself. I understand and respect that."

Her jaw dropped as he left the room. Nothing he could have said would have surprised her more. Jess had never treated her like an equal, someone who could care for herself.

She heaved herself awkwardly to her feet and followed him down the corridor to the living area.

What the hell was going on in his mind now?

* * * * *

Jess sat down in front of the public data terminal. Bethany was back on the ship, sleeping. She hadn't gotten sick again, but he'd still decided it would be better if he caught a shuttle to the main port by himself. He needed to find out if Logan had contacted him. He was just paranoid enough that he didn't want to use the ship's communication equipment to check. If something had gone wrong, if someone were looking for him, he didn't want to lead them back to Bethany.

So there he sat, hands flitting across the interface, trying to remember the code words Logan had given him.

I'll set up a mailbox for you at Dalaron Station, his bunkmate had told him before they'd left the asteroid belt. *Your keyword will be Calla, after your sister. I'll leave the message in the name of "Jess Freedman". If you don't hear anything from me by the time three months have passed, then don't expect anything.*

Jess had wondered many times what had happened to Logan. Now that he was poised to find out, he found himself strangely reluctant to check for the message. The bulk of survivors from the Pilgrim mining asteroid, women, children, and escaped slaves, had all gone with Logan. Were all those people dead now? Had things gone terribly wrong for them? Or were they living new lives now?

Bethany had a friend with them, a woman named Moriah. She might want Moriah there when the baby was born. In fact, if she had Moriah, she probably wouldn't need him.

That was the real problem, he admitted to himself. Part of him was actually hoping things hadn't worked out for Logan. If they didn't have a place waiting for them with him, then Bethany would still need Jess to take care of her. Or at least he hoped she would. After her outburst on the ship he wasn't so sure anymore.

For so long he had thought of her as being dependent on him. He *liked* her dependency. It meant that she couldn't leave him, not as long as she needed him to take care of her. When she'd tried to leave him before, it had been like a knife stabbing though his heart. The kind of pain he'd felt when he'd realized Calla was gone…

Once upon a time he'd had Calla in his life. He had taken care of her, they had always been together. He knew his purpose in life. Then he failed Calla and she died. He had sworn to himself that he wouldn't fail Bethany. He would keep her safe and provide for her. But now that he was in the position to do so, she didn't need him.

She could go to Logan, to Moriah, and she would be safe and happy. She wouldn't need him at all. He shook his head, forcing the thoughts away. He didn't like acknowledging that a part of him actually hoped Logan hadn't left a message because the implications were impossible to consider. It was better to simply check for the message and get it over with.

He touched the keys and the terminal flickered to life. Within seconds he navigated through the main station menu to the traveler's bulletin board. He typed in his query, and then a message icon appeared before him. Holding his breath, he typed in the keyword, and the message opened.

* * * * *

Bethany woke as Jess slipped under the covers. She gave a sleepy whimper, protesting the cold air he brought with him. His arms came around her, and then he was rolling her to her back. His hand came down to touch her stomach, fingers dancing lightly across the skin.

His head dropped down, lips whispered against the mound of flesh. What was he doing?

He was talking to the baby, she realized. She lay still, not wanting to do anything to disturb him. It was the first time he'd displayed any real interest in the child within her. Against her will, moisture built up in her eyes. He really did care…

He stayed that way for several minutes, whispering and rubbing her stomach. Then he moved back up the length of her body. He kissed her mouth gently and pulled her body against his. She started to speak, to tell him how much it meant that he wanted to communicate with their child. He cut her off, lifting one finger and pressing it against her lips.

"Shhhhhhhh…"

His mouth grazed her chin, smoothing kisses along her jaw and cheek. He kissed her eyelids, her forehead, her ears — each touch soft and light as a whisper of silken fabric. A shiver of sensation wafted through her. How she loved his touch!

His body was warm and naked against hers beneath the covers, bare flesh pressed to bare flesh. There was a special kind of heat to him, one that called her body in a way that no other source of warmth ever could. She stretched, enjoying the slide of her skin against his. Every hair on his legs, the calluses on his fingers, told the story of their time together. She could remember the first time she'd touched him like this. The excitement she'd felt when she'd seen his body on the floor in the mining complex.

Everything about him was precious to her.

She shifted, rolling into his body and raising one knee to hook his leg with hers. His thigh slipped between hers, and she could feel the rise of his erection against her side.

She ran one hand down his back, feeling the taut muscles of his shoulders as they tapered down to his lean hips. His butt was tight and firm in her grasp. She could feel his strength everywhere she touched him. She trailed her hand back up again, raking him lightly with her nails, reveling in the power she held over him. With that one gesture he stilled, every nerve strung tight in anticipation of her next move.

She froze for several heartbeats, stopping time for a moment. Then she pushed him back, pressing him to one side. He followed her unspoken directions, rolling on to his back.

He laid back his head, closing his eyes.

It seemed a signal of submission to her, as if he were giving himself to her this time. He put his faith in her, his pleasure in her hands. He trusted her.

She took a deep breath, then sat up beside him. She reached out with both hands, gripping each of his shoulders with firm fingers. She squeezed, hoping to ease some of his tension by massaging him. Letting go in any way was a big step for him and she would do whatever she could to make it easier.

After several minutes of working his shoulders she allowed herself to move lower. Each of his nipples stood taught as she rubbed the strong, smooth muscles beneath them. Squeeze and release. Squeeze and release. The rhythm mirrored another rhythm, that of their bodies moving together in sex. She closed her eyes, allowing herself to relax into the comfort of the motion. How many times had they moved together like this? Sometimes it was passion, sometimes comfort. At least once in grief.

Now she tried to infuse each touch with the love and need she felt for him, the unity that had come between them in the conception of this child. They were bound together with ties that could never be broken, ties that made them stronger and better. They were more than the sum of their parts.

His flesh grew warm beneath her hands and she felt some of his tension draining away. He looked less tense, too. He had draped one arm up and over his head, his breathing was slow and steady. Even his erection looked less urgent. He was still hard, but without the tightness that she associated with his greatest need. He was content in the moment.

She moved her hands lower, rubbing his upper stomach.

A new tension was building in him now. His muscles were tightening back up. He threw one arm over his eyes, and allowed other hand to grip the sheet. She continued her slow, steady motions and the skin of his fingers grew white with tension. His stomach muscles hardened with every touch, then he gasped.

"I can't take too much more of this."

She laughed, bracing her hands against his chest and swinging one leg over him.

"I'll be the judge of how much you take," she said lightly. He grunted.

She positioned herself so that the head of his erect penis just brushed her opening. Then she lowered herself just a bit, teasing him with her touch. He shuddered and tried to thrust up at her. She pulled away.

"None of that."

He nodded beneath his arm, lips tightening. Bethany paused, waiting for him to settle down.

She lowered herself over him again, once more teasing his most sensitive spot. He shivered, but this time managed to keep still. Encouraged, she pushed down slightly.

She could feel the wide head pushing into her, and for one moment she nearly sat straight down on him. It would be so easy, so fulfilling to simply swallow him with her body. She knew that if she did, his hands would come up around her hips, guiding her movements. They had done this what seemed like a thousand times — he always ended up in control, bringing her to pleasure. She had insisted earlier today that they be partners. This was her chance to express that partnership. His needs would come first. She couldn't just let him take over and do the work for her.

So she gritted her teeth, lowering herself once more. She could feel him slowly sliding up into her body. His length pushed her open, inch by agonizing inch. She paused again, forcing herself to stay controlled. *Breathe,* she reminded herself. *Remember to breathe.*

She started moving a third time, sinking down over him until the pressure from within was almost painful. He was so large, filled her so completely, that she wondered for an instant if she'd be able to take him. But just when she thought it was too much she hit bottom. She sat across his hips, his length fully embedded within him. She paused, allowing herself to adjust to the tight fit.

She opened her eyes, unable to remember closing them. She was startled to see her own fingers braced against his chest, clutching him so tightly that her nails were white. She forced herself to release them, one finger at time, and was shocked to see the tiny, half-moon shaped marks that were left there.

"I'm sorry," she whispered. He grunted, and lifted the arm away from his face. His eyes met hers, steady and serious, then he spoke.

"It felt good."

She giggled, made suddenly nervous by the intensity of his gaze. He was so big, so much stronger than her. He could pick her up and break her without even thinking about it, yet he lay before her submissively. Every muscle in his body was tight with tension, ready to take her and make her his. Instead, he was giving her a choice. He wasn't allowing his instincts to control the situation.

He really was willing to trust her.

She closed her eyes and flexed her fingers against his chest. Then she deliberately squeezed him from within. He grunted, quivering with need.

"Please…"

She pushed herself up, then plunged back down over him. His cock rasped against her, filling her with chills that were almost more than she could handle. How could one man give her so much pleasure? Everything about him—his smell, his skin, the sound of his breathing—aroused her. She pulled back and plunged down over him yet again.

Taking him into her body was much easier this time. He still felt big, but her fluids eased his way. Braced against his chest, she pumped again. This time his hips pushed up at her involuntarily, as if he could no longer keep himself from joining in the dance they had started between them.

Earlier she had wanted full control, but now she no longer cared how they came together. It was enough that they did, their bodies smacked against each other with every stroke. Perspiration broke out across her skin, and she opened her eyes to look at him. He was covered in a fine sheen of sweat, too. It seemed to bind them closer together, her wet flesh sliding across his with every stroke. Her entire body filled with tension, and every time her clit slid down his length it grew stronger. Her heart pounded, her breath grew ragged. Moving became harder. She desperately wanted to go faster, harder, but coordinating her thrusts with him was difficult. Then her hand slid off his sweat-slicked chest, and she collapsed against him. They both stopped moving, each sucking in air in with deep gasps.

"Why don't we change positions?" he said softly. "You've been doing all the work. Why don't you let me take over for a while?"

She laughed, then pushed herself upright.

"Nope, I started this," she said, "I'm going to finish it. Remember, I can take care of myself."

He chuckled too, and she narrowed her eyes in mock anger.

"Tease me?" she asked. "I'll show you what it means to tease."

She squeezed him from within again, taunting him.

"You win," he said. "Stop, you win. I'll just lie back and let you take advantage of me."

She giggled, then moving slowly on him, ground her hips against his in a circle. She kept it up for thirty seconds, but by then it was backfiring on her. With each slow rotation, her clit moved across his pelvic bone with tantalizing force. She closed her eyes, trying to concentrate, but it was too much.

She orgasmed suddenly, body stiffening and clutching him fast. Through her own release she heard him shout his. Then his hips spasmed against her and she could feel his seed spurting up within her body. Wave after wave of pleasure coursed through her until she collapsed against his chest, spent.

They lay there in silence, and she listened to his heartbeat slow as he calmed down. He wrapped both arms around her and held her close. She fell asleep, happier than she'd even been in her life.

Finally, she had found her partner.

* * * * *

Jess held Bethany for several hours. For the first time, he understood how she could have left him on Berengaria. She had done it because she didn't have a choice. She had seen their situation so clearly even though he'd been oblivious. There was a tiny being, a new life growing within her. That child deserved a safe, happy and healthy life. It deserved love, it deserved protection.

Everything he had failed to provide Calla. Bethany wanted those things for their child.

Sure, he had managed to take care of Bethany. But she had made it abundantly clear that she didn't need him. She really was capable of caring for herself. She even had a safe place to go. Logan would provide her with more than Jess could ever hope to give her. Bethany didn't need him, and he hadn't given her the opportunity to choose to be with him. From the beginning he had forced himself on her, taking what she wasn't willing to give freely and holding her captive when she wanted to go.

He'd put her in a cage. What kind of animal was he?

He couldn't hide the truth from himself any longer. She deserved more than he had to give and she deserved choices in life. He lowered his head, allowing himself to drink in the scent of her hair one last time. He kissed the top of her head and slid out from under the covers. She would be free now.

* * * * *

Bethany woke up and stretched, enjoying the delicious looseness in her arms and legs. Everything was finally all right.

Jess was already up, nothing unusual in that. He usually woke before her, especially now that she was pregnant. She needed more sleep than she ever had before. Her stomach growled, and she rolled out of bed feeling light and happy. Had Jess eaten yet? She felt like a big breakfast… Maybe they could even go out to eat on the station. At one of those restaurants she liked so much.

There was no sign of Jess out in the main room, so she ambled up toward the cockpit. He spent much of his free time up there, studying the piloting tables. She called his name as she walked down the hallway, not wanting to startle him.

There was no response, and sudden chill hit her. Where was he?

The cockpit was empty, so she jumped when the computer's soft voice spoke.

"Message waiting."

"What?"

"There is a message waiting," the computer repeated. "Would you like to play the message?"

"Yes, play the message," she said slowly. Tension built within her, and a slow burning started in the pit of her stomach. With a whirring noise, a small vid screen rose from the control panel and flickered to life. Jess' beloved face looked down at her. His expression was grim.

"Bethany, I'm sorry to do this without talking to you first," he said slowly. "I didn't want to just disappear on you, but I also wanted to give you the freedom to make a choice for yourself. To be honest, I wasn't sure I could trust myself to do that if I spoke to you face to face."

Suddenly it was hard for her to breathe. She sat back in the pilot's chair heavily, forcing herself to listen as he continued speaking.

"I understand now that you don't need me, that you can take care of yourself. I've never given you a choice to be with me, and I haven't even listened to you when told me how foolish it was to chase Jenner halfway across the sector.

"I realize that you were right about that. Killing her was a waste of time. Calla is still dead, and I'm still a failure. You and the baby deserve more."

She shook her head, wondering how he could be so stupid. He never listened to her, not when she told him he was wrong, and not when she told him she wanted a partner. Why couldn't she communicate with this man?

"I've programmed the ship to take to you Logan," Jess continued. "You'll be there in less than three weeks. He'll be expecting you. I'm staying here on the station. I've got half of our money, and I'm ready to apply for my pilot's license. You don't have to worry about me any more."

His hand in the image reached toward her, almost as if he were trying to touch her through the screen. She reached one arm up toward him, then pulled it back, feeling foolish. He was just reaching out to end the recording…

But instead of flicking off, he pulled his hand back and looked out once more.

"I know it's weak of me to even tell you this, but there's a part of me that isn't ready to give up hope. If you want to get in touch with me, I've got a room at the Pilot's Hostel in Quadrant Four. I'll be here until I get word that your ship has left."

He reached out again, and this time the image disappeared. The vid screen rolled silently back down into the control panel, leaving Bethany to stare thoughtfully at the space it had occupied.

She stood up and stretched. *How could he misunderstand like this?* she asked herself again. *Hadn't they been through enough?* She sighed and walked slowly back to their room. She needed to take a shower and get dressed. Goddess only knew how long it would take her to find this Pilot's Hostel place…

Chapter Eighteen

છ

Jess sat in the bar, drinking a rich, dark glass of beer. It was good stuff, some of the best he'd ever tasted. Every few moments he would check his message box on the counter-top terminal. He wasn't quite sure what he was expecting. Every time it showed up blank he was filled with both relief and fear. Relief that the ship hadn't left the station yet, fear because she hadn't tried to contact him.

What was she thinking? When would she be out of his life for good? Would he ever be able to forgive himself for losing her? He was so caught up in his thoughts that he didn't even notice it when someone slid into the seat next to him.

"Can you please bring me a glass of water?" a familiar voice asked the bartender, and for a moment he thought he was dreaming. He turned to look at her, trying to keep the longing he felt out of his face. He'd pressured her too much already, the last thing she needed from him was more force. She had to make her own decisions.

"How are you doing?" he asked, doing his best to sound casual. As if his entire life didn't rest on her answer.

"Not too good, Jess," she said softly. She looked at him, those beautiful cat eyes that he'd loved from the first minute he'd seen them gazing deeply into his own face. "I woke up this morning and found myself all alone. Now, instead of eating breakfast I had to come hunt you down. Why are you doing this to us?"

He opened his mouth, then closed. What was he supposed to say?

"I was pretty angry when I first got your message," she said softly. The bartender brought a glass of water over and she took it, murmuring, "Thanks."

He waited as she drank deeply. She put the glass down, them lightly traced the rim with one finger.

"But I realized something," she continued. "Being angry with you wasn't the solution. I love you for who you are, Jess."

His heart froze.

"And I guess that means loving you even when you do things I can't understand."

"What are you saying?" he asked, trying to keep his voice steady.

"Oh, Jess," she said, turning to him. "I really don't get why you're doing this to yourself. How many times have I told you I love you? How many times have I made it clear I want you for my partner?"

"You've also made it very clear you don't need me," he said, shaking his head.

"Of course I don't *need* you," she replied. "I'm a grown woman. I'm capable of living without you. I'm not a child. But that doesn't mean I don't *want* you, Jess. You're my man, we're a family now. How could I ever be happy without you? I love you."

She leaned forward, kissing him on the mouth. He didn't respond, still trying to process what she was telling him. She really did want to be with him.

She pulled back, sliding off the barstool and standing beside him.

"Let's get back to our ship and get out of this place," she said, holding out one hand to him. He nodded slowly, and took it.

"That sounds like a good idea to me," he replied. "Where are we going? To Logan?"

"We'll see," she said, a strange little grin playing across her face. "I think it's my turn to pick where we go. Some place warm, maybe. And definitely no Pilgrims or slaves."

"Yes m'am," he replied, smiling back at her. "I'm up for anything you want."

"Good," she replied, laughing and shaking her head. "Brace yourself, Jess. I'm in a strange mood, so things could get interesting. Let's see what kind of future we can find for ourselves, hmm?"

Epilogue

Logan stood alone on his balcony.

He could see his entire city from here, the shining capital that his family had ruled for centuries. Once his father had stood here too, telling his young son stories of the star system that would one day be his to rule. He had always imagined doing the same with his own son, Soren.

Instead he had spent five years as a slave, less than a man.

For all that, his return to power had been almost laughably easy. His people had rallied to him upon his return, turning on the revolutionaries and slaughtering them as Logan strode through the city toward his palace. Millions had followed him, singing songs and throwing flowers in his path. Several times he had been forced to stop. They all wanted to touch him, to hear his voice and remember the good times. Nobody could have guessed how bad life would get once revolutionaries had crept into his palace wearing gas masks five years ago. Every electronic security system had been subverted, and loyal guardsmen were slaughtered as they lay unconscious. A reign of terror had followed and millions suffered.

Many of the conspirators were already dead. Thousands more waiting in the prisons below the castle, damp, dark pits his earliest forefathers had carved out of the living rock to encase their enemies. Now his men were questioning those prisoners, demanding answers and ripping the truth from the very fabric of their brains.

So far no one had been able to give him the information he sought. Somewhere, out in the city or in the hills beyond, his son still lived.

Every other member of his family was dead. His brothers, sisters...his lifemate, Linnea. They were all gone, but Soren still lived.

Those of his loyal friends and counselors who had survived the assault thought he was crazy. There was no reason to believe the child had survived. He had been less than a year old when the revolutionaries had struck the palace. His caretakers were all slaughtered, and while the child's body was never found, there was no reason to hope. The destruction in the nursery had been terrible, many bodies completely destroyed before they could be identified. How could a child survive something like that? Entire sections of the palace were ultimately vaporized during those tense, horrible hours...

Despite that, Logan knew in his heart Soren lived. He could hear the child's heart beating deep within his soul, just as he had been able to hear Linnea's heart stop beating. He had felt it the instant his lifemate had perished. Her dying screams echoed in his dreams, though they had been miles apart when the attack came. A part of him died with her and only the hope of finding his son had kept him alive. Logan leaned forward, willing himself to feel the life of the city, calling out silently to his son to answer him.

Of course, there was nothing. He was no sorcerer to reach outside his body for the truth. Even the priests and priestesses of the Goddess, many with powers beyond his ability to comprehend, believed his son was dead.

Logan sighed, closing his eyes. His son was alive. He was out there, waiting for his father to rescue him. Logan's grip on the railing grew tight, anger welling up within him as he made a silent promise.

When he did find whoever held his son captive, not even the Goddess would be able to stay his hand. He or she would die slowly and terribly for their part in this revolt. He vowed it on his Linnea's cold and lonely grave.

Enjoy this excerpt from
JERRED'S PRICE
© Copyright 2004 Joanna Wylde

Note: The events in Jerred's Price occur before Price of Pleasure and Price of Freedom.

"How's Giselle this evening?" Vetch asked expansively as he walked into the bar. Giselle winked at him, used to his flirting. The station was part of the freighter captain's usual run, and he came in at least once every other week. She gave him a big grin and leaned forward across the bar, flashing her cleavage at him.

"I'm fine, Vetch," she said. "Getting better all the time. What can I do for you?"

"My friend and I needed a comfortable place to talk, and naturally we thought of Manya's," Vetch said, gamely attempting to maintain eye contact with her. Every few seconds she caught his glance darting downwards. Men always looked at her chest first. She was used to it by now.

"They're still there, hon," she whispered conspiratorially. "Don't worry, I check on 'em first thing every morning, just for you."

Vetch blushed, and she gave a deep, rich laugh. Then he started laughing, too, and to her surprise he leaned forward and gave her a quick kiss on the cheek.

"You're one in a million, Giselle," he said. "But I have business to take care of this evening. Can you set up me and my friend with a pitcher? Talking business is thirsty work."

"Is there anything that's not thirsty work for you, Vetch?" a man asked. Giselle looked up, startled.

Her breath caught.

Vetch had always seemed tall to her, but this man towered over the friendly freighter captain. His face was hard, angular, and a nasty scar twisted one side of it, pulling his features into a permanent snarl. Startled, she looked down quickly, but she couldn't seem to take her eyes off him. He wore tall, black boots that seemed to be made of leather, of all things. Leather was expensive... Her eyes moved slowly upward following a roughened pair of black breeches that clung to every lean muscle of his legs. A loose, black shirt draped his upper body, and he carried a leather jacket cradled in one arm.

His gaze met hers coolly as her eyes reached his face. That scar caught her attention again, and she found herself looking at it with morbid fascination. What kind of wound would do damage like that, and why hadn't he gotten it fixed? He cleared his throat meaningfully. Embarrassed, she flashed a smile at him. She had been rude. He didn't smile back. In fact, he didn't respond to her at all. Instead he looked away, checking out the room as if he was expecting trouble. Her intuition prickled, and she made a mental note to keep an eye on him. If there was going to be trouble this evening, she'd bet her last credit it would come from him.

"Find a seat, and I'll be right with you," she said to him, trying not to let him see how uncomfortable he made her. She'd be damned if she'd show him weakness.

"Thanks, Giselle," he said softly. He rolled her name across his tongue slowly, as if savoring its taste and sound.

He nodded to Vetch, indicating a table against the wall. As they walked over together, she watched out the corner of her eye as he took a seat against the wall. Definitely dangerous. She might want to warn Manya...

She brought them their pitcher and some glasses, and tried flashing another smile at him. But even Vetch's expression was sober now, and it was clear her presence wasn't wanted. Then a group of Debsian traders came in talking loudly, and her attention was taken up filling their drink orders. Still, she pointed the man out to Manya when he came out from the back office to tend bar. She didn't like Black Leather's attitude one little bit.

The bar filled steadily over the next two hours, and while she checked regularly on the two men, they didn't want anything more from her. She had to admit, the way Vetch's friend ignored her piqued her interest. She was used to men noticing her, used to them paying attention when she flirted and smiled at them. She was getting nothing from him, although at times she felt as if he might be watching her.

After she stopped by the table to check on them a third time, something flickered in his eyes as she brushed him—she knew she was on to something. He noticed her, but he didn't want to show it. She smiled to herself, wondering why she was bothering to play this little game with him. Boredom? Maybe. A little flirting would make the shift go faster. After all, if he were going to cause trouble, he would have by now. She reached one hand to her already low neckline and pulled it down just a bit. Manya gave her a pointed look, which she ignored. Cleavage sold drinks—he knew that. She was just doing her job.

On her next pass through the tables she ignored Black Leather, focusing on the Debsians instead. She leaned over as she served the traders, flashing them a wide expansion of soft, sloping breast littered with ginger-colored freckles. Out of the corner of her eye, she caught Black Leather's stare. She pretended not to see, and then leaned forward even further.

"Anything else I can get you boys?" she asked in a low voice, winking at the loudest of the traders. He was a bluff, friendly looking man who didn't seem used to getting attention from women. His friends hooted, and one slapped him on the back.

Encouraged, the man leaned forward and held out two fingers with a credit chit between them.

"This is all yours, darlin'," he said. "I don't suppose you want to come back to my hostel with me?"

"Nope," she said with a wink, "I'm not really that kind of girl. But I appreciate the offer."

The men groaned, and then, to her surprise, their leader reached out and tucked the credit chit between her breasts. She drew in a breath, about to let him have it, when she caught a movement out of the corner of her eye. She had Black Leather's full attention now. Feeling pleased with herself, she laughed and stood up.

"Thanks, sweetie," she said, picking up her tray and balancing it against one full hip. "I appreciate the tip."

"Another round!" one of the traders said in a loud voice, face flushed from drink. "We'll keep you busy tonight!" They all broke into a round of cheers, thumping the table for emphasis. Feeling pleased with herself, she sashayed away from the Debsians toward the two men against the wall. Vetch waved her away from them, but she came over, pretending to misunderstand his gesture.

"Can I get you boys anything?" she asked. Black Leather shook his head, darkness filling his face. Vetch looked a little nervous, and Black Leather leaned back in his chair, lifting one arm casually and laying it on the seat back behind him. Her eyes ran down his body languidly. Then they stopped. He had a blaster holstered against his side. The jacket had hidden it from her sight when she'd first come in.

Damn.

Manya had a security screen on the door. Why hadn't it picked up his weapon? She felt the smile fade from her face, growing uncomfortable under his steady, cold gaze.

"We ask our customers to check their weapons before coming in here," she said uncertainly, looking toward the bar for backup. Manya was deep in conversation with Kisti, the other barmaid. Neither looked in her direction. "It's against station regulations to have a blaster in an establishment that serves alcohol. It's a serious offense."

"I prefer to keep my blaster with me," he replied in a cool voice. She glanced at Vetch, saw him swallow, and then nodded her head, feeling sick. Black Leather was trouble. She had

sensed that from the start, why hadn't she trusted her instincts?
Damn men.

"All right, then," she said, trying to smile. "I'll leave you to
your drinks."

About the Author

෨

Joanna Wylde is a freelance writer who has been working professionally for more than eight years as a journalist and fund-raiser. In April 2002, she branched out into fiction with The Price of Pleasure, a futuristic romance published by Ellora's Cave. She is 29 years old, married, and lives in north Idaho.

Joanna welcomes mail from readers. You can write to her c/o Ellora's Cave Publishing at 1056 Home Avenue, Akron Ohio, 44310-3502.

Why an electronic book?

We live in the Information Age — an exciting time in the history of human civilization in which technology rules supreme and continues to progress in leaps and bounds every minute of every hour of every day. For a multitude of reasons, more and more avid literary fans are opting to purchase e-books instead of paperbacks. The question to those not yet initiated to the world of electronic reading is simply: *why?*

1. *Price.* An electronic title at Ellora's Cave Publishing runs anywhere from 40-75% less than the cover price of the <u>exact same title</u> in paperback format. Why? Cold mathematics. It is less expensive to publish an e-book than it is to publish a paperback, so the savings are passed along to the consumer.

2. *Space.* Running out of room to house your paperback books? That is one worry you will never have with electronic novels. For a low one-time cost, you can purchase a handheld computer designed specifically for e-reading purposes. Many e-readers are larger than the average handheld, giving you plenty of screen room. Better yet, hundreds of titles can be stored within your new library — a single microchip. (Please note that Ellora's Cave does not endorse any specific brands. You can check our website at www.ellorascave.com for customer recommendations we make available to new consumers.)

3. *Mobility*. Because your new library now consists of only a microchip, your entire cache of books can be taken with you wherever you go.

4. *Personal preferences are accounted for*. Are the words you are currently reading too small? Too large? Too...ANNOYING? Paperback books cannot be modified according to personal preferences, but e-books can.

5. *Innovation*. The way you read a book is not the only advancement the Information Age has gifted the literary community with. There is also the factor of what you can read. Ellora's Cave Publishing will be introducing a new line of interactive titles that are available in e-book format only.

6. *Instant gratification*. Is it the middle of the night and all the bookstores are closed? Are you tired of waiting days—sometimes weeks—for online and offline bookstores to ship the novels you bought? Ellora's Cave Publishing sells instantaneous downloads 24 hours a day, 7 days a week, 365 days a year. Our e-book delivery system is 100% automated, meaning your order is filled as soon as you pay for it.

Those are a few of the top reasons why electronic novels are displacing paperbacks for many an avid reader. As always, Ellora's Cave Publishing welcomes your questions and comments. We invite you to email us at service@ellorascave.com or write to us directly at: 1337 Commerce Drive, Suite 13, Stow OH 44224.

THE
⚨ ELLORA'S CAVE ⚨
LIBRARY

Stay up to date with Ellora's Cave Titles in
Print with our Quarterly Catalog.

To recieve a catalog,
send an email with your name
and mailing address to:

CATALOG@ELLORASCAVE.COM

or send a letter or postcard
with your mailing address to:

Catalog Request
c/o Ellora's Cave Publishing, Inc.
1056 Home Avenue
Akron, Ohio 44310-3502

COMING TO A BOOKSTORE NEAR YOU!

ELLORA'S CAVE

Bestselling Authors Tour

UPDATES AVAILABLE AT

WWW.ELLORASCAVE.COM

MAKE EACH DAY MORE *EXCITING* WITH OUR

ELLORA'S CAVEMEN
CALENDAR

WWW.ELLORASCAVE.COM

erridwen, the Celtic Goddess of wisdom, was the muse who brought inspiration to storytellers and those in the creative arts. Cerridwen Press encompasses the best and most innovative stories in all genres of today's fiction. Visit our site and discover the newest titles by talented authors who still get inspired - much like the ancient storytellers did, once upon a time.